Noble

William Pitt, the Younger

BOOKS BY

PHILIP WHITWELL WILSON

THE UNMAKING OF EUROPE

THE CHRIST WE FORGET

THE CHURCH WE FORGET

THE VISION WE FORGET

THE LAYMAN'S CONFESSION OF FAITH

AN UNOFFICIAL STATESMAN
(Life of Robert C. Ogden)

GEORGE PEABODY, ESQ.

AN EXPLORER OF CHANGING HORIZONS
(Biography of William Edgar Geil)

Editor of

THE GRÉVILLE DIARY

William Pitt, the Younger

BY P. W. WILSON

DOUBLEDAY, DORAN & COMPANY, INC.

GARDEN CITY   MCMXXXII   NEW YORK

PREFACE

FOR *this book, there is, perhaps, an opportunity. No man ever lived a more remarkable life, and few men made more of a difference to other lives than the younger Pitt. Yet the story of his career is to-day virtually inaccessible to this present generation. The fragment of a biography, attempted by Bishop Tomline, has become an archive. The fascinating four volumes by Earl Stanhope are unobtainable. What Macaulay wrote on Pitt for the* Encyclopædia Britannica *was no more than a brilliant essay. Lord Rosebery's little book is a monograph. The massive tomes of Dr. J. Holland Rose contain an elaborate analysis of Pitt's period, but are only incidentally biographical of Pitt himself.*

A book is needed, therefore, which will enable the reader of this twentieth century to see William Pitt as he was— the man, his environment, the situations that he had to face, his triumph at the outset, the tragedy that overwhelmed him at the end. It is after many years, spent in the parliamentary and administrative atmosphere, that I have attempted this task.

v

*In the United States, the importance of the younger Pitt
has been obscured by the dramatic part which his father,
Lord Chatham, played during the American crisis. Yet,
as it seems to me, the qualities of the son were fully as
astonishing as the genius—let us add, the idiosyncrasies—
of the father. In William Pitt, the younger, we see the
very quintessence of the English character, its virtues and
its limitations, its sentiment and its solidity. He was a
patriot, yet without boasting. He had pride without conceit. His rectitude was immaculate, but his income was
mismanaged. His courage made it easier for him to die in
defeat than to acknowledge that defeat had been suffered.
Without Chatham, Pitt would never have had his chance.
But when the chance came it was the son, not the father,
who had the patience, the judgment to make full use of it.*

P. W. WILSON.

CONTENTS

CONTENTS

William Pitt, the Younger

IN WILLIAM PITT, the younger, we are confronted by a miracle of precocity. At the age of twenty-three years, a barrister, glad of a brief, he was appointed Chancellor of the Exchequer and arbiter of British finance; he was offered and, more astonishing still, he refused the yet more glittering prize of Prime Minister. When he was twenty-four years old the office of Prime Minister was again pressed on him and he accepted the responsibility.

Nor was this the full extent of the achievement. Having attained to the greatest of all appointments open to a subject of the King, he held that appointment, with one brief and voluntary intermission, for the rest of his life, being in power for nineteen years, a longer period than any other recorded, whether of his predecessors, amongst whom was included Sir Robert Walpole, or of his successors, amongst whom were included a Gladstone and a Salisbury. In their forty-seventh year, most public men are satisfied to find themselves in a Cabinet. But in his forty-seventh year, this man, after an unprecedented domination over the Cabinet, was borne with all the honours of the highest eminence to his inevitable resting place in Westminster Abbey.

It is by one standard alone, and this the greatest, that William Pitt is to be measured, yet even so, the more closely we survey his achievement, the more perplexing appears to be the problem which is involved in it. By temperament and by training it was for the guidance of the nation through a period of tranquil progress that he was fitted. He was the Asquith of his time. Yet for the latter half of his administration, about ten long and bitter years, Great Britain was engaged in a war with France which swept away all that, whether in finance or in reform, Pitt cared about. He hated the struggle. Yet he had to persist in it.

As a rule there is one and only one condition laid down for a minister in charge of war. If he wins, his vices are forgiven. If he loses, his virtues are forgotten. Vices and virtues alike are subordinate to victory. The astonishing fact about William Pitt is that without success he was able to survive. Though he was the Asquith of his day, yet there was never a Lloyd George to supersede him. The apotheosis of Napoleon at Austerlitz might kill him, but it did not destroy the confidence which he inspired. Through a second, a third, a fourth, a fifth term of supreme vicissitudes, his reputation, though fiercely assailed, had endured, and an England, still a dozen long years distant from the final decision at Waterloo, mourned in Pitt the one leader of the nation whose infallibility was fortified by failure. If, at the end, he was defeated, even at Westminster, it was because, for many weeks, he had ceased to be a whole and healthy man, and a successor was essential.

★

We belong to the Twentieth Century. The century to which Pitt belonged was the Eighteenth, and it has been the Eighteenth Century in which mentally his biographers and his commentators still lived and moved and had their being. If we look upon him only with their eyes, he may appear to us as a figure, remote from life, even from life as, in fact, he lived it. What the Eighteenth Century meant by Great Britain is not what we mean by Great Britain. Their Parliament is not our Parliament. We do not eat as Pitt ate. We do not drink as Pitt drank. We do not travel as Pitt travelled. We do not think as Pitt thought. We need to correct the instinctive anachronisms which arise out of chronological astigmatism.

It would be an interesting and perhaps an instructive experience for the academic historian to live even a single day of his life as every day of Pitt's life had to be lived. It was a hundred years before Edison drove electricity through the first of his illuminating filaments that Pitt became Prime Minister. Even the era of gas had not begun, nor was the use of oil in lamps as yet perfected. Out of doors, people carried torches and rudimentary lanterns. The light in which Pitt had to pore over his Greek and his Latin was the light of a candle.

So with heat. The fire was an open fire. The bathroom, with its hot and cold water, had yet to be elaborated. It was an open fire that served for cooking in the kitchen, with an oven for baking bread. The fire was still stoked with wood and the supply of wood had been diminished by deforestation. It was the discovery of coal and its uses that was becoming the salvation of the country from a famine in fuel.

During the boyhood of Pitt the era of machinery had but just begun. It was only in 1759, the year of his birth, that James Watt looked upon steam as a possible motive force. Pitt was in his tenth year when Arkwright set up his spinning frame, and before Cartwright had used the steam engine, Pitt had become Prime Minister. It was thus into a world as dependent on hand labour as the more backward provinces of China that the future statesman was born.

For economic reasons it was taken for granted that, in such a world, it would only be the few who could enjoy the comforts of an elaborated civilization. To-day, every home has or wants an automobile. Those were days when a carriage was a social distinction. Between the few and the many there lay an impassable distinction, expressed in behaviour, costume, education, and authority. But if you belonged to the few, as did Pitt, you had every opportunity of cultivating your powers to their full range of activity.

For the very fact that the comforts derived from labour of hand were limited in quantity meant that they were superfine in quality. In not many homes were there many books. In many homes not all could read them. But the binding of books was leather, the paper was permanent. There was no photography. Even the daguerreotype was only achieved after the accession of Queen Victoria. But a portrait in the Eighteenth Century, multiplied by engravings, was a work of art, the value of which has increased with time. So with furniture and porcelain. Chippendale immediately preceded Pitt; for years Wedgwood was his contemporary, and Wedgwood was the patron of Flaxman, the sculptor and exponent of a restraint at once classical and characteristic of his period.

· It was thus amid a culture, dignified and secluded within the frontiers of caste, that William Pitt was reared. According to the accepted creed of his generation, Providence placed people in allotted "stations." The upper classes enjoyed advantages to which were attached corresponding obligations. The "lower orders" had not and ought not to have either voice or vote in the government of the country. If they entered into the calculations of statesmen at all, it was only on those rare occasions when there was a mob, either enthusiastic over victories attributed to a Chatham, or enraged by some fanatic of ultra Protestantism like Lord George Gordon, or by some Radical like Wilkes; or repentant under the thunderous preaching of a Whitefield. A statesman of Pitt's day would speak of the nation approving or disapproving this or that, and historians repeat the phrase. But in that sense there was no nation, what was meant by "the nation" was a small and close oligarchy floating on the surface of an underworld, somnolent, at times, or sullen or seething.

William Pitt, like his successor, Stanley Baldwin, held himself to be answerable to public opinion. But the public opinion acknowledged by the earlier statesman was the very reverse of the public opinion which has since developed. To us, public opinion, organized in the press, through the radio, even on the screen, is a daylight shining into the windows of the eminent and flooding their most secret domiciles. But to Pitt, public opinion was created by the eminent and shone out through their windows on to a pavement that could be seen by no other illuminant. The press was still in its infancy and barely tolerated. The politician did not consult his constituency. The constituency consulted the politician. The only people who mattered were the people who did matter, and these people could have been gathered, one and all, in a single auditorium. It was possible for Pitt's cousin, Lord Camelford, to boast that, if he wanted, he could nominate his Negro butler for a seat in the House of Commons.

In order to understand William Pitt we must suppose ourselves to have been transported into a world where not one newspaper, comparable with our own, had been published, where not one telegram had been despatched or received, where not one railway had ever been built, where not one automobile had ever been licensed, where the roads themselves were but ill-maintained by the receipts of the toll-bar and were not to be paved by McAdam until years after Pitt's death. Deep in mud, carts and carriages crawled along, and distances had still to be measured by the day. It is a fact, actual yet incredible, that Britain, reckoned in terms of locomotion, was larger in the days of Pitt, far larger, than are the United States in the days of President Hoover. To proceed from London to Aberdeen took longer than to proceed by ocean liner from London to Bombay, and with no telegraphic means of communication to supplement physical transit, the true measure of the remote was indefinitely multiplied.

In a world thus lacking vital communications aristocracy

was something more than a citadel of privilege. It was an organized network of power. The families thus united held the country as well as the capital.

The peerage was thus no mere dignity. It was a legislature which could say Yes, and what is of more importance, No. So with the landed nobility. The squire was a magistrate, possibly a lord-lieutenant of his county, the agent of the few exercising authority within his jurisdiction over the many. Nor was the Church merely or, indeed, mainly spiritual. The Tory parson might differ in politics from the Whig prelate, but on the main issue parson and prelate stood firm for the established oligarchy. John Peel of Cumberland, with his coat so gray, might turn that coat this way and that, supporting now King George and then Prince Charlie from over the water, but if there had been a Reform Bill before the country John Peel would have forgotten all about rival dynasties and remembered only his conservatism.

The organization of the few extended throughout the world. It was the parsonage which contributed Horatio Nelson to the navy. It was Irish land that sent Arthur Wellesley, afterward Duke of Wellington, into the army. The governors of colonies, the ambassadors accredited to foreign courts—they were all selected from families, themselves select—from an inner circle as clearly defined as nationality itself.

The whole of this elaborate and—to use the current yet singularly accurate phrase—"well-connected" social, naval, and military system revolved like a wheel around an axle that consisted of certain institutions. There was the Court;

there was the Cabinet; there was Parliament; there was the Judiciary, and they all lived and moved and had their being in one small area which included the Palace of Westminster, Buckingham House, as it was still called, Whitehall, and Downing Street. Any man who could control that square mile of palace and park could control the destinies of Great Britain. No opinion that was not uttered within these precincts of power was an opinion of which notice need be taken. When we say that William Pitt governed Great Britain as Prime Minister, it is to this concentrated and exclusive empire that we refer.

★

It was thus into a privileged omnipotence that William Pitt, the younger, was born, and if we are to envisage the England that lay open to his political subjugation we must glance, if only for a moment, down the long perspective of history. As a nation the English are numbered by foreigners among the incomprehensibles. A people, at once so autocratic and so democratic, so imperial and so liberal, so patriotic and so self-critical, presents a paradox to which the clue has never been obvious; nor do we suggest that, in what follows, we have found it. Yet what follows is certainly pertinent to the problem of William Pitt.

England is the product of two subconscious memories. Within her citizenship, living side by side, even inter-marrying, there are the conquerors and the conquered, the rulers and the rebels, the silk hat and the red tie. In name, the duality changes; in substance, it is ever the same—

Norman and Saxon, Catholic and Lollard, Cavalier and
Puritan, Tory and Whig, Conservative and Liberal, with
Labour as the ultimate.

To say that the patrician and the popular are eternally
opposed would be misleading. On the island of Runnymede
it was the barons who in 1215 expressed their demands in
popular terms, and compelled a King to sign the Magna
Carta. So was it a baron, Simon de Montfort, who gave his
name to the earliest of England's Parliaments. In the annals
of England there has been no crisis, involving privilege and
the rights of the people, in which a body of the privileged
classes has not stood for the cause of reform.

In the Seventeenth Century the issue to be decided was the
acceptance or the repudiation of the divine right of kings.
The cause of mystical autocracy was embodied in the
Stuart dynasty. It was upheld by the Tories. It was resisted
by the Whigs. By summoning William of Orange and the
Hanoverians to the throne, the great Whig nobles recon-
stituted Runnymede, supplemented Magna Carta by a Bill
of Rights, and so led the nation into a wider liberty.

As the party responsible for the glorious Revolution, the
Whigs found themselves in a position of permanent power.
It was with an exiled dynasty that the Tories were allied,
at any rate by sentiment and tradition, and it was only by
changing the succession that they could come into favour at
Court. Indeed, the invasions of successive pretenders—
"the Fifteen" and "the Forty-Five"—while they were
futile, served none the less to keep alive the revolutionary
issue, and so consolidate the prevailing faction. It was to the

Whig Party that, as a matter of course, the family of Pitt belonged.

About Pitt's ancestry there is more than a touch of romance. The little town of Blandford in Dorsetshire has various claims to distinction. It is the birthplace of Alfred Stevens, the sculptor of Wellington's Monument in St. Paul's Cathedral. It is a Marquess of Blandford who, son to father, grows up to be the next Duke of Marlborough. It was a Rector of Blandford who founded the family of Pitt; and what raised the family to eminence was wealth.

The Gladstones were merchants in Liverpool; the Peels spun cotton; Thomas Pitt, reared in the rectory, sought and found a fortune in India.

In the Seventeenth and Eighteenth centuries oversea commerce was unrestricted by the Ten Commandments. Even the Gladstones owned slaves. Thomas Pitt was hunted down, fined in England, and imprisoned in India as a smuggler.

What he had infringed was the monopoly of the East India Company, and as "an interloper," to use the phrase then current, the parson's son had proved himself to be a "desperate fellow"—an adventurer who was "cool in action, saw what to do and did it."

Baffled by his enterprise, the company invited "the interloper" to enter its service, and Thomas Pitt was sent out to India as President of Fort St. George in Madras, that outpost of Western civilization which—glacis, ditch, basement, and the ancient Protestant Church—remains to this day substantially unchanged. For ten years Thomas Pitt was known in Madras as "the Great President."

Among his innovations was a new method of sending remittances of value to London. The currency that he adopted was neither gold nor the equivalent of gold, but diamonds, and among his jewels there was one which was to achieve a world-wide fame. In the rough it weighed 410 carats, and cutting reduced the stone to 137 carats. It cost Governor Pitt the sum of £12,500, and there is a portrait of him which shows the gem, worn as an ornament in his hat.

As Regent of France, the Duke of Orleans purchased the stone for £135,000 or its equivalent in other gems and, in 1792, it was stolen from the Tuileries but soon recovered. In the Louvre there may still be seen this historic jewel, and it is, indeed, a strange reflection that a diamond acquired by the great-grandfather of William Pitt, the younger, should have flashed its light from the hilt of Napoleon Buonaparte's sword.

In *Vanity Fair* Thackeray's nabob, Joseph Sedley, was "a very stout puffy man, in buckskins and Hessian boots, with several immense neckcloths that rose almost to his nose, with a red striped waistcoat and an apple-green coat with steel buttons almost as large as crown pieces," who gave Cashmere shawls to his sister Amelia. Governor Pitt was the Anglo-Indian nabob *in excelsis*, and he invested his profits in politics, so conferring on his posterity two prime ministerships.

★

A mile and a half from the spire of Salisbury Cathedral there may be seen a large mound which carries one of the few derelict towns in England. A British camp, a Roman fort, a Saxon village, and a Norman city have successively occupied Old Sarum and disappeared. The hillock, almost untenanted, emerged as a rotten borough and returned two members to the House of Commons.

Governor Pitt had the shrewdness to purchase this and similar constituencies, and, as member for Old Sarum, he elected himself to Parliament. His son Robert inherited the father's political assets and Robert had two sons. The younger of them was William Pitt, Earl of Chatham and father of that William Pitt whose life concerns us.

By Norman tradition the aristocracy was vested in the ownership of land. To this day the title to a peerage includes a local name. It is not enough to be Viscount Haldane. It must be Viscount Haldane of Cloan.

But if the aristocracy persists it is because land has been allied with commerce. Like the Gladstones, the Pitts married into what we may call "the set." William Pitt's mother was Lady Hester, in her own right Countess Temple. His sister was married to the third Earl of Stanhope. It meant that he himself, his father, Lord Chatham, his uncle, George Grenville, his first cousin, Lord Grenville, and at a later date, his great-great-grand-nephew, Lord Rosebery, were associated—all five of them—in the office of Prime Minister. Of officers, minor to the prime ministership yet important, these "welded" families held their full share, and their record indicates—in Lord Rosebery's words, applied to the Temple family—"a disciplined and formidable force which lasted as a potent factor in politics for at least two generations."

It was George Grenville who by the Stamp Act lost the American Colonies. It was his brother-in-law, the Earl of Chatham, who was credited, at any rate, with winning India.

If the aristocracy accepted alliances by marriage with commerce, the reason was not only the cash. Aristocracy also needed the initiative which commerce develops. Doubtless there were periods of tranquillity when the son of a duke could do no great harm. But it did not follow that the son of a duke would be able to foil the intrigues of France and master the mariners of Holland. The first of Prime Ministers in the modern sense, Sir Robert Walpole lived to preserve peace. When war broke out he made the famous remark, "They are ringing their bells now. Soon they will be wringing their hands." The Whigs did not want to have to wage war.

The death of Walpole in 1745 and the accession of George III in 1760 tended to disintegrate the solidarity of the Whigs. What had held them together was the fear of a Stuart reaction. That fear was now at an end and the Court itself could afford to flirt with the Tories. A prolonged tenure of office, with a practice of corruption which was based on the axiom that every man has his price, had weakened successive administrations to an extent rapidly to be revealed.

In the year 1756, when the Prime Minister was the Duke of Newcastle, there began the Seven Years' War with France, and England was startled by news of a disaster. In the Mediterranean, she had held the island of Minorca— an island that loomed as large in her strategy as does the naval base at Malta in our own day. Minorca fell to the enemy.

The admiral who was held to be responsible for the calamity was John Byng. It was a piquant coincidence that he was the son of George Byng, Viscount Torrington, who, in the year 1704, had played his part in the capture of Gibraltar, which, indeed, was but one of a number of his gallant exploits in the Mediterranean Sea. The good fortune of the father did not mitigate the ill fortune of the son. Byng, the younger, acquitted of cowardice, was condemned to death for neglect of duty. The King refused a pardon and, on board the *Monarque* at Portsmouth, March 14, 1757, the disgraced admiral was shot, as Voltaire put it, "to encourage the others."

At the moment of humiliation there arose among the Whigs themselves a demand for a man who could win the war. The choice fell on William Pitt, the elder. "My Lord," said he to the Duke of Devonshire, "I am sure that I can save this country and that nobody else can." His view of his destiny was precisely that entertained in 1916—and at a crisis infinitely more serious—by David Lloyd George.

Why it should have been supposed that he could command victory is a question that it is not easy to answer. His only service in the army had been as a cornet and even this had not been active service. He could not steer a ship. He could not aim a gun. His only ammunition was the spoken word, and the spoken word did not carry a yard beyond the walls of a chamber already convinced on the main issue.

Nor was this all. From the days of his boyhood at Eton to

his final collapse in the House of Lords the elder Pitt was a martyr to the most virulent form of gout. It was a disease which confronted the patient with a dreadful dilemma. If he allowed it to run its course he suffered an agony of physical torture. But if he took a cure at Bath and restrained the malady by strong drugs he fell a victim to what can only be regarded as a derangement of intellect. He had to hold to a narrow course between a Scylla of suffering and a Charybdis of insanity. Sometimes he sacrificed the body. At other times it was the brain that had to pay the price.

It might be supposed that what the elder Pitt meant by saving England was defending England from danger. But England was in no danger. With the France of King Louis XV drifting rapidly from insolvency to revolution, it was possible for England to wage war for eleven weeks without any government at all. To the elder Pitt the salvation of England meant the conquest of Canada and the expulsion of the French from India.

★

It is indeed difficult at first sight to understand how it came about that a nation, apparently so sedate as it is revealed to us in the pages of *Cranford* or Jane Austen, was able to explode, as it were, into an empire wide as the world. The country was not then overcrowded, nor was there any physical need for emigration. The impulse was of the very spirit itself.

It is true that life was simple and restrained. But it was this very simplicity of restraint that led to a curious extravagance of fashion. The fact that an educated minority could not travel as we do, could not read the newspaper as we do, could not attend the places of entertainment as we do, meant that they could and, where there was money, did dress as we would not dream of dressing. A man was shaven, not on his chin alone but on his pate, and he wore a wig tied at the nape of his neck by a riband and powdered profusely. There were periods when a woman's hair was dressed so high over cushions and adorned with flowers, ships, and other erections of so lofty an altitude that she could not sit in her travelling chair with the lid closed, and had to wear her coiffure all night. Gambling and the duel were also an outlet for energies not fully employed.

This taste for finery and extravagance extended to troops. Coats might be ragged but they were red. Epaulettes might be tarnished but they were gold. Flags were the more honourable when tattered and torn by shot and shrapnel. The ideal of an army was to face the enemy as if on parade.

To Pitt, the elder, and his generation war was thus a game. To fight the French was as fashionable an occupation as to hunt the fox. In the army and the navy there were to be observed the same distinction between the Few and the Many which was so evident in society. The officer had to be a gentleman, and promotion from the ranks was unthinkable. But the risks of the officer were the risks of the men he commanded. Wolfe was shot down at Quebec; Moore at Corunna; Abercrombie in Egypt; Nelson at Trafalgar; Wellington was hit in Spain; Angelsey lost a leg at Waterloo. As for horses, the player at polo does not need an ampler reinforcement of mounts than did a general who fought a hotly contested engagement.

The elder Pitt was an actor. If he remained in seclusion for days at a time, one reason, so it was suspected, was his dislike of appearing before the footlights of Westminster except at his best. There were occasions when in his extravagance and passion for display he rivalled the Indian rajahs with whom his grandfather had struck such shrewd bargains. At the Castle Inn at Marlborough, to give one instance, he created an immense sensation by insisting that, during his presence, the waiters and the stableboys should wear his livery. It was with the spectacular panoply of war, the drama of it, that the imagination of this strange man was apt to be fascinated, and in his zeal for military display he shared an emotion with the common people who were dazzled by the glint of the sun on the helmet of a lifeguard. In the person of the elder Pitt the fervours of bellicosity, which at a later date were dignified by the name of jingoism, were splendidly embodied.

There was a different and a worthier sentiment which he was able to evoke. For many years he held the office of Paymaster of the Forces. It was an office considered to be lucrative and with good reason. On large balances credited to the paymaster he was permitted by custom to draw the interest for his private use. The elder Pitt did not hesitate to tolerate a rotten borough but, in that case, the property was private. He drew the line at the misuse of public funds, and his correctitude was so unusual as to create a sensation, especially in the City of London, where such virtues are appreciated.

When he held the subordinate position of paymaster the elder Pitt had opposed a system of subsidies to European allies of Great Britain. As Secretary of State, responsible for the war, he threw all such economy to the winds. On the recruiting and equipment of expeditions he lavished money which the nation, knowing his personal rectitude, was ready to provide. The weapons of war might be few, cannon loaded through the muzzle, flintlock muskets, bayonets, horse pistols, and the like. But with the ease of a spendthrift Pitt provided whatever was needed.

It is here that we are confronted by an astonishing situation. The various expeditions set sail and were lost to view. For months at a time not a word of their fate could reach London, whether by cable, by wireless, or any other means. Over the operations on land and sea Pitt had no more of an influence than had his footman. Yet when news of victory was received it was the elder Pitt who was the victor. Wolfe might die on the Heights of Abraham, but it was the Great Commoner who captured Quebec. It was his eloquence and not the humdrum heroism of Admirals Hawke and Boscawen that twice defeated the French Fleet in the Biscay. It was his well-turned sentences that arrested the progress of the French in Westphalia. Clive crushed Suraja Dowlah on the Hooghli, but it was the Great Commoner whose eagle eye subdued Bengal. Sir Eyre Coote might defeat the French forces at Wandewash, but it was the politician at home who established the power of England over the Carnatic. In the year 1759 the popularity of the elder Pitt transcended the bounds whether of logic or of justice. "One is forced," wrote

Horace Walpole, "to ask every morning what victory there is for fear of missing one."

★

It was in this most glorious year, 1759, that two boys were born whose lives will occupy our attention. The one was William Pitt, the younger; the other was his friend, William Wilberforce.

At that supreme moment when, as it seemed, the nation was awakened for the first time to the consciousness of an imperial destiny the popularity of the name of Pitt, the symbol at once of patriotism and of political purity, was unprecedented. But in the nature of things, no such fervour of enthusiasm could be expected to last. In the exuberance of victory there was a reason why the people should cheer the minister. Who other than he was there to receive their plaudits? But the mood of the nation changed. On the elder Pitt, disliked by King George III, there fell that kind of reaction which drove a Lloyd George, a Woodrow Wilson, and a Clemenceau into the background.

Indeed, it was the elder Pitt himself who committed political suicide. On resuming office, in 1766, he quitted that House of Commons which had been his realm. For reasons which may have been reasons of health he accepted the Earldom of Chatham and entered a House of Lords, small in numbers, conservative in temper, which in very truth was a lethal chamber for his fervid eloquence. "I am glad I am not the eldest son," remarked the younger Pitt, when he was little more than an infant. "I want to speak in the House of Commons like Papa."

During the boyhood of William Pitt, the younger, the Earl of Chatham played a great part as an individual in the politics of the period. But these were years when fame had arrived at its aftermath. Eagle-eyed, eccentric, and eloquent as he appeared to the world, the elder Pitt was to his family at once a tender husband and a solicitous father. Of the three sons, the eldest was designed for the army, and the youngest for the navy, but the second among the boys was dedicated to the law, and the law was intended to be, from the outset, no more than a stepping stone to Parliament. In letters to his wife Chatham referred to the favourite of his old age as "eager Mr. William," as "the philosopher," and his "counsellor." Indeed, the "sweet boy" himself was told that he was "the hope and comfort" of a father's life. "The fineness of William's mind," wrote the mother, "makes him enjoy with highest pleasure what would be above the reach of any other creature of his small age."

Between the elder Pitt and the younger Pitt there was this contrast. The one was the Elijah, calling down fire from heaven onto his country's reconstructed altar and, in a chariot of fire, ascending to the heaven which he had so often invoked. The other was the Elisha, clad in a father's mantle, endowed with his father's gift of eloquence, yet more than a dazzling dervish from the political desert, incomparably majestic yet irritably unaccountable. William Pitt, the younger, was genius in harness.

T HE details of the childhood of great men," writes Lord Rosebery, "are apt to be petty and cloying. Hero worship, extended to the bib and the porringer, is more likely to repel than to attract." Yet even Lord Rosebery, thus defying the dictates of education, has to admit that the childhood of the younger Pitt contains "the key to his career."

First, let us allude to his health. "My poor William is still ailing," was the complaint of his fondest of fathers, nor was there any question of sending "my poor William" to school. He had to be taught at home.

Of his proficiency there is no doubt. He seemed—so we are told by his tutor, the Rev. Edward Wilson—never to learn but merely to recollect. Not more fully acquainted in Latin and Greek than Pitt were Pope and Milton themselves. At sight he would translate half-a-dozen pages of Thucydides— this with but two or three errors, nor, as Lord Harrowby has testified, did he ever lose the facility. Waiting for the Prime Minister in his library—they were bent on a ride—he and Lord Grenville opened Thucydides and were floored by a passage. On entering the room Pitt immediately construed it.

It was in the morning that Pitt studied the classics with his tutor. During the evening his education was continued by a more inspiring—some would say awe-inspiring—method. The boy would join his father and would recite in English what he had been reading in the Latin and Greek. It was by one of the greatest orators of all time that, day by day, this lad was trained in the art, if it be an art, of public speech. In later years it was the sneer of the rivals who were confounded by his rhetoric that he was "taught by his dad on a stool."

His education in literature was not confined to the classics. Every day Lord Chatham instructed his children in the Bible, and to the Bible Pitt owed his fine sense of rhythm. An instance of the boy's accurate memory has been recorded. His tutor was expounding the Thirty-Nine Articles and, in support of them, quoted certain texts. Suddenly, Pitt stopped him. "I do not recollect," said he, "that passage and it doesn't sound like Scripture." The passage came from the Apocrypha, with which, at the time, he was unacquainted.

It was thus a perilous possibility that the boy, brought up in a world that seemed to circulate around his interests as an axis, might grow up to be a prig. That from the first he took himself seriously is evident from his juvenile contributions to literature, prose and poetry. "From the weather we have here," so he wrote at the mature age of eleven, "I flatter myself that the sun shone on your expedition, and that the views were enough enlivened thereby to prevent the drowsy Morpheus from taking the opportunity of the heat to diffuse his poppies upon the eyes of the travellers."

Of his verses, composed in Johnsonian style, a few lines
will suffice:

> *Ye sacred Imps of thund'ring Jove descend,*
> *Immortal Nine, to me propitious, bend*
> *Inclining downward from Parnassus' brow;*
> *To me, young Bard, some Heav'nly fire allow.*
> *From Aganippe's murmur strait repair,*
> *Assist my labours and attend my prayer.*
> *Inspire my verse. Of Poetry it sings.*
> *Thro'* HER, *the deeds of Heroes and of Kings*
> *Renoun'd in arms, with fame immortal stand.*
> *By* HER *no less, are spread thro' ev'ry land*
> *Those patriot names, who in their country's cause*
> *Triumphant fall for Liberty and Laws.*

It will be noted that the couplets are in no sense original
in idea but merely derivative. Sacred Imps, inclining a
propitious ear to the young Bard, are engaged in an employ-
ment which has been familiar to Parnassus for three thousand
years. To a student of Pope or Dryden such "click-clock
tintinnabulum of rhyme," as Cowper called it, should be
no more puzzling than the solution of an acrostic.

Pitt's education was thus, in a sense, negative. He did
not create ideas. He translated them. It is true that at about
the age of seven years, when his juvenile calligraphy was still
enclosed between parallel lines, he inscribed to his father a
Latin letter, signed:

> *Sum, mi charissime Pater,*
> *tibi devinctissimus,*
> *Gulielmus Pitt.*

But with serious composition in Greek or Latin, including what Lord Stanhope has called "the laborious inutilities of the ancient metres," he did not concern himself. In elegiacs, says the allusive Macaulay, he was outclassed by a Wellesley and in hexameters by a Canning.

With some asperity Macaulay complains that, as Prime Minister, Pitt omitted to patronize the arts and letters. Neither Porson as a scholar nor Gibbon as a historian nor Johnson as a lexicographer obtained a farthing from the public purse. To Pitt, literature, like linen or steel, was a commodity, the price of which must be fixed by the laws of supply and demand. Indeed, his own studies were strictly utilitarian in their objective. Like Woodrow Wilson, he regarded learning less as a means of life than as a weapon of power.

It is by a simile that the curriculum can best be appreciated. The gunfounders of the Renaissance, bred in the tradition of statuary, were ill satisfied unless their cannon were embossed with the lineaments of cherubs, saints, and angels. If Pitt mastered the available poetry of ancient Greece, including the obscurities of Lycophron's *Cassandra*, it was for some such reason. It was by tags from Virgil and Homer that discussion in the House of Commons was decorated. It was not what you said that alone was important. It was how you spoke. From the paternal instruction, Pitt emerged with a facility in the use of words which has never been surpassed. On any occasion and without hesitation he could utter sentences, sonorous, dignified, and precise, which captured and indeed charmed the ear. To resume our simile, the cannon, decorated on the exterior, was accurate to a hair's breadth in its aim.

To the Pitts, literature was merely the raw material of rhetoric. What they studied was style. The son disliked Johnson's, much preferring Robertson and Hume. Like his father, he greatly admired Lord Bolingbroke, and deplored the fact that, of his speeches in Parliament, scarcely a trace is extant.

★

Among the houses with which he was familiar there still remains the seat of the Stanhope family at Chevening, near Seven Oaks in Kent. Of the régime there maintained, Lady Hester Stanhope, Pitt's niece, has given one of her usual vivacious descriptions, how at festivals it required two men to carry the plum puddings and how the barons of beef were dressed in mediæval style. The footmen behaved like gentlemen ushers and their masters were treated with the etiquette due to ambassadors. A lady's maid was not allowed to wear white nor curls nor heels to her shoes beyond a certain height, and in her room Lady Stanhope kept scissors to cut the curls and a rod to whip the maid.

At the birth of a child in the village two guineas were paid to the mother and there was a gift of baby linen, a blanket, some posset, and two bottles of wine. In the hopping time the vagrants and Irish hoppers were locked up in a barn by themselves and so kept in quarantine. Every week 1,000 pieces of linen were washed, and the wash-house had four different stone troughs from which the linen was handed piece by piece, by the washerwomen, from the scalder to the rinser. In the laundry a false ceiling, let down and raised by pulleys, served to air the linen after it was ironed. There was a mangle to get up the table linen, towels, etc., and three stoves for drying on wet days. The tablecloths were of the finest damask, covered with patterns of exquisite workmanship. At set periods of the year, pedlers and merchants from Glasgow and Dunstable and other places passed with their goods. The housekeeper's room was surrounded with presses and closets, where were arranged stores and linen in the nicest order. An ox was killed every week and a sheep every day.

At what appears to us to have been the early age of fourteen years "the long lank stripling" called William Pitt was considered to be ready for Pembroke College, Cambridge. It is significant that, on entering the university, he was accompanied by a nurse, Mrs. Sparry, the housekeeper at his father's residence, Burton Pynsent in Somerset. He was taken so seriously ill that four days were required to get him back to London, and he was put in charge of a certain Dr. Addington, of whom, with his son, we shall hear later. Addington told the boy to go early to bed, to ride daily on a horse, and to be careful of his diet. He also prescribed port wine, and hence it was that throughout his career Pitt was sustained by and was able to sustain not one but more than one bottle of this stimulant daily—an allowance that, beyond doubt, cost him many years of his life. A Victorian Prime Minister was asked how it was that statesmen, so inspired, managed to command a great legislative assembly. "You must remember," so he is reported to have replied, "that others may have been in the same condition." That Pitt's health began to improve is undeniable. Whether the improvement was due to his doses or not will always be a matter of alcoholic argument.

In the University of Cambridge there is a School of Mathematics dignified by the name Tripos and led by Wranglers, of whom the Senior Wrangler enjoys the fame that properly belongs to a champion, either athletic, mental, or physical. In 1772 the honour fell to George Pretyman, born at Bury St. Edmunds in 1750 and thus Pitt's senior by about ten years. He it was who acted as "governor" or tutor to the distinguished undergraduate.

Pretyman tells us that, during his earlier years at Cambridge, Pitt was seldom out of his rooms. "I never knew him spend an idle day," writes the tutor, "nor did he ever fail to attend me at the appointed hour." Unfortunately, Pitt's attainments were never tested by a competitive examination. The sons of peers enjoyed the privilege of taking the degree of Master of Arts without any such ordeal, and at the age of seventeen years, Chatham's son claimed a formal graduation.

Alternately reading classics and mathematics, it was by mathematics that Pitt appears to have been fascinated. The Moderators were delighted by the facility with which Lord Chatham's son could solve problems. In later life Pitt alluded frequently to the value of this instrument of education. But his tutor, though himself a mathematician, restrained within customary limits a study, which, if unduly developed, would have been so unbecoming to a prospective statesman. Into the vulgar mysteries Pitt was admitted with due caution, and when parting from Pretyman in his capacity of tutor, the hope that Pitt expressed was that, during a summer, they might find time again to read a book so elementary as Newton's *Principia*. That he had an excellent head for figures is indicated by the remark that he was the only Chancellor of the Exchequer who could introduce the budget of the year without dependence on notes. It was an ability that, in later years, was to be rivalled by a successor, Andrew Bonar Law, whose habit of memorizing a speech was no less extraordinary.

★

For his tutor Pitt never lost the respect which, as a boy, he had paid to the older man. Indeed, as Prime Minister, he who could face without flinching a House of Commons led by Charles James Fox, retired after the fray and took counsel—we might almost say refuge—with his authoritative friend. Pretyman was appointed Canon of Westminster and acted as Pitt's private secretary, the keeper of his conscience.

In 1803 Pretyman inherited a large estate and changed his name to Tomline. He was elevated successively to be Bishop of Lincoln and Bishop of Winchester. If, indeed, Pitt had had his way, Tomline would have been an Archbishop of Canterbury.

It was King George III who robbed the bishop of the Primacy. Hearing that Pitt intended this recommendation, His Majesty determined that his own candidate should have the preference. At eight o'clock one morning Dr. Manners

Sutton, Lord Bishop of Norwich, happened to be indulging in his bath. He was told that a gentleman was downstairs who insisted on seeing him. He sent a message that the gentleman must go away, but despite the message the gentleman refused to leave. Clad in his bathrobe, the bishop descended the stairs and was greatly astounded to see his sovereign, who, with the butler and housemaid for witnesses, there and then appointed the perturbed prelate to the chair of St. Augustine. In private, Pitt referred to the artifice as "a scurvy trick." But in the royal presence he was able, none the less, to smile and congratulate His Majesty on the wisdom of his choice. In the *Rolliad*, Tomline is satirized as

> *Prim preacher, prince of priests and prince's priest,*
> *Pembroke's pale pride, in Pitt's præcordia placed.*

It was this prelate who honoured his pupil, his friend, and his patron with what Macaulay called "the worst biographical work of its size in the world." The work consists largely of letters, speeches, and extracts from the *Annual Registers*, and is thus the product—to quote the *Edinburgh Review*— less of His Lordship's pen than of "His Lordship's sharp and faithful scissors." Lord Rosebery thinks "there are worse books" but shrewdly observes that it had become the fashion for private secretaries to indulge in memoirs, not always with welcome results. Over Canning, as Greville tells us, Stapleton caused no end of worry. On Napoleon, despite Lord Rosebery's suggestion to the contrary, Bourrienne, as we think, achieved a respectable success.

★

Of friends at Cambridge, prior to his graduation, Pitt had few. Once a day he dined in hall. Twice a day he attended chapel. For the rest of his time he was usually to be found with Pretyman.

Pitt's residence at the university continued for nearly seven years. Yet, in our sense of the words, he could not be called a typical Cambridge man. He was a boy to whom the competition of the classroom was unknown. Remote from his experience, moreover, were the dust and heat of athletics. His only cricket was a hexameter, and his only football, an ablative absolute. Not once was he bowled out first ball. Not once was he rolled in the mud. Not once was he sworn at from the towpath. Not once had he to race for a train. Not once did he meet his superior. The fact, the only fact that impressed his contemporaries was that young Pitt excelled in the classics. That was the recognized standard of excellence, and the circumstance that others excelled young Pitt, let us say, in music or science was immaterial.

The qualities of conceit and pride are frequently confounded. A man who is conceited seeks from others a recognition of his own achievements. There was no such conceit in William Pitt. His was the deeper emotion which is indifferent to what others may think. He guarded his own worth as a shrine is guarded by a priest, asserting nothing on his own behalf, but assuming everything. Putting on himself so high a valuation, he compelled the world to accept it.

After his graduation and with his health restored, Pitt began to emerge from his shell. His manners, now as later, were as gentle and unassuming in private life as they were, or could become, haughty in public. His wit was playful. At repartee, he was ready. Yet he was able to avoid giving pain to others or causing offence. He began to meet other men. He made friendships, none the less important because they were few. He was standing at last on the threshold of his destined stage.

On every occasion that was possible to him, and especially when his father was to speak, young Pitt would listen to debates in Parliament. It was in January, 1775, that first he heard his father and the subject was an appeal for conciliation with the American Colonists. Among that audience there was, it will be remembered, Benjamin Franklin. So, on a number of occasions, we may see Pitt on the steps of the throne in the House of Lords, and there it was that he was introduced to his senior by eleven years, Charles James Fox, even then unsurpassed in debate and scarcely surpassed in oratory. It is from Fox himself that we learn how, as he listened, Pitt would turn to him and remark, "But surely, Mr. Fox, that might be met thus," or "Yes; but he lays himself open to this retort." Already the youth was measuring his wits against the Parliamentarians of his time.

On the 7th of April, 1778, Chatham intended to deliver a speech in the House of Lords. "Burning in the feet" had reduced him to a mere wreck of his former splendid presence. His son, William, and his son-in-law, Lord Mahon, afterward Earl Stanhope, supported the old man as he tottered into the Chamber. It was against the final secession of the American Colonies that he raised his voice, but when the moment came for him to reply he fell back stricken, his son and son-in-law aided by peers carried him forth, he was removed to his home at Hayes, and on the 11th of May he died. In an empty England there was now but one William Pitt, and he not yet of age.

All parties were associated in the honours showered upon the memory of Lord Chatham. The House of Commons granted £20,000 for the payment of his debts and added an annuity of £4,000 to his earldom. Unanimously, there were voted a public funeral and a monument. From the obsequies, the succeeding earl was absent and it was William Pitt, a slim, lonely youth, who as chief mourner followed his father's body into Westminster Abbey. The spacious and splendid comradeship was only interrupted. The day was to come when the death that divided this father and this son would again unite them within those splendid aisles.

BY THE law and custom of primogeniture the titles and the emoluments of an ennobled family were reserved for the eldest son. The generous provision voted by Parliament to the Pitts left William, therefore, as a mere cadet of the house, with an income of no more than £300 a year. By the eternal want of pence he was thus afflicted, and we find him writing to his mother for drafts of fifty pounds, or sixty pounds, which would enable him to meet "the current expenses of this quarter."

Hence, he had to undertake a profession, and, as arranged by his father, it was to the law that he applied himself. At Lincoln's Inn he kept his terms, investing £1,100 in the purchase of his chambers, "a frightful sum," as he called it, which was advanced by his uncle, Lord Temple.

A career at the bar, had it been prolonged, could scarcely have failed to break down the proud reserve with which Pitt came to regard mankind. Barristers are dependent on solicitors for their briefs, on juries for their verdicts, and on judges for their points of law. The profession consists of pleading, and often of pleading before minds inferior to the

33

mind of the advocate who presents the plea. Pitt's apprentice-ship was merely a passing phase.

Still, it is worth a word. That it was of interest to the bench to see and to hear a son of Lord Chatham may be assumed. Yet the son of Lord Chatham had to set his foot on the lowest rung of the ladder. For seven days his fidelity to obligation held him at the Court of Common Pleas with a junior brief to which was attached a fee of one guinea.

When work came to him it need hardly be said that he did it well. Speaking on a motion for habeas corpus in a case of murder, he won the admiration of the bar and the praise of Lord Mansfield. On an election petition "Mr. Pitt's observations had great weight" with the judge Mr. Baron Perryn. There is evidence, too, that he could cross-examine.

What, however, created the deepest impression on his brethren of the bar was a speech that he made at a mock debate held at the Crown and Anchor Tavern on an occasion when the Western Circuit Club, to which he belonged, was dissolved. For Pitt, that debate was what speaking at the Oxford and Cambridge Union societies was for the statesmen of the Nineteenth Century. The subject was trivial. The audience was merely ephemeral. But he put forth all his powers and it was recognized that here was the gift which is prized by deliberative assemblies.

It was to no court of law that his eyes were directed. His destination was the High Court of Parliament itself. To enter the House of Commons was his absorbing ambition, and it might be supposed that, for a man bearing the name of Pitt, this ambition would have been immediately gratified. But it was not so. The name was indeed a noble inheritance. But to the name there was attached a host of memories, not only glorious but embittered. Pitt inherited at once the prestige of the Great Commoner and his controversies.

To fight those old battles over again would be to write the life not of the younger Pitt but of the elder. Yet it is essential that we appreciate broadly the personal issues which, implied rather than expressed, the younger Pitt had to face. The year 1779, which we are considering, was the twentieth, only the twentieth, since the accession of King George III. It was into a drama still proceeding that Pitt was about to plunge. And what was the drama?

On assuming the throne the King found a Whig Party which had drifted into a situation not unlike that of the Republican Party of the United States in the early years of the Twentieth Century. Both parties had been born of a national emergency. Both parties had been accustomed to dominance. In both parties there was "the old gang." In both parties there were admitted abuses. In both parties there was a progressive movement, and both the progressive movements were embodied in powerful personalities—the elder Pitt in the one case, and in the other case, Theodore Roosevelt.

The Progressives, some would call them the repentant Whigs, were resolutely opposed to corruption, to the interference of King George III in politics, to restraints on the liberty of the press, and, last but not least, to a policy imposing taxation on the American Colonies. Macaulay tells us confidently that they were "worthy to have charged by the side of Hampden at Chalgrove or to have exchanged the last embrace with Russell in Lincoln's Inn Fields." Assuredly that was true of the elder Pitt.

But he was, first and foremost, an orator. His speeches were politics, declaimed as opera, and like a great singer, he was the creature of temperament. To seek an explanation for his whims and fancies, and especially an explanation in writing, would be to falsify his entire character. To no opinion but his own was he answerable. No one could share his feelings. But there was one excess of caprice that affected the career of his son.

Largely as the result of the eloquence of which the elder Pitt was so consummate a master, the Progressive Whigs were called to power. The date was 1776 and the younger Pitt was seventeen years old. The Prime Minister was the Marquis of Rockingham. He was a statesman who made no pretense of genius. But he was honest. He discouraged the practice of bribing members of Parliament. He repealed the Stamp Act imposed on the American Colonies. It is significant that he should have selected as his private secretary a young Irishman called Edmund Burke.

On any terms the Great Commoner might have entered the administration of Lord Rockingham. He insisted on standing aloof. Indeed, he went further. In the Cabinet, the least desirable of the ministers was the Duke of Grafton, a near descendant of King Charles II. "Let me return to your Grace," wrote Junius. "You are the pillow upon which I am determined to rest all my resentments." The concise *Chambers* describes him adequately as "indolent, vacillating, obstinate, and immoral."

The Duke of Grafton resigned, broke up the Rockingham government, was appointed Prime Minister, and the elder Pitt, as Earl of Chatham, agreed to serve under him. It is true that the chief minister was really Chatham. But why had he preferred a Grafton to a Rockingham?

In the game of politics, however keenly played, there must be rules or the game becomes a mere scramble. This chicanery was disastrous. After a brief experience of Lord Chatham's scarcely credible eccentricities when in office the country resigned itself to twelve years of royalism, represented by Lord North; and in 1779, when the younger Pitt was seeking a constituency, Lord North was still in power. The Whigs were still paying the penalty.

★

During the whole of this long sojourn in the wilderness Lord Rockingham remained the leader of the Opposition. It was thus to the very statesman whose administration had been destroyed by Chatham that the son of Chatham applied for a constituency. The letter was dated July 19, 1779. The reply, dated August 7th, was what Pitt might have expected:

I am so circumstanced from the knowledge I have of several persons who may be candidates, and who indeed are expected to be so, that it makes it impossible for me in this instance to show the attention to your wishes which your own as well as the great merits of your family entitle you to.

The cold courtesy of the rebuff was not only admirable but, in a hereditary sense, richly deserved. At the same time, its

result must not be underestimated. If Pitt had entered
Parliament as an official protégé of the Whigs, his immediate
leader in the House of Commons would have been Charles
James Fox, and his career might have been far different
from what it became. Lord Rockingham's letter meant
that Pitt had to start as a free lance.

It was to the University of Cambridge that he next submitted himself for election. Neither his name nor his abilities
sufficed to break down the barriers raised by others who stood
ahead of him. On this occasion he came out bottom of the
poll. It was a humiliation which he did not forget.

He discovered that he had nothing to depend upon except
whatever was left, in an ungrateful world, of personal affection for his father. In that glorious year, 1759, when Pitt
himself was born, the Commander-in-Chief of the British
Forces in Germany was the Marquis of Granby. Later Lord
Granby was appointed Master General of Ordnance and
Commander-in-Chief of the Army as a whole. "Brave" and
"lamented" are the adjectives bestowed by Lord Stanhope
on this "friend and follower of Chatham," but Junius was
less complimentary. "If," wrote he, "it be generosity to
accumulate in his own person and family a number of
lucrative appointments; to provide at the public expense,
for every creature that bears the name of Manners and,
neglecting the merit and services of the rest of the army, to
heap promotions upon his favourites and dependents, the
present commander-in-chief is the most generous man alive."
Those were the days when the press could still ignore the
shackles known as the law of libel.

It was Lord Granby's son who, five years senior to Pitt, became his warm friend at Cambridge. In 1779 he succeeded his grandfather as Duke of Rutland and expressed concern at Pitt's failure to arrive at Westminster. Among the political allies of the young duke was Sir James Lowther of Westmoreland, whose family is to-day represented by the Earl of Lonsdale. It is a family of magnificent tastes, of lavish hospitality, of immense political influence. It was Mr. Speaker Lowther who, in the Twentieth Century, presided over the Parliaments where Mr. Asquith and Mr. Balfour were the friendly rivals.

Sir James Lowther had also been among Pitt's contemporaries at Cambridge, and wielding what used to be called his "cat-o'-nine tails," he could be of great assistance to a rising politician. For by this expressive phrase was meant nine close boroughs, returning his nominees to Parliament. It was Appleby that he offered to Pitt and, in a letter from Pitt to his mother, Pitt explained what precisely were the terms:

Lincoln's Inn, Thursday night, Nov., 1780.

My dear Mother,

I can now inform you that I have seen Sir James Lowther, who has repeated to me the offer he had before made, and in the handsomest manner. Judging from my father's principles, he concludes that mine would be agreeable to his own, and on that ground—to me of all others the most agreeable—to bring me in. No kind of condition was mentioned, but that if ever our lines of conduct should become opposite, I should give him an opportunity of choosing another person. On such liberal terms I could certainly not hesitate to accept the proposal, than which nothing could be in any respect more agreeable. Appleby is the place I am to represent, and the election will be made (probably in a week or ten days) without my having any trouble, or even visiting my constituents. I shall be in time to be spectator and auditor *at least* of the important scene after the holidays. I would not defer confirming to you this intelligence, which I believe you will not be sorry to hear.

I am, my dear Mother, &c.,
W. Pitt.

This was what was meant in Pitt's own words by a member enjoying "independence." It was independence not of a patron but of the people. About the procedure there was entire candour. Sir James Lowther, wrote Pitt, "had to settle an election at Haslemere before he went into the North." But when he went North, he settled the election at Appleby. Pitt thus entered Parliament as the acknowledged nominee of a great ruling family and without so much as a glimpse of the electors who were supposed to have returned him as their representative. On January 23, 1781, he took his seat. On the twenty-fifth anniversary of that date, January 23, 1806, he died.

★

In the year 1781 the House of Commons consisted of 558 members. Like the House of Lords, it was included in that Palace of Westminster which, save for the famous hall, certain cloisters, and a few other fragments, was swept away in 1833 by fire. The chamber was oblong—a mere box— with narrow galleries at the side, but none at the ends, and a plain roof. Behind the Speaker's chair there were windows, which, however, could be of little use during the climaxes of debate in the small hours of the morning. What lighted the House, what added to its temperature, was a vast chandelier hung from the ceiling.

In this chamber there was little, if any, provision for the public, and reporters, such as there were, could be asked to "withdraw," like other "strangers." Parliament was an intimate affair. Members, knowing one another, did not need to know anyone else. With their hair powdered, and wearing elaborate waistcoats, knee-breeches, and buckled shoes, they sat in serried ranks, as if debate were a levée. They did not applaud, for applause is of the hands. But the collective voice of the Commons—Aye. . . . No. . . . Hear! Hear! . . . Laughter. . . . Oh! Oh!—was an instrument of political music as varied and as expressive as oratory itself. Most eloquent of all were the silences. Grief, blame, surprise —they would produce, all of them, a stillness which was formidable indeed to the member whose duty it was, amid that stillness, to say his say.

When informed that *Punch* is not as good as it used to be, the editors of that vivacious journal replied that "it never was." Like *Punch*, every great British institution flourishes by chronic deterioration. The House of Commons in which a Snowden and a Churchill introduce budgets yearns for the great days of Gladstone and Disraeli. In those days Gladstone and Disraeli, no less humble, looked back longingly on the great days of Peel and Canning. Need it be added that

Peel and Canning were the unworthy successors of Fox and Pitt?

Compared with the House of Commons, now sitting at Westminster, the House which Pitt entered and conquered was but a rudimentary legislature. Owing to what Lord Brougham has called a "scanty political acquirement," there were few members who spoke or were desired to speak, and few were the topics that were raised for discussion. It was possible for law-abiding crofters in Scotland to have their homes burned over their heads, for the peasantry of England to see their common lands enclosed, for the owners of mines to chain children to the wagons in their coalpits, for the press gang to seize citizens in the streets and ship them to the ends of the earth, for towns to be built with homes which even as cells of a prison would have been a disgrace, and for debtors to languish out their lives in jail, to say nothing of thieves to be hanged and girls to be flogged, without a ripple, or scarcely a ripple, of comment disturbing the bibulous vivacity of the Parliament of Pitt and Fox. For the aged, for the sick, for the babe unborn, for the mothers of the nation, for education, for the unemployed, for the injured by accident—the Parliament of the Eighteenth Century did not even pause to disclaim responsibility. Such obligations on a legislature lay outside a limited if acute intelligence, and even the raiding of Africa for slaves, though debated, was allowed to continue.

Indeed, over the great issue that had to be discussed, the rebellion of the American Colonies, the House, though stirred, failed. It was a failure that was felt first in New England. But in due course old England also, suffering from the same inefficiency, was to be brought to the verge of revolution.

★

There was, however, one function, distinct from the legislature, that the House did discharge. If its measures were few and inadequate, it did at least select men—and by a process of which the severity is seldom appreciated. On the one hand, the House was "the best club in Europe." On the other hand, it was "a talking shop" or debating society. A member was thus estimated according to his personality as seen from every point of view. His demeanour in the lobby, his habits, his conversation—all these were included in the account. He might be wholly silent in debate yet exercise an influence by means of what he was in himself.

We are able to reconstruct the very aspect of the parties with which William Pitt had to deal. To the right of Mr. Speaker sat the government and they on whose support as a rule the government could rely. To the left of the chair there were to be found all who, for whatever reason and under whatever name, formed an opposition.

In these days a visitor to the House of Commons during questions is impressed by the appearance of a ministerial bench, greatly prolonged since the time of Pitt, yet crowded to the very gangway with a vast miscellany of ministers, eminent and obscure, hopeful of the future, disappointed with the past, secretaries, under secretaries, whips, and even a lady. But in 1780 a government as presented in the House of Commons was little more than a one-man show, and the government that Pitt addressed may be summed up in the personality of Lord North.

No man—so it may be safely said—who, like Lord North, holds the office of Prime Minister for a period of twelve years, can be devoid of ability. Indeed, the ability of Lord North, as a Parliamentarian, ranks high. He was excellently educated. In the forms of the House he was perfectly instructed, and to the feelings of the House he was wholly responsive. Not only was he cool, courteous, and courageous. He had humour. Blessed with the invaluable gift of slumber on the front bench, he was not the less but rather the more witty when awakened.

Addressing the House, no member likes to see the Prime Minister asleep, and, at times, there were protests. On such an occasion Lord North observed how very hard it was that he should be grudged so very natural a release from considerable suffering; but, as if recollecting himself, added that it was somewhat unjust in the gentleman to complain of him for taking the remedy which he had himself been considerate enough to administer. If an irate member demanded his head on a charger he would agree blandly to surrender it, but on condition that he did not have to accept the honourable member's head in exchange.

Lord North was opposed by two men much more eloquent than he, much more illustrious, yet for the moment much less influential. The older of these men, now over fifty, was Edmund Burke. To say that his effect on the House at this date was negligible would be impious. It was still great and, as we shall see, it was to become still greater. But it was the influence of the written, not the spoken, word. Burke had become "the dinner bell of the House of Commons"—too eloquent with the pen to be persuasive with the tongue.

It was Charles James Fox, then in his thirty-first year, who led the opposition. Fox was the son of Henry, the first Lord Holland, and during the earlier Nineteenth Century his memory was cherished at Holland House as a sacred cult. That he was utterly lovable is due in part to the fact that, whereas he had learned his vices from his father, his virtues were his own. On the one hand, he was a gambler, a bankrupt, and a rake. On the other hand, he was a scholar, a gentleman, a friend of the oppressed, a soldier of peace, and an upholder of liberty whether of the white man in his colony or the black man in his compound.

It is customary to describe Fox as the founder of British Liberalism. More accurate is it to say that, like the curate's egg, his Liberalism was good in parts. Fox was descended from the ducal House of Richmond. In his veins there flowed the warm blood of the Merrie Monarch. His very names, Charles and James, reminded him that he was a Stuart. Half royal and half radical, he frolicked with the Prince of Wales and was fervent for Robespierre.

We see this strange man in the House, massive, corpulent, overwhelming, a man who, after a night of exhausting dissipation, with the bailiffs claiming his furniture, could elaborate an ample argument on a great constitutional issue and evoke thunders of cheering by his passionate, yet usually effective, periods. As his mind strained under the intensity of his thought, a voice that could be soft and persuasive would rise to a note almost strident, yet the more compelling of attention.

The issue that divided Lord North from Fox and Burke was an issue on the merits of which the three of them were agreed. Not one of the three was a fool. Not one was a knave. All of them knew that the treatment of the American Colonies by Great Britain was fatuous. Where they parted company was in the application of this wisdom. Fox and Burke went frankly into opposition and spoke their minds. Lord North, clad in the gratitude of George III, as in a shirt of Nessus, retained office on condition that he enforce a policy which he knew to be suicidal. With pathetic insistence, he entreated his sovereign to release him. The sovereign only drew the gratitude yet more closely around his victim. It was the certainty that Lord North, by his acquiescence in the royal folly, was driving the British Empire to disruption that stirred Fox and Burke to paroxysms of denunciation.

★

Into this atmosphere of fierce acrimony, yet of keen and daily observation, the two young men, Pitt and Wilberforce, born the same year, and both educated at Cambridge, were plunged. Slim and clean-shaven, their very youth rendered them at once conspicuous; their manners and their dress emphasized the sensation. It was not only for Fox that "the town" was a synonym for indulgence. There was the Prince of Wales and his entourage, openly defying the proprieties. That two young men should appear on the scene, of an age when to-day they would be at college, and should avoid the customary excesses, evoked a smile.

It is true that the Puritanism of Wilberforce was not yet fully developed.

Indeed, he and Pitt did not hesitate to enjoy the reasonable pleasures and even the gaieties of an amusing period. "You will have the goodness," so Pitt wrote his mother on February 11, 1779, "to excuse the haste of a letter written on my way to the opera." Again:

> Nerot's Hotel, Wednesday night (1779)
> I have heard no news of any kind. James is gone with my sisters to the ball as a professed dancer, which stands in the place of an invitation; a character which I do not assume, and have therefore stayed away.

We read of "a ticket for the Duchess of Bolton's," and this:

> Grafton Street, April 4, 1780.
> Last night was the masquerade, the pompous promises of which the newspapers must have carried to Burton. Harriot went with Lady Williams to Mrs. Weddel's (who is, I believe, a sister of Lady Rockingham's) to see masks. She was very much pleased with it, principally, I fancy, because it was the first thing of the kind she has seen. I was there as well as at a much more numerous assemblage at a magnificent Mr. Broadhead's, to which *some few* ladies did not like to go, from little histories relative to the lady of the house. These did not prevent its being the most crowded place I ever was in. The company I was not conservant enough in masks to judge of. I concluded my evening at the Pantheon, which I had never seen illuminated, and which is really a glorious scene. In other respects, as I had hardly the pleasure of plaguing or being

plagued by anybody, I was heartily tired of my domino before it was over.

A number of the young men, including Pitt and Wilberforce, formed a club of their own called Goosetree's, from the name of their host in Pall Mall. Of Pitt's behaviour at this resort we have word from Wilberforce:

He was the wittiest man I ever knew, and, what was quite peculiar to himself, had at all times his wit under entire control. Others appeared struck by the unwonted association of brilliant images; but every possible combination of ideas was present to his mind, and he could at once produce whatever he desired. I was one of those who met to spend an evening in memory of Shakespeare at the Boar's Head in Eastcheap. Many professed wits were present, but Pitt was the most amusing of the party, and the readiest and most apt in the required allusions.

That Pitt knew his Shakespeare is attested by other witnesses.

At Goosetree's, as at other clubs, the peril was play. Even Wilberforce, when he went to Boodle's, won twenty-five guineas the first day from the Duke of Norfolk, and more than once lost a hundred pounds at the faro table. The statement is that he interrupted the practice, not because of what he lost but because he was pained at others losing to him. Anyway, he gave it up, as did Pitt. And wisely. Wilberforce tells us of the "intense earnestness" which Pitt displayed when joining in these games of chance, and adds, "he perceived their fascination and soon after suddenly abandoned them forever."

Not less rigid was their view of another indulgence. To the end of his life Pitt was a celibate of the strictest sincerity. Peter Pindar ridiculed an undergraduate virtue which repelled the flower girls in Cambridge "who came fresh from the country, and who only endeavoured to sell to the young gentlemen their roses and lilies." The House of Commons suggested that, as Chancellor of the Exchequer, Pitt should flirt with a few maidservants instead of taxing all of them.

Pitt and Wilberforce thus appeared to be, as indeed they were, paragons of virtue. Over their care for conduct cynics might sneer. But even the cynic could not but agree that, in public life, there is no factor so potent as personal character. It is an argument to which, in the nature of things, there can be no reply. Over William Pitt the House began to exhibit an impatient curiosity. If Chatham's son so behaved, how would Chatham's son speak?

This is, we take it, the explanation of the unusual circumstances in which, when the moment came, Pitt had to intervene in debate. In the House of Commons the new member is given one chance. At whatever hour he rises, it is customary, for any minister, however important, to give way to him. To Pitt, without doubt, that courtesy would have been extended.

What happened, however, was far other than this. On February 26, 1781, the House was debating Burke's Bill for Economical Reform. Mr. Byng, member for Middlesex, urged the young member for Appleby to reply and appears to have understood that he was prepared so to do. Pitt, however, had decided in his mind not to take such a chance and did not realize that Mr. Byng had told the friends around him to expect his intervention. When, therefore, the previous speaker, Lord Nugent, sat down, the member for Appleby, to his surprise, was assailed by cries of "Mr. Pitt! Mr. Pitt!" It followed as a matter of course that no other member rose to continue the debate. Every eye was thus directed to Pitt alone. He had to accept what was the challenge of destiny.

A tall, slim man rose. Not by a gesture, not by a hesitation, did he betray what he must have felt. At once there was revealed in him that "Parliamentary manner" which Mr. Gladstone declared to be perfect in Sir Edward Grey. In Grey, as in Pitt, it was a manner inborn. After all, Pitt belonged to the fourth generation of fathers and sons who made the House of Commons their home. To him, the House was as familiar as his fireside.

To this perfect poise there was added a voice, clear and musical, to which, whatever he said, it was a delight to listen. The speech aroused the deeper astonishment because it was delivered *ex tempore*. The sentences were accurately constructed. The phrases were precise. The argument was to the point. From that moment, Pitt took his place among the greatest who have ever addressed the chair.

What Pitt wrote to his mother about the speech was as follows:

Tuesday night, Feb. 27, 1781.

MY DEAR MOTHER,

. . . I know you will have learned that I heard my own voice yesterday, and the account you have had would be in all respects better than any I can give if it had not come from too partial a

friend. All I can say is that I was able to execute in some measure
what I intended, and that I have at least every reason to be happy
beyond measure in the reception I met with. You will, I dare say,
wish to know more particulars than I fear I shall be able to tell
you, but in the meantime you will, I am sure, feel somewhat the
same pleasure that I do in the encouragement, however unmerited,
which has attended my first attempt.

"The reception" accorded to the maiden effort must have
meant a loud and prolonged cheering, again and again renewed. In such cheers, politics are for the moment obliterated.
The House of Commons, as a House, welcomes an addition
to its historic yet ever-growing prestige.

Lord North was the leader of Pitt's political opponents.
He said at once that Pitt had delivered the best first speech
that he had ever heard. When someone said to Burke that
here was "a chip of the old block," Burke exclaimed, "He
is not a chip of the old block: he is the old block itself."

But what the House noticed with an especial attention was
the response of Charles James Fox. Here were two men, both
young, one very young, who belonged to the same political
faith. They were comrades but, because they were comrades,
they were also or might be rivals.

★

There is an anecdote which, dated earlier, we have reserved
for this place because it reveals the atmosphere of vigilance
over the prospects of their youngsters in which the political
families lived and moved and had their being. The authority
for the story is the Duchess of Leinster, sister to the first
Lady Holland and aunt to Charles James Fox. It seems that,

on one occasion, Lady Holland remonstrated with her husband on the excessive indulgence with which he brought up his children, and Charles James Fox in particular. "I have been this morning with Lady Hester Pitt [Lady Chatham]," said she, "and there is little William Pitt, not eight years old, and really the cleverest child I ever saw; and brought up so strictly and proper in his behaviour that, mark my words, that little boy will be a thorn in Charles' side as long as he lives." The mother of Fox meeting the mother of Pitt was able at a glance to foresee the probabilities of the future.

It was "little William Pitt, not eight years old," who had grown to be the William Pitt now sitting after his maiden speech with the House cheering him. Charles James Fox, anticipating no thorn in his side, hurries from his front bench to Pitt's less prominent seat and warmly congratulates him. Indeed, he loses no time in putting up the name of Pitt for election to Brooks's, the club of the day for a Whig politician.

Yet even as he grips Pitt by the hand there occurred one of those strange incidents, trivial in themselves, which yet seem to be omens. An old member, said to have been General Grant, joined the two young men. "Aye, Mr. Fox," said he, in a bustling fashion, "you are praising young Pitt for his speech. You may well do so; for, excepting yourself, there is no man in the House can make such another; and, old as I am, I expect and hope to hear you both battling it within these walls, as I have heard your fathers before you."

By this allusion to the dissensions among the Whigs of a previous generation, Fox was disconcerted. He stood silent.

But Pitt was equal to the occasion. "I have no doubt, General," said he, with a ready tact," you would like to attain the age of Methuselah."

For a young member who makes a pleasant impression in the House, it is a wise rule to let well alone. But here again Pitt had to be an exception. There were many who, like Wilberforce, recognized that Pitt, like his father, was "a ready-made orator" who had made a "famous speech." But it needed more than one speech to establish him as "the first man in the country." To hear Pitt a second time became the desire of a curious House. On May 31, 1781, the House was debating a financial matter and he rose. Fox rose at the same time but at once gave way. Pitt repeated his earlier success.

"Mr. Pitt," said a member to Fox, "seems to be one of the first men in Parliament." Without a touch of jealousy Fox replied, "He is so already." Indeed, as Pitt continued to establish himself in the House, Fox declared in debate that he could no longer lament the loss of Lord Chatham, for he was again living in his son, with all his virtues and all his talents. In the journal of Horace Walpole we have this entry:

December 14th, 1781. Another remarkable debate on Army Estimates, in which Pitt made a speech with amazing logical abilities, exceeding all he had hitherto shown, and making men doubt whether he would not prove superior even to Charles Fox.

Such a Parliamentary honeymoon could not last forever. In the usual course of debate Pitt began to give and to receive the usual cuts and thrusts. That real issues were discussed, is true enough. But in the main the argument was a fight for power, in which it was the personalities that counted, and it is the personalities in such debates that are so difficult to reproduce. In order to appreciate their flavour we have to know the men—it may be quite obscure men—who were part of the scene. We have to see the actual incident as it happened. We have to be ourselves included in it.

One illustration of these Parliamentary intimacies may be attempted. Pitt is speaking. Lord North is sitting on the front bench opposite. His colleague, Lord George Germaine, is sitting beside him, and talking to Lord North. Two days earlier Lord George Germaine had declared that he would never agree to sign a declaration of independence for the Colonies. Lord North was less resolute and Pitt was exposing these ministerial differences of opinion. A little placeman called Welbore Ellis, ridiculed by Junius, as Grildrig, inter-poses his head between the two statesmen. Pitt pauses. He looks at the scene in front of him. The House also looks."I will wait," says Pitt, "until the unanimity is a little better registered. I will wait until the Nestor of the Treasury [meaning Grildrig] has reconciled the difference between the Agamemnon [meaning Germaine] and the Achilles [mean-ing North] of the American War." The aptness of the allusion —its spontaneity, its acid humour was the talk of London. Not for nothing had Pitt conned his classics.

So for a brief interval William Pitt was a member, not holding office but earning his living at the bar. To those who saw him only on public occasions he was, to quote the *Rol-liad*, a man of dignity who, even at the tea table, would

Pass muffins in Committee of supply
And buttered toast amend by adding dry.

But in private he was wholly human. His colleague on
the Western Circuit, Mr. Jekyll, wrote:

Among lively men of his own time of life Mr. Pitt was always the
most lively in the many hours of leisure which occur to young un-
occupied men on a circuit, and joined all the little excursions to
Southampton, Weymouth, and such parties of amusement as were
habitually formed. He was extremely popular. His name and reputation of high acquirements at the university commanded the
attention of the seniors. His wit, his good humour, and joyous
manners endeared him to the younger part of the Bar.

In the summer of 1783 we find him frequently at the villa of
his friend Wilberforce, at Wimbledon, there expecting, as he
wrote, "an early meal of peas and strawberries." Indeed, he
could indulge in a practical joke. "One morning," writes
Wilberforce, "we found the fruits of Pitt's earlier rising in
the careful sowing of the garden beds with the fragments of
a dress-hat with which Ryder had over night come down
from the opera." Precisely what was the point of the jest
history has yet to elucidate.

IF EVER the field of politics merited the description of Matthew Arnold—

> . . . a darkling plain
> Swept with confused alarms of struggle and fight,
> Where ignorant armies clash by night—

it was in those days of the Eighties in the Eighteenth Century when Pitt and Burke, Fox and North, fought for whatever it was that they were fighting. The strife in the foreground, the intrigues behind the scenes, may be compared with the ancient labyrinth where Theseus himself would have been lost had he not been guided by a thread which led him to the inwardness of the maze. The thread, here to be followed, is twisted in two strands, distinct yet never apart. On the one hand, there was a genuine conflict over principle. On the other hand, there was a genuine struggle for power. There were the measures; more significant than the measures were the men.

It is with a man that we are here dealing. Amid the uproar he is to be seen, solitary, self-possessed, and central. As to his position, we need be in no doubt. He defined it himself, and in terms which could not have been more explicit.

To be precise, we find two declarations. In January, 1782, there was an attack, led by Fox, against the Admiralty, where the First Lord was the Earl of Sandwich. Pitt allied himself with Fox but with a significant reservation: "I support the motion," he said, "from motives of a public nature, and from those motives only. I am too young to be supposed capable of entertaining enmity against the Earl of Sandwich; and I trust that when I shall be less young it will appear that I have early determined, in the most solemn manner, never to allow any private and personal consideration whatever to influence my public conduct at any one moment of my life."

It was a promise, proud and even pompous, that he would forswear all the petty motives which were swirling around him and guide himself solely by what he conceived to be the national interest.

The second ultimatum issued by this young man, scarce entered into his twenties, was not general but specific, and the occasion on which it was promulgated, for that is not too strong a word, should be clearly understood.

When Pitt entered the House in January, 1781, Lord North was still in power. Debate was raging over the war with the Colonies, over reform, over the authority of the Crown, over scandals, and over personalities. The language was heated. The air was electric. But Lord North survived.

In November, 1781, news reached London which transcended argument. At Yorktown, Lord Cornwallis with his entire army had surrendered to General Washington. Lord North threw up his arms, paced up and down the room, and on this occasion at least, fully awake, cried, "O God, it

is all over!" There was nothing now to be done save to recog-
nize the independence of the United States. Over the manner of that hard necessity there continued to be infuriated
and futile discussions which every day weakened the government to whose folly the situation was attributable. In March,
1782, it was known that, at last, Lord North was on the point
of compelling the King to accept his resignation and that at
an early date politics, so long stagnant, must be thrown in-
evitably into the melting pot.

It was immediately in advance of North's retirement that
William Pitt, still a new member, interjected into one of his
speeches a placid but startling announcement:

For myself, I could not expect to form part of a new administration; but were my doing so more within my reach, I feel myself
bound to declare that I never would accept a subordinate position.

It was pleasantly, even modestly, expressed. But the
meaning was clear and clearly understood. It was that if
Pitt were to accept any office at all in the forthcoming government, it must be nothing less than a seat in the Cabinet.

Even in these days it would be regarded as unusual for a
young member, however great his success, to state his terms
thus candidly in a legislature of older men, every one of
whom, in a sense, is a rival of everyone else. But in the year
1782 the attitude of Pitt, deliberately confessed, was scarcely
credible. To-day the Cabinet consists of at least a score of
statesmen, amongst whom even the Air Minister may be
included. But the Cabinet to which Pitt, in effect, demanded
admittance, did not exceed seven, and of the seven, the great

peers must form a majority. Even Sheridan, even Burke, were never invited to that sacred table. Yet in no other seat of responsibility was William Pitt, the younger, willing to take his place.

That there were smiles over the egotism may be taken for granted. A test soon revealed that, whoever smiled, Pitt was serious. He had meant what he had said.

★

When Lord North resigned it was the Marquis of Rockingham who was asked by the King to form an administration. He who a dozen years before had been confronted by the aloofness of Pitt, the father, was now faced by the aloofness of Pitt, the son. To "the boy," as he was still called, there was offered the vice treasurership of Ireland. It was the office that, at one time, had been held by Lord Chatham himself. It was practically a sinecure and the salary was £5,000. To the astonishment of the House, Pitt refused the office and continued, a struggling barrister, with a private income of no more than a nominal amount. He stood to his terms.

The refusal was quixotic. But, none the less, it was shrewd. Pitt emerged once more into the limelight. Here was a poor man who could not be bought. Here was a proud man who would not be subordinate. Here was a young man too patient to be hurried. Here was a bold man, who declined to play for any save the highest stakes. Here was an independent man who would be held responsible for no decisions to which he was not himself actively a party.

The Opposition, thus returning to power, consisted broadly

of two groups. There were the orthodox Whigs led by Fox. There were the Whigs who had followed Chatham, and these were led by Lord Shelburne. The Cabinet of Lord Rockingham united these factions. Both Fox and Shelburne were included in the same administration.

But their association in office only accentuated the bitterness between them. On the one side we see Fox, hated at Court, eager for reform, temperamental, flagrantly dissolute, yet a genius. On the other side there lurked a statesman to whom Mr. Trevelyan applies the epithet, "mysterious."

★

Let us endeavour, as best we may, to identify this intriguer, as he was regarded, who slid through the jungle of politics like a snake in the grass. In the year 1623 there had been born at Romney, in Hampshire, a lad of enterprise called Henry Petty, the son of a clothier. He went to sea, studied under the Jesuits at Caen, also studied at Utrecht, Amsterdam, Leyden, Paris, and Oxford, where he taught astronomy. Appointed physician to the army in Ireland, he started iron works, lead mines, sea fisheries, and other industries on estates that he had bought, and was knighted by King Charles II. In 1647 he invented a copying machine.

Just as William Pitt himself was the descendant of Governor Pitt, the clergyman's boy who went to India, so was Lord Shelburne the descendant of Sir William Petty, the son of the clothier, who also dared the seas. Shelburne was the very reverse of Fox. What Fox squandered Shelburne amassed, and Bowood, with its pictures and library, remained a monument of his taste. He was created the first Marquis of Lansdowne, and of him we are again reminded by that regal mansion of Piccadilly, Lansdowne House. Lord Shelburne, then, was the partner of Charles James Fox in the Whig Cabinet. The two of them were the Secretaries of State.

After less than four months of office Lord Rockingham died and his administration had to be reconstructed. Realizing that they were themselves detested at Court, Fox and Burke proposed that the Prime Minister should be a second Rockingham, that is, the Duke of Portland. But the man for whom the King had sent already was Lord Shelburne and, having selected his man, the King refused to give way.

Fox and Burke insisted that the decision lay with the Cabinet. It is a nice point in constitutional law. What can be said with certainty is that on frequent occasions the sovereign, left without a Prime Minister, and faced by divided parties, has exercised his discretion in choosing a prospective adviser. To this day the King, if, on the death of a Prime Minister, a Cabinet were in dissension, would summon the statesman who seemed to be most suited to the emergency. Against the claim of Sir William Harcourt, Queen Victoria thus sent for Lord Rosebery; King George V thus sent for Mr. Stanley Baldwin.

But in 1782 it was not easy for Fox and Burke so to regard the matter. It was but two years before that the House of Commons had asserted Dunning's famous resolution, "that the power of the Crown has increased, is increasing, and ought to be diminished." It was a motion, carried by 233 votes to

Lord Shelburne pressed home a yet more damaging point. Appealing to the memory of the Earl of Chatham, he insisted that "the Great Commoner had always declared that the country ought not to be governed by any oligarchical party or family connection, and that if it is to be so governed, the Constitution must of necessity expire." Challenging Fox on his own ground, Shelburne declared, "On these principles I have always acted."

The charge that Fox had sacrificed the party to the Whig nobility—had been willing to serve under a Duke of Portland, willing to serve under a Marquis of Rockingham, but unwilling to serve under an Earl of Shelburne—was reinforced by a dramatic blow. With Fox there had resigned the Chancellor of the Exchequer. Personally undistinguished, Lord John Cavendish, like Rockingham, like Portland, belonged to the greater nobility, the House of Devonshire. It was to the high office, thus vacated, that William Pitt was appointed. Charles James Fox, of all men alive at that date, was placed in the position of preferring hereditary privilege to personal ability in the control of the nation's finances. With their talk of reform, the orthodox Whigs were, apparently, opposing the recognition of the very merit, apart from the claims of mere birth, on which their cause depended.

It was with an imperturbable nonchalance that Pitt accepted his already amazing destiny. "With regard to myself," he wrote to his mother on July 2, 1782, "I believe the arrangement [of the administration] may be of a sort in which *I may*, and probably *ought* to take a part." There was "great uncertainty" but his "lot" would be either the Exchequer or the Home Department as Secretary of State. Also, we have this:

Grafton Street, July 16, 1782.

Our new Board of Treasury has just begun to enter on business; and though I do not know that it is of the most entertaining sort, it does not seem likely to be very fatiguing. In all other respects my situation satisfies me, and more than satisfies me, and I think promises everything that is agreeable. . . . Lord North will, I hope, in a very little while make room for me in Downing Street, which is the best summer town house possible.

"I expect," he adds, "to be comfortably settled in the course of this week in a *part* of my vast, awkward house." There follows certain curious information:

Grafton Street, Aug. 10, 1782.

. . . My secretary, whom you wish to know, is a person whose name you may probably never have heard, a Mr. Bellingham, an army friend of my brother. You will wonder at a secretary from the army; but as the office is a perfect sinecure, and has no duty but that of receiving about four hundred a year, no profession is unfit for it. I have not yet any private secretary, nor do I perceive, at least as yet, any occasion for it.

Among other details, he settled the arrears of his mother's pension which, in the strange fashion of the day, had been constantly left unpaid.

To-day there is a rule, unwritten indeed but of increasing stringency, that the Prime Minister must sit in the House of Commons. Lord Shelburne was a peer and, though a capable Parliamentarian, could only address the House of

Lords. Hence it followed that, as Chancellor of the Exchequer, William Pitt, almost single-handed, had to meet the attacks of Fox, of Burke, of Sheridan, and of North. Entering the House only eighteen months before, he had passed from a back bench in Opposition, not only to the front bench, but to the leadership on that bench.

The House was now in a more deeply divided condition than ever. There were not two parties but three. The Tories were led by Lord North. Some of the Whigs were led by Fox. Others supported Pitt and the government. It could not be said that any administration would have had a clear and a defined majority.

The embitterment among the Whigs can be best understood by comparison with the internecine feud which, for some years, divided Liberals who followed Mr. Asquith from Liberals who followed Mr. Lloyd George. Burke denounced the "duplicity and delusion" of Shelburne, likened him to a serpent with two heads, and declared him to be "a Borgia" and "a Catiline." They were compliments characteristic of the Eighteenth Century sage.

The real question was whether Lord North and the Tories would enter this domestic fray, and in such a situation there are always emissaries, acting on their own initiative yet not wholly without a higher authority, who set about playing the great game of fusion. A colleague of Pitt was Henry Dundas. He had several talks with William Adam, a friend of Lord North. The result was negative. "There is no longer any prospect," wrote Dundas, "none at least for the present, that there will be any overture for a coalition to Lord North from the present ministry. Lord Shelburne and I have pushed for it, but we could not get the other ministers to agree to it."

★

What Pitt urged was an approach to Fox. Reluctantly Shelburne agreed, and at once there occurred what may be fairly called one of the most important five minutes in the history of England. On February 11, 1783, Pitt called on Fox by appointment and at his house. When Fox heard what was the reason of the visit he asked one question—was Lord Shelburne still to be Prime Minister? Pitt answered in the affirmative. "It is impossible for me," replied Fox, "to belong to any administration of which Lord Shelburne is the head." It was a rebuff but not a rebuff that closed the door to further negotiation. Amid the uncertainties of the moment, an administration composed of Whigs, including Shelburne and Fox, might have been devised. But there was an electricity in that room which would not be denied the lightning. "Then we need discuss the matter no further," said Pitt. "I did not come here to betray Lord Shelburne." Then and there the men parted, and from that day onward, so it is stated, never were they to be found together alone in the same room.

Unable to make terms with Fox, the government had a difficulty in holding office. That Lord Shelburne sent a message to Lord North is history. There arises the question whether Pitt, as his leading colleague, was a party to this overture. The assumption is that if Shelburne and North had joined hands Pitt would have resigned. Not that we need discuss the assumption, for, in fact, the situation never arose.

"I cannot meet Lord Shelburne now," so Lord North replied to the wire pullers, "it is too late." While Shelburne had been considering the matter something unforeseen had happened.

It was, indeed, the incredible. Having refused pointblank to accept office under Lord Shelburne, a Whig, Charles James Fox—of all men living on this planet—had entered into a partnership with the archpriest of Toryism, the very mouthpiece of King George III, the oppressor of the American Colonies, the enemy of reform, Lord North himself.

As lately as that very year, 1782, Fox had said of North and his government:

From the moment when I shall make any terms with one of them, I will rest satisfied to be called the most infamous of mankind. I would not for an instant think of a coalition with men who in every public and private transaction as ministers have shown themselves void of every principle of honour and honesty. In the hands of such men I would not trust my honour for a minute.

Yet, on the discovery of the Coalition, Fox, having used such language, coolly observed:

It is not in my nature to bear malice or live in ill will; my friendships are perpetual, my enmities, not so.

For Pitt, with his still slender Parliamentary experience, it was a situation that strained the nerves. The merely physical circumstances were a kind of third degree. When the truth of what had been perpetrated dawned on the House there arose a debate which continued, hour after hour, until midnight, and still continued, hour after hour.

It was not until four o'clock in the morning that it came Pitt's turn to speak. He was exhausted. The House was exhausted. Also, it is clear that he was upset. He had not expected the surprise, and the surprise had put him in a minority. Under such a stress men are not always at their best. Forgetting his more cautious instincts, Pitt rounded on Sheridan and told him to reserve his epigrams for the stage where they would obtain, as they always deserved, the plaudits of the audience. Sheridan sprang to his feet. He wished "only to explain." He then "explained" as follows:

If ever I again engage in those compositions to which the Right Hon. Gentleman has in such flattering terms referred, I may be tempted to an act of presumption. I may be encouraged by his praises to try an improvement on one of Ben Jonson's best characters in the play of the *Alchymist*—the Angry Boy!

It was a retort that endangered Pitt's career. It was a retort that almost justified the Coalition.

A day or two later the debate was renewed. Fox spoke from the front Opposition bench. Pitt was ill of the nerves and actually had to stand behind the Speaker's chair while he battled with what, in a rough sea, the French call *mal de mer*. Yet this was the man, overcome with excitement, who, returning to the House in such a condition, delivered a speech of three hours' duration, and one of his best.

The pretext for the Coalition was the anguish over the terms of peace with the United States. Yet, as Macaulay has said, there is not the slightest reason to suppose that Fox, had he remained in office, would have hesitated for a moment in concluding the treaty. It was in trenchant fashion that Pitt dealt with the point:

I repeat then that it is not this treaty, it is the Earl of Shelburne alone whom the movers of this question are desirous to wound. This is the object which has raised this storm of faction—this is the aim of the unnatural Coalition to which I have alluded. If, however, the baneful alliance is not already formed, if this ill-omened marriage is not already solemnized, I know a just and lawful impediment, and in the name of public safety, I here forbid the Banns!

Of the Coalition, Wilberforce, mildest of men and most respected, said that it was a progeny that partook of the vices of both its parents—the corruption of the one (Lord North) and the violence of the other (Charles James Fox).

Fox defended the arrangement by comparing it, in a splendid simile, with "the junction of the Rhone and the Saone," which rivers—the one calm, the other turbulent—were yet mingled in a broad stream that "adorns and benefits the country through which it passes."

Faced by the Coalition, Shelburne's days were numbered, and in February, 1783, he found it impossible to carry on. One of those occasions arose when custom compels the wire pullers to be busy, and accomplished among these experts, as we have seen, was Henry Dundas. He was a Scot who talked no other language and talked it plainly. In his pocket he had the votes of his countrymen, whether peers or members of the Commons, and serious for an administration was any day when it was, as the phrase went, "deserted by the Thanes." Dundas thus served under North, under Rockingham, under Shelburne, under Pitt, with a political impartial-

ity, not to call it perseverance, which commands the admiration. Of his ultimate fate we must say nothing as yet.

It was Dundas who suggested to Shelburne that he should
see the King and advise the King to send for Pitt and offer
him the office of Prime Minister. Shelburne jumped at this
plan for dishing Fox and North.

But would the King agree? On May 7, 1782, Pitt had denounced "the corrupt influence of the Crown—an influence
which has been pointed at in every period as the fertile
source of all our miseries—an influence which has been substituted in the room of wisdom, of activity, of exertion, and of
success—an influence which has grown up with our growth
and strengthened with our strength, but which unhappily
has not diminished with our diminution, nor decayed with
our decay." These were words that King George III was not
the man to forget.

Enough that the King, tolerant to an occasional and youthful indiscretion, greatly preferred Pitt to Fox and at once
fell in with Shelburne's advice. Dundas wrote to his brother:

                                        February 25, 1783.
. . . Not a human being has a suspicion of the plan, except those
in the immediate confidence of it. It will create an universal
consternation in the allied camp the moment it is known. Still,
secrecy!

                            ★

To reconstruct even one day of human life is beyond the
utmost ability of the most eager historian. Yet, in Pitt's life,
here, indeed, was a great day. Consider his actual position—
a young man, a very young man, surrounded by admiring

friends, clothed for the first time as privy councillor in the panoply of gold lace; receiving for the first time that peculiar and indescribably flattering deference which is only paid to the higher and the official statesmanship of the country; enjoying for the first time the sense of power; and undergoing for the first time the exhilaration of a political hurricane well calculated to sweep the most hardened politician off his feet.

To this man of twenty-three years there is delivered a brief note, brief but unmistakable in its meaning, a note in the writing of the King himself. It read:

Queen's House, March 23, 1783, 8.50 A. M.

Mr. Pitt is desired to come here in his morning dress as soon as convenient to him.

G. R.

At 11.55 A. M. the King wrote again:

I desire Mr. Pitt will be here after the Drawing Room.

Next day, the royal urgency was thus expressed:

Queen's House, March 24, 1783, 11.10 A. M.

Mr. Pitt's idea of having nothing announced till the debate of to-day meets with my thorough approbation. I have just seen the Lord Chancellor, who thinks that if Mr. Pitt should say, towards the close of the debate, that after such conduct as the Coalition had held, that every man attached to this Constitution must stand forth on this occasion, and that as such he is determined to keep the situation devolved on him, that he will meet with an applause that cannot fail to give him every encouragement.

I shall not expect Mr. Pitt till the Levee is over.

G. R.

Windsor, March 24, 1783, 5.12. P. M.

I am not surprised, as the debate has proved desultory, that Mr. Pitt has not been able to write more fully on this occasion. After the manner I have been personally treated by both the Duke of Portland and Lord North, it is impossible I can ever admit either of them into my service: I therefore trust that Mr. Pitt will exert himself to-morrow to plan his mode of filling up the offices that will be vacant, so as to be able on Wednesday morning to accept the situation his character and talents fit him to hold, when I shall be in town before twelve ready to receive him.

G. R.

Under circumstances less exciting, and after an experience of as many years almost as Pitt's brief months, Fox had lost his head. Not for a moment did Pitt's judgment waver. He neither accepted with alacrity nor refused without deliberation. After sleeping over the matter he wrote to the King:

March 25, 1783.

Mr. Pitt received this morning, the honour of your Majesty's gracious commands. With infinite pain he feels himself under the necessity of humbly expressing to your Majesty, that with every sentiment of dutiful attachment to your Majesty and zealous desire to contribute to the public service, it is utterly impossible for him, after the fullest consideration of the situation in which things stand, and of what passed yesterday in the House of Commons, to think of undertaking, under such circumstances, the situation which your Majesty has had the condescension and goodness to propose to him.

As what he now presumes to write is the final result of his best reflection, he should think himself criminal if, by delaying till to-morrow humbly to lay it before your Majesty, he should be the cause of your Majesty's not immediately turning your Royal mind to such a plan of arrangement as the exigency of the present circumstances may, in your Majesty's wisdom, seem to require.

The King's disappointment was outspoken:

> Windsor, March 25, 4.35 P. M.
> Mr. Pitt, I am much hurt to find you are determined to decline at an hour when those who have any regard for the Constitution as established by law ought to stand forth against the most daring and unprincipled faction that the annals of this kingdom ever produced.
>
> G. R.

Pitt left Downing Street, once more a private member, with no more than a nominal income and whatever he could add to it by his practice at the bar.

To Dundas, he stated his reason for declining to be Prime Minister. He held that his government, had he formed one, could only have existed in hope of support by Lord North. "In point of honour to my own feelings"—as Pitt put it—he refused "unalterably" to be dependent on such support. "I write this," he said, "while I am dressing for Court. I have to beg a thousand pardons for being the occasion of your having so much trouble in vain. This resolution will, I am afraid, both surprise and disappoint you. . . ." He signed himself "with the deepest sense of friendship you have shown me in all this business."

It was a friendship that lasted, and ultimately the price of it was to be pain.

CHAPTER FIVE

INTERLUDE

IN THE life of William Pitt, whereon not a day was wasted and few days fully enjoyed, there was one and only one interlude when it could be said that he was marking time. On March 25, 1783, he refused to form a government, and on December 19th of that same year he became Prime Minister. For nine months he was out of office.

The situation was chronic crisis. With Pitt unwilling at that date to form a government, the King left the country for thirty-seven days without this encumbrance, and it was with utter disgust that he submitted to the nominee of the Coalition the aristocratic but colourless Duke of Portland, sitting among his peers in the House of Lords. The desire of the King, his sole desire, was to get rid of the rascals at the earliest moment.

The Commons had to become accustomed to a strange sight. It was as if Theodore Roosevelt and Woodrow Wilson had shared the White House. Side by side on the ministerial bench sat Fox and North, the one vehement, the other adroit, and together claiming that they had laid aside party in order to vindicate popular right against royal encroachment. To quote Lord North's tribute to Fox:

In the early part of that gentleman's career, when I had the happiness to possess his friendship, I knew that he was manly, open, and sincere. As an enemy I have always found him formidable and a person of most extraordinary talents, to whatever Minister he may be opposed. But in proportion as I had reason to dread him while his principles were adverse to mine, now that they are congenial we shall, with the greater certainty of success, unite with one mind and one heart in the cause of our common country. And let me hail it as an auspicious circumstance in our country's favour, that those who were divided by her hostilities are cemented by her peace.

Immediately opposite, there sat Pitt, the third element in that eternal triangle, now leader of the Opposition, a spare, proud man, grave, clear of eye, tight of lip, haughty in his every glance, courteous but never so crushing in his superiority as when, with a frigid bow, he acknowledged a courtesy. What Pitt said of Lord Buckingham was true of himself. He had "the condescension of pride."

The issue that had arisen between Fox and the King was clearly an issue that had to be determined by public opinion. Unless public opinion outside the House supported Fox, he was impotent. Yet it was precisely this public opinion that Fox had alienated. People could understand his quarrel with the King. They could not understand his quarrel with Shelburne. They could not understand why he preferred a North to a Pitt. The Coalition, intended to be a national party, merely embodied a personal pique.

So young a man as Pitt had time on his side. With life

ahead of him, he could afford to wait. For every day added to
his prestige. He was at once independent and indispensable.
He had resisted the Court, yet the Court had not dared to
quarrel with him. Encroachments of the Crown? Who had
denounced them more strongly than he? Yet the King
was inconsolable without him. Subservience to the Court?
He had refused a higher office than the office at which
Fox had snatched. "I desire," said he, "to declare that I
am unconnected with any party whatever. I shall keep myself reserved and act with whichever side I think is acting
right."

It is the business of an opposition to oppose. But even in
opposition there should be reason. It should not be merely
playing politics. Pitt as a critic was the more deadly because,
on the whole, he allowed the Coalition to be its own inevitable
retribution. No blow that he struck was at random. Every
blow went home.

It is for this place that we have reserved a narrative de-
scribing Pitt's attitude toward reform. It is a narrative
which will cover the period between January 23, 1781, when
he entered the House, and December 19, 1783, when he
became Prime Minister. We shall be able thus to approach
this aspect of his career as a whole.

There were two kinds of reform. In the language of the
day, it might be "economical" or "constitutional." Along
each of these avenues of improvement Pitt—mischief in his
eye—gaily set forth.

In these days, when governments command the time of

the House, it is not easy for a private member, whoever he may be, to submit legislation to a full-dress debate. But in Pitt's day, when governments had less business to transact, there were these opportunities, and it was on Burke's Bill for Economical Reform that, in February, 1781, Pitt had delivered his maiden speech. In such discussions all the miscellaneous paraphernalia of graft, of pensions, of sinecures came under the lash.

Having served as Chancellor of the Exchequer, Pitt had been able to look into things for himself. And on June 2, 1783, he introduced a bill dealing with Abuses in Public Offices.

To a generation accustomed to think in hundreds of millions, the sums indicated in this discussion are amusingly small. The saving to be effected was £40,000 a year, and one extravagance to be pruned was stationery. Actually, the item came to £18,000—this in days when statesmen wrote their own letters! Lord North—personally, the most blameless of men—learned that his stationery had cost the nation a sum of £1,300 a year, of which £340 had been devoted to packthread.

Lord North, stung by remorse, protested his astonishment. Said he:

I had given the most positive direction that no stationery ware should be delivered for my use without the express order of my private secretary. If therefore any fraud has been committed, it must have been by a breach of this direction. I assure the House that I will make a most rigorous inquiry into this business, and if I find delinquency, I will leave nothing in my power undone to bring the delinquents to punishment. . . . As to coals and candles, I found when I was placed at the head of the Treasury that my predecessors had been supplied with those articles at the expense of the public, and it was according to an old and established custom. But I declined to avail myself of this custom, and I have supplied my house with coals and candles at my own expense.

★

Over constitutional reform there was a skirmish which, perhaps, deserves a more serious attention. In the struggle with successive sovereigns, maintained over several centuries and pressed to an issue under the Stuarts, the powers of Parliament had been asserted. But in the year 1783 the structure of Parliament was essentially the same as it had been in 1283 or thereabouts, that is, in the remote reign of King Edward I. Scotland had been added, but that was the only substantial change.

In a country still agricultural there were only 122 county members. Also London had only the four members which had been assigned to the metropolis by King Edward II. But the boroughs had 432 members, and all save five of them sent two members apiece to Westminster. A nation of 8,000,000 inhabitants had only 160,000 electors—a percentage of enfranchisement no more than comparable with what, in 1928, India enjoyed.

Before Pitt entered the arena there had been three discussions on reform. In 1745 Sir F. Dashwood had moved an amendment to the Address. In 1776 a motion by Wilkes had been lost without a division. In 1780 the Duke of Richmond, in the House of Lords, had proposed a similar motion and with a similar result.

The keen eye of Lord Chatham, piercing into the realities of England's industrial expansion, had foreseen that reform was inevitable. As quoted by his son, Chatham had held that "unless a more solid and equal system of representation were established, this nation, great and happy as it might have been, would come to be confounded in the main of these when liberties were lost in the corruption of the people." Chatham's proposal was to add 100 to the number of county members.

For some years the demand for reform had been audible outside Parliament. With that demand Fox had been identified. He had even committed the unpardonable offence of attending public meetings. With an acute taste for strategy, Pitt proceeded, at once, to demonstrate his own consistency as a reformer and to test the sincerity of the Coalition.

On May 7, 1782, the leader of the Opposition, for this, in fact, Pitt had become, brought forward an artful motion. Knowing well that no two persons would agree over what the word "reform" should mean, he proposed a select committee to examine the subject. Considering the manner of his own election for Appleby, his speech was not wanting in courage, for he spoke about members entering the House, "under the control of the Treasury or at the bidding of some great Lord or Commoner, the owner of the soil," and he asked the famous question, "Is this representation?"

In a House dominated by Lord North it is no wonder that this motion was opposed. There were hundreds of members whose seats were affected. What does astonish us is the hostility of Edmund Burke.

With his wig awry, his round spectacles, his pockets bulging with papers, his uncontrollable vocal chords, his unwieldy body and careless dress, Burke was a sage, as grotesque in aspect, as gorgeous in genius as Dr. Johnson. What Burke believed in was the nation as a coherent organism, and it was a great belief, often nobly expressed, yet sometimes it was defined in terms of a violence and an obscenity which are incredible and unquotable. Not since the days of Diogenes had there been a more quaint incarnation of a sagacity, at once profound and uncertain.

Over the American Colonies Burke had been dead right. In them he saw the social organism growing to its due stature. But the liberties which he demanded for Englishmen at a distance Burke denied to Englishmen at his own doors. He would admit that evils like bribery and corruption should be remedied, that extravagance should be corrected, and that the King should know his place. When, however, it came to constitutional reform, Burke's vision was obstructed by a blind spot. If England had lived under a written constitution there would have been reason in insisting that such a constitution be respected. But it was in the growth of English institutions that Burke himself had gloried. It was as the long result of time that he had defended them. Yet, in effect, he insisted that, at a given date, selected by himself, this growth must cease. The Revolution of 1688 was quite correct. But there must be no other. With the departure of King James II, England as a country was completed.

Even anomalies must be reverently cherished. Tennyson was to write:

> *Better a rotten borough or so*
> *Than a rotten fleet and a city in flames!*

But to Burke the rotten borough, even if it resulted in the rotten fleet, must be tolerated. "The equilibrium of the Constitution," said he of the oligarchy, "has something so delicate about it that the least displacement may destroy it." Hence, "it is a difficult and dangerous matter even to touch so complicated a machine."

With difficulty, yet with ample reason, Fox persuaded Burke to stay away from the debate on Pitt's motion. It was thus nearly carried. In a full House, the division was 141 votes in favour, 161 against, an adverse majority of only 20. Macaulay reminds us that never did the reformers have so good a division until that year of upheaval, 1831.

A few days later Burke broke loose. Parliaments then sat for seven years. The period was not fixed by any constitution. It depended merely on an act, passed in 1716, which Parliament was entitled at any time to amend. Indeed, in 1911 the period was reduced from seven years to five.

Yet when, on May 17, 1782, a certain Alderman Sawbridge, a veteran in the cause of reform, brought forward a bill "to shorten the duration of Parliaments," Burke exhibited himself as a man, best described by Sheridan, who wrote:

On Friday last Burke acquitted himself with the most magnanimous indiscretion, attacked William Pitt in a scream of passion, and swore Parliament was and always had been precisely what it ought to be, and that all people who thought of reforming it wanted to overturn the Constitution.

★

In the year 1783 Pitt had held office as Chancellor of the Exchequer. But on May 7th, exactly a year after his previous motion, he returned to the crusade for reform, and this time he did not deal in generalities. He proposed three resolutions. The first condemned bribery and undue expenditure at elections. The second provided that a borough convicted of gross corruption should be disfranchised and that the minority, not so convicted, should be allowed to vote in the county; the third increased the number of county members. Lord Chatham's proposal had been to add a hundred of these to Parliament. Pitt supplemented his father's views by suggesting a larger representation also for London.

The resolutions drove a wedge into the very vitals of the Coalition. Fox supported them; North denounced them; and it was made manifest by the division—293 votes to 149 —that Fox, by joining North and holding to Burke, had smashed his own cause. This was the situation that, as Prime Minister, Pitt was to inherit.

★

During that summer we see Pitt, with his friends, enjoying one another's company. First, there was William Wilberforce who, on Sunday, "persuaded Pitt and Pepper to Church." Secondly, there was Edward Eliot, who had his own reasons for cultivating the connection. Two years later he married Pitt's sister, Lady Harriot.

With a light heart then, and not a thing in the world to worry him, Pitt welcomed the month of September and the chance of a holiday. Together the three of them made their way in all gaiety to the seat of Henry Bankes, Pitt's friend at Cambridge and now a member of the House, who lived in Dorsetshire on an estate where there were partridges whose sole purpose in life was to get shot. The friends roundly alleged that Wilberforce, who was more interested in slavery than in shooting, and in sermons than either, nearly shot Pitt. But Wilberforce, with his adroit pen, explains that his accusers indulged "a roguish wish, perhaps, to make the most of my shortsightedness and inexperience in field sports." On the 10th of September Pitt was back in London for gold lace and the Levee.

It is assumed to-day as a matter of course that an education, to be complete, must include travel. Only the perspicacity of a George Bernard Shaw is equal to the paradox that the best way to see a country is not to go there. If any man needed to travel, it would appear to have been William Pitt. He hoped to be Prime Minister one day of that empire over which already the sun had no little difficulty in setting. Yet never had he put his foot on soil other than English.

Hence, when he entered his "chaise" for Dover, he contemplated an entirely novel experience. Indeed, not only was it to be novel. It was to be unique. The friends set sail from Dover on September 12th. At Dover they landed again on October 24th. The trip thus lasted for only six weeks, and, apart from this brief trip, Pitt did not spend one hour at any time outside his own country. To the end of his life Pitt's

eyes were England's eyes. He saw nothing beyond England—
not Scotland, not Ireland—save through a telescope, and
even in England he travelled nowhere north of Northamptonshire nor west of Weymouth.

The limitation of his outlook was, in one sense, the secret
of his success. What he had to deal with was the House of
Commons, and the idea that the House is an international
unit of democracy would not be true, even to-day. The House
is ineradicably English. About its atmosphere there is a
continual intimacy. In the times of Pitt, statesmen might be
friends, they might be foes, but in either event they were
familiars. No one dreamed of discussing foreigners except
by hearsay and with a certain implied apology for having to
acknowledge that such people existed. It was an immense advantage to a Parliamentarian, leading a legislature, to be
himself completely insular.

The three tourists did not attempt to go beyond France
and, even in France, they limited themselves to the three
royal citadels: Rheims, Paris, and Fontainebleau. The year
was 1783; within six years the Bastille was to be stormed;
within ten years the guillotine was to be applied to King
Louis XVI. Yet apparently these young men of culture,
of intelligence, could perceive not a hint of the storm. Their
education had rendered them incapable of the larger foresight. It had drawn a veil before their eyes.

It had been education in forms, not facts, and by these
forms Pitt himself was surrounded. Take his correspondence.
Compared with others of the period, his letters were laconic.
Compared with letters of our own day, they were luxurious

in their loquacity. Yet letters are now dictated to and are typed by a stenographer. Pitt—when he so far condescended —had to write his letters with his own hand. He had to transact business, at any rate with the King, in a special costume. Whatever the rubbish that might be talked, he had to attend the House. He had to maintain the due style which was the very life of the system that he was called on to administer.

What he wrote home will illustrate his powers of observation:

Calais, Sept. 12 [1783].

My dear Mother,

Lest any howling at Burton should have given you the idea of a storm, I am impatient to assure you that we are arrived here after a rough but a very prosperous passage. We shall set out to-morrow and reach Rheims Sunday night or Monday morning. A letter, directed to a Gentilhomme Anglais à la Poste Restante, will, I find, be sure to reach me. I hope I shall have the pleasure of hearing from you very soon.

Your dutiful and affectionate
W. Pitt.

Rheims, Sept. 18, Thursday, 1783.

My dear Mother,

We arrived here after a journey which had little but the novelty of the country to recommend it. The travelling was much better than I expected, and the appearance of the people more comfortable, but the face of the country through all the way from Calais the dullest I ever saw. Here we are in very good quarters, though as yet we have not found much society but our own. The place is chiefly inhabited by mercantile people and ecclesiastics, among whom, however, I suppose we shall by degrees find some charitable persons who will let us practise our French upon them. At present, when I have told you that we are here and perfectly well, I have exhausted my whole budget of news. The post is also not well suited for a longer letter, as it goes out at nine in the morning, and I am writing before breakfast. This, however, is not so great an exertion as in England, for the hours are uncommonly early, to which we easily accustom ourselves, at night, and in some measure in the morning. I hope I shall have the happiness of a letter from Burton soon. You will probably have received one which I wrote from Calais. Kind love to Harriot, and compliments to Mrs. Stapleton.

> Your ever dutiful and affectionate
> W. PITT.

To Lady Harriot Pitt

Rheims, Oct. 1, 1783.

MY DEAR SISTER

. . . This place has for some days been constantly improving upon us, though at this time of year it has not a numerous society. We are going to-day to dine at a countryhouse in the midst of vineyards, which, as this is the height of the vintage, will furnish a very pleasant scene. To-morrow we are to dine at a magnificent palace of the Archbishop's, who lives about five miles off, and is a sort of prince in this country. Most of those we see are ecclesiastics, and as a French Abbé is not proverbial for silence, we have an opportunity of hearing something of the language. . . .

> Your ever affectionate
> W. PITT.

To Lady Chatham

Rheims, Monday, Oct. 6, 1783.

This will be the last time of my writing from this place, which we leave on Wednesday for Paris. The time has passed not unpleasantly or unprofitably, and I flatter myself has furnished a stock of French that will last for ten days or a fortnight at Paris. We shall arrive there on Thursday, and do not mean to be tempted by anything to prolong our stay much beyond the 20th of October. Parliament I hear meets on the 11th of November, and a fortnight or three weeks in England first is very desirable.

The direction I sent became, from my manner of expressing it, more mysterious than I meant, as I had no intention to leave out my name. It is some proof of French politeness that they do not bear it any enmity, though they seem to know the difference between this war and the last. I believe you may venture to direct to me at full length at Paris, adding Hôtel du Parc Royal, Rue du Colombier, Faubourg St. Germain.

> Hôtel de Grande Bretagne, Paris,
> Wednesday, Oct. 15 [1783].

I am just setting out to Fontainebleau for two or three days, where I shall find the Court and all the magnificence of France, and with this expedition I shall finish my career here. Since I have been here I have had little to do but see sights, as the King's journey to Fontainebleau has carried all the world from Paris except English, who seem quite in possession of the town.

At Rheims, the Abbé de Lageard, soon to be *emigré*, put to Pitt a searching question. All human things, he argued politely, are perishable. Then, in what part might the British constitution first decay?

Pitt had to pause at this. However, he answered, "The part of our constitution which will first perish is the prerogative of the King and the authority of the House of Peers."

"I am much surprised," said the abbé, "that a country so

moral as England can submit to be governed by such a spendthrift and such a rake as Fox; it seems to show that you are less moral than you claim to be." "The claim is just," Pitt replied, "but you have not been under the wand of the magician."

Anticipating De Tocqueville, Pitt said to the abbé, "Sir, you have no political liberty; but as to civil liberty, you have more of it than you suppose."

Like ships that pass in the night, the three friends and their French hosts caught glimpses, but only glimpses, each of the others. At Rheims the archbishop had a young nephew who, had he known what was to come, might have interested William Pitt. His name was Charles Maurice Talleyrand de Périgord. He was five years older than Pitt and he survived Pitt by nearly a quarter of a century. Whether Pitt noticed Talleyrand is doubtful. But Talleyrand never forgot noticing Pitt.

At Fontainebleau Pitt went stag-hunting, while Eliot and Wilberforce in a chaise saw the King, a "clumsy, strange figure in immense boots." The son of Chatham became a social lion. Everyone looked at him. "Men and women crowded round Pitt in shoals; and he behaved with great spirit, though he was sometimes a little bored when they talked to him of Parliamentary reform."

We see him, slim, erect, holding high his head, yet deferent to others who had a right to deference. We also see that "more delightful vision," as Burke described her, "just above the horizon, decorating and cheering the elevated sphere she just began to move in—glittering like the morning

star, full of life, and splendour, and joy." To Marie Antoinette, Pitt bowed as only Pitt could bow.

In October Pitt returned, as he said, to his profession at
the bar. But there was that in Parliament which was to
claim him for the rest of his life.

IT WAS the events of two short months, November and December, 1793, which drew William Pitt again to Downing Street; and this time, not only as Chancellor of the Exchequer but as Prime Minister. They were months when the sincerity of statesmen was subjected to what President Wilson used to call an acid test, from which test, it may be, not one of them emerged wholly without a scar.

Over the crisis that developed, historians have argued and may be expected still to argue as long as history is read. On the issues involved, men differed at the time; and where a Pitt, a Burke, a Fox, and a Sheridan failed to agree, it is idle to suppose that any jury of a later date will bring in a unanimous verdict.

The Coalition, including Tories as well as Whigs, might be compared with a convoy, of which the speed of the whole is no faster than that of the slowest ship. Only if the convoy held together could it be safe from external attack; and with Parliamentary reform, therefore, the Coalition was thus impotent, as we have seen, to deal.

But it was not only at home that reform had become urgent. Oversea, there was also ample room for improvement, and here, as it seemed, lay the opportunity for the Coalition to render an immense service to mankind.

In the year 1783 Great Britain was still astounded by the loss of the American Colonies. But there was a region, to this day three times as populous as the United States of America, over which the dismembered sovereignty was rapidly extending its grip. In India, the energies of Clive and Warren Hastings had already founded the Empire of the East.

In the brief government of Lord Rosebery there was included a statesman whose name, once familiar, is already forgotten. Ennobled later as Viscount Wolverhampton, Sir Henry Fowler served in the House of Commons as Secretary of State, in which capacity, on one occasion, he uttered what has become a memorable saying. "We are all of us," said he, "members for India." With the vision of the East looming mysterious on a far horizon, interested or uninterested, every member had to be a member for India. He could not help himself.

Of all the members for India, the most zealous, the most faithful by far, was Edmund Burke. Of America and of India the physical eyes of Burke saw nothing. But he knew those countries better than did the Indians and the Americans themselves. Of bluebooks from India, as we should now call them, he had absorbed libraries. Whatever he absorbed was illuminated by his genius. Statistics were translated into vitalities. It was no small part of Burke's task in life to acquaint his fellow members for India with the significance of their stupendous constituency. The subject was not one that could be avoided. For the great dependency a tolerable constitution had somehow to be provided.

The interests of Great Britain were still vested in the commercial undertaking called the East India Company. But responsibilities had accumulated which far exceeded the usual obligations of a trading venture. Impoverished by war, the company itself, if not bankrupt, was financially embarrassed and unable to discharge its indebtedness to the Treasury on account of duties on imported goods.

Behind this situation there lay a dim hinterland of abuses in India herself. To quote Macaulay, India was subject to "English power," as yet "unaccompanied by English morality"; there was to be seen "the most frightful of all spectacles, the strength of civilization without its mercy." With the retirement of Clive, that robbery of the people of which Governor Pitt himself had been by no means innocent raged rampant in its unashamed rapacity.

Against these abuses Fox and Burke had declaimed for years. On the Select Committee which examined the facts Burke had sat side by side with Dundas, and over the facts there was no serious dispute. Even Lord North, however reluctantly, had to admit that it was time for something to be done. As long ago as 1773 his Regulating Act, as it was called, had asserted the right of Parliament to intervene in Indian affairs on grounds of high policy, and this act had been flouted.

It was Warren Hastings who, under the act of Lord North, was appointed to be the Governor General of India, with a council of four to advise him. Over this autocracy there began

to be grave misgivings, and in 1782 Parliament by vote of
censure demanded his recall. The Court of Directors embodied this decision in an order.

But, with the capital standing at about four million pounds,
there was also a Court of Proprietors, consisting of about
two thousand shareholders, each holding stock to an amount
not less than £500; and the Court of Proprietors voted
against the Court of Directors and, in effect, reinstated
Warren Hastings. Whatever view be taken of the charges
against Hastings, here was a flat repudiation of the will of
Parliament.

It was with this situation that any government, whatever
its complexion, would have been compelled to deal; and at
first sight it seemed as if the Coalition was especially well
equipped to make the most of the necessity. It included the
highest authority on the constitution, Burke himself. It
included Fox, the critic of the company. It included North
who had already been responsible for an important measure
affecting the direction of Indian policy.

★

The bills which Fox introduced were by no means devoid of
merits. They would have swept away certain abuses that had
become a gross scandal—for instance, the acceptance of
presents by the company's servants, and the holding of
monopolies, of which one, ominously opium, had been cor-
ruptly awarded to the son of a former chairman of the company. Against all this there might be opposition in interested
quarters but there could be no open resistance. It is thus the

more astonishing that in the bills there should have been embedded what can only be described as a gross and wilful blunder.

For the bills did not merely remedy abuses. They readjusted the relations between the company and the crown. A clear distinction was drawn between the commercial enterprises of the company and its political authority. Commerce was left to a committee of directors appointed by the proprietors. Authority was transferred to seven commissioners —in due course named in the bill—who would sit for four years, after which their successors would be nominated by the crown, or in effect, the government of the day. It was this proposal that caused the trouble.

The outcry raised against it was based, like all agitation, on arguments, both good and bad. To begin with, it was protested that the bill cancelled a charter, and affected the sanctity of contracts. Every corporation with a charter professed alarm.

Merchants argued that, if the most powerful of existing corporations could be thus roughly handled, a precedent would be created which might be applied in other directions. A charter? cried the Attorney General. It was "only a parchment with a seal of wax dangling at one end of it, compared with the happiness of thirty millions of subjects." It was a sentence that, like Bethmann Hollweg's "scrap of paper," evoked emotions.

Mere prejudice, however, could have been overcome if the bill itself had been above suspicion. But it was roundly asserted, fairly or unfairly, that the motives which animated its authors were far other than a desire for the abstract good of India. During the whole of their public life Fox and Burke suffered from the adverse use of an immense patronage by King George III. Promotions in the army and navy, advancement in the church and the law, pensions, jobs, titles—all these had rewarded "the King's friends"—all these had been withheld from the King's enemies. Now, at last, there was a chance to get even with the hostile sovereign. By means of the India Bill—to apply Canning's later epigram—a new world was called in to balance the corruptions of the old. As Pitt wrote to the Duke of Rutland:

. . . The Bill which Fox has brought in relative to India will be, one way or other, decisive for or against the Coalition. It is, I really think, the boldest and most unconstitutional measure ever attempted, transferring at one stroke, in spite of all charters and compacts, the immense patronage and influence of the East to Charles Fox, in or out of office. I think it will with difficulty, if at all, find its way through our House, and can never succeed in yours. [The] Ministry trust all on this one die, and will probably fail.

When the names of the commissioners were announced, the inwardness of the situation ceased to be in doubt. The chairman of the board was to be Earl Fitzwilliam "whom," as Horace Walpole said, "the Cavendishes are nursing up as a young Octavius, to succeed his uncle Rockingham." The seven commissioners also included Lord North's son, and were all supporters of the administration. Whatever happened to the Coalition, these men would remain in office, irremovable, and for a period of four years, uncontrolled by Parliament, they would be in a position to hand out jobs to the friends of their party.

As a whole, the London of that day was illiterate. But in the latter years of Sir Robert Walpole there began to be devised a language which even the illiterate could read. The art of caricature, associated later with journals like *Punch*, was consecrated to satire.

For such caricature, Fox, the flagrant, and Pitt, the precise, seemed to have been designed by Nature herself. Fox appeared as Samson carrying off the ruins of the East India House, and a penman called Sayer set the world laughing over pictures of "A Transfer of East India Stock" and "Carlo Khan's Triumphal Entry into Leadenhall Street," in which latter satire Fox rode on an elephant with the face of Lord North, while Burke marched ahead as trumpeter. A man about town himself, Fox was quick to appreciate the importance of these deadly skits. "They have done me more mischief," said he, "than the debates in Parliament."

★

Satire—verse and picture—was inevitable. Ostensibly the Coalition had been formed to resist the encroachments of the royal power. Ostensibly it was as the tribune of a free and independent legislature that Charles James Fox stood forth, defying the royal lightning. But, strip the situation of phrases, and what was the fact? At the very moment when Fox was making himself responsible for the India Bill we have this from Horace Walpole:

Fox lodged in St. James's Street, and as soon as he rose, which was very late, had a levee of his followers, and of the members of the gaming-club at Brook's—all his disciples. His bristly black person and shagged breast quite open, and rarely purified by any ablutions, was wrapped in a foul linen night-gown, and his bushy hair dishevelled. In these Cynic weeds, and with Epicurian good humour, did he dictate his politics, and in this school did the Heir of the Crown attend his lessons and imbibe them.

Fox, as everyone knew, was as deeply involved as Bute himself in the intrigues of the Court. If he was not numbered among the King's friends, it was only because he preferred to be "Dear Charles" to the Prince of Wales, and if a choice had to be made between the occupant of the throne with his domestic virtues, and the heir to the throne with his notorious excesses, there was no doubt on which side popular sentiment would be found. The first gentleman in Europe was not even one of those attractive rakes in whom—as Burke was to put it—"vice itself lost half its evil by losing all its grossness." His indulgences, which might have been delicate, were in fact detestable.

In May, 1783, the significance of the partnership between Fox and the Prince was made only too clear. As Secretary of State, Fox urged that Parliament grant to the Prince an income of £100,000 a year. Proportionate to the revenue of Great Britain in the year 1926, it represents a sum no less than about six million pounds. Even Lord North was staggered by the demand which, largely at the King's instance, was cut to £50,000 a year from the Civil List and a lump sum of £60,000.

This was the entourage, to the tender mercies of which, as it was believed, the patronage of India was to be handed over. A bill which ought to have been passed without contention aroused a desperate if wordy warfare.

Many were the speeches. But here, in the drama of it, was a single combat. "Giants stand like Titans face to face," wrote Byron of Pitt and Fox, whom, in a splendid simile, he compared with mountains:

> *Athos and Ida, with a dashing sea*
> *Of Eloquence between.*

The rivals were, indeed, a contrast. Fox was all exuberance. As he boasted, he needed naught save a spoonful of rhubarb to keep him in health. He entered the House, every inch of him, and there were many inches, the good fellow; revelling in the exhilaration of popularity; not an exact speaker but spontaneous, ample, and of a generous eloquence.

But Pitt—how different!—a man who had to husband his strength, reserved, keeping his distance, and insisting that others keep theirs. Writes a critic, Sir Nathanael Wraxall:

In the formation of his person he was tall and slender, but without elegance or grace. In his manners, if not repulsive, he was cold, stiff, and without suavity or amenity. He seemed never to invite approach, or to encourage acquaintance, though when addressed he could be polite, communicative, and occasionally gracious. Smiles were not natural to him even when seated on the Treasury Bench. . . . From the instant that Pitt entered the door-way of the House of Commons, he advanced up the floor with a quick and firm step, his head erect and thrown back, looking neither to the right nor to the left, nor favouring with a nod or a glance any of the individuals seated on either side, among whom many who possessed £5,000 a year would have been gratified even by so slight a mark of attention. It was not thus that Lord North or Fox treated Parliament.

While, however, the matter of Pitt's speeches was dignified, his manner suggested excitement. Lord Lyndhurst tells us that he would bend forward until his body nearly touched the table. To quote another eyewitness, Francis Horner, Fox "saws the air with his hands" while Pitt saws the air "with his whole body."

"In conversation with me," writes Bishop Tomline, "I always noticed that Mr. Pitt considered Mr. Fox as far superior to any other of his opponents as a debater in the House of Commons."

★

Two lawyers emerged, as they usually do. John Scott made himself ridiculous by talking about Desdemona and comparing the bill with the Beast in the Book of Revelation which has seven heads and ten horns. Sobered by Sheridan's sarcasm, he decided to talk sense for the future and so became Lord Eldon. Erskine met with a harder fate.

His success at the bar had been phenomenal. But over the doors of the House of Commons there has always been inscribed the sentence—"Abandon reputation [that is, your professional reputation] ye who enter here." Of Erskine there were indeed great hopes, but it was incumbent on him to fulfil them.

Erskine rose. But it was at once apparent that the House

was less interested in his speech than in Pitt's reception of the speech. With Erskine on his feet, it was to Pitt that the eye wandered.

Preparing to answer the great advocate, Pitt had taken up pen and paper. He jotted down a word or two. Then, as Erskine proceeded, he seemed to pay less attention to his notes. At length, with a contemptuous smile, he drove his pen through the papers and threw them on the floor. The gesture was the sensation of the day. Erskine faltered, his speech was ruined. From that day onward Erskine, most flamboyant of orators, dreaded the eye of William Pitt.

In the House of Commons the India Bill was safe enough. It was passed by 208 votes to 102. In very truth, it seemed as if Fox were, as Burke exultantly declared, at "the summit."

When, in these prosaic days, a measure, however important and however contentious, passes the Commons, a clerk of the House ties around the document the usual tape, walks with it coolly to the other House, and hands it to the clerk thereof, usually exchanging that weary smile which so often relieves the face of a permanent official.

But what awaited Fox was a Roman triumph. None but he must bear the bill to the House of Lords, and on December 8th, followed by a multitude of his enthusiastic supporters, he presented the measure at the bar. It was not merely a formality. It was a challenge.

In the Upper House, the King's friends, not quite sure of the King's wishes, were in full force. But so were the Prince of Wales and his friends. The Court, jealous of patronage, was fully represented by rival agents.

For a measure about to be obliterated there was available a perfect executioner. In the government of Lord Shelburne, the Lord Chancellor had been the redoubtable Lord Thurlow. Brougham has described his predecessor, Thurlow, as a man with "eyebrows formed by nature to convey the abstract idea of a perfect frown." To the scowl on his face this grizzly bear of the legal bench added a growl of the voice, and in December, 1783, his temper was not improved by the recent memory of ejection from the Woolsack where Lord Chancellors usually sit with comfort.

Rising with his accustomed and portentous deliberation, Lord Thurlow faced the Prince of Wales and proceeded to emit his grim anathemas. "I wish," said he, "to see the crown great and respectable, but if the present bill should pass, it will be no longer worthy of a man of honour to wear. The King will, in fact, take the diadem from his own head and place it on the head of Mr. Fox."

It was a direct thrust—repeated in effect by Dr. Johnson —yet despite it—possibly, encouraged by it—the Prince of Wales registered a vote in favour of the bill at that early stage.

★

There was now to be achieved what in those dignified days was called "a transaction." To begin with, Lord Thurlow had drawn up a private memorandum. In this important and long secret paper he stated that the India Bill was "a plan to take more than half the Royal power and by that means disable His Majesty for the rest of the reign." It was an interesting thesis, and on December 1st the thesis was

communicated by Lord Thurlow to another statesman, who
by a coincidence was closely associated with a young and
ambitious Parliamentarian called William Pitt.

The connection should be clearly appreciated. Pitt's
mother, still living and long to live, belonged to the able and
acquisitive family of Temple. She was the sister, an intimate
sister, of the first earl. In Buckinghamshire there still stands
that great Stowe House, with its lavish gardens, which is a
monument to the pride and extravagance of a clever but
foolish family. At Stowe House, William Pitt—himself half
a Temple—was an occasional and a welcome guest.

Pitt and the second Lord Temple were thus near cousins.
Nor was this all. When Shelburne was Prime Minister, and
Thurlow was Lord Chancellor, and Pitt was Chancellor of
the Exchequer, Temple had been Lord Lieutenant of Ireland.
The cousins had thus been colleagues and the cousins expected in due course to be colleagues again. Under these circumstances it was not easy for anyone in the year 1783 to
believe that any action taken by Lord Temple would be unknown in some way or other to William Pitt.

During the summer there had been a curious incident. On
returning from Ireland, Temple had been received in the
usual audience by the King who, much incensed by the
friendship between Fox and the Prince of Wales, had talked
of dismissing the Coalition. As Stanhope puts it, "Lord
Temple, however, though one of the keenest of party men,
had sagacity enough to see that here neither the juncture
nor the pretext would be favourable, and he strongly advised
the King to await a better time." Pitt was not "consulted

in this affair" but—and the sentence is of great importance—"he must have been fully apprized of it in subsequent conversations with Lord Temple." In other words,
Pitt knew that the King would go all lengths to get rid of
Fox and that he was only waiting for a favourable opportunity. He also knew that the King had discussed such matters with his cousin.

When the India Bill reached the House of Lords there
arose the question whether the favourable opportunity had
not at last arisen. Temple and Thurlow, both of them, were
Pitt's political colleagues and, presumably, in full sympathy
with his intentions. No one who had been in close touch
with political happenings at Westminster will doubt for one
moment that this must have been the situation. Indeed, the
coöperation could not have been more skilful. Each actor
stepped onto the stage precisely at his appointed cue.

To begin with, Temple and Thurlow sent their memorandum to King George III, for whose eye, needless to say, it
had been designed. The paper created the stronger impression
on the intellect of the King because it supported his own
views. It was a memorandum, moreover, tendered to him
by statesmen who, only yesterday, had been his constitutional advisers.

The memorandum indicated to the King that the India
Bill could be defeated in the House of Lords. But in order
that this most desirable result might be put beyond doubt,
it would be well if the peers were "acquainted with his
wishes." In effect, the King was invited to issue a whip
against the government of the day.

On more than one occasion the sovereign has influenced a vote in the House of Lords. It was the intervention of King William IV that secured the passage of the Reform Bill in 1832. It was a similar intervention that saved the Parliament Act of 1911. But in both these cases the King acted on the advice of ministers—Earl Grey in the one instance, Mr. Asquith in the other. What King George III was asked to do was to rally the House of Lords against his ministers. He was to act on the advice of the very men who wished to turn his ministers out of office.

In all these cases the King has to consider a simple question. He can afford to part with one government if he can obtain an alternative government, but not unless. It was essential, then, for King George III to know whether, in the event of his quarrelling with Fox and North, he might depend on Pitt.

★

It was, as we have seen, Pitt's colleague and cousin who had communicated the memorandum, and when, on December 11th, Lord Temple requested of the King an audience, it was immediately granted. The one man who, of all others, was best qualified to disclose to the King the attitude of William Pitt met His Majesty alone. Stanhope assures us that Pitt "had taken no part in these transactions." He did not need to take a part. It was the business of his colleagues to keep him out of it. "So far as we can trace," adds Stanhope, "he had not even been apprized of them beforehand." Naturally. It is not usual to put such apprizals into writing. In January, 1784, Pitt was accused of using secret influence. His disclaimer was vigorous rather than convincing. "I came up no back stairs," he said. "When I was sent for by my sovereign to know whether I would accept of office, I necessarily went to the Royal Closet. I know of no secret influence, and I hope that my own integrity would be my guardian against that danger. This is the only answer I shall ever deign to make to such a charge." It left a good deal unsaid.

In the *Rolliad*, where "Buckingham," of course, stands for Temple, and Brunswick for the King, the decisive audience was thus satirized:

> *On that great day when Buckingham, by pairs,*
> *Ascended, Heaven-impelled, the King's back stairs,*
> *And panting, breathless, strained his lungs to show*
> *From Fox's Bill what mighty ills would flow;*
> *Still, as with stammering tongue he told his tale,*
> *Unusual terrors Brunswick's heart assail,*
> *Wide starts his white wig from the Royal ear,*
> *And each particular hair stands stiff with fear!*

In concert with Temple, the King decided to act. On a card there was written, apparently in the King's own hand, a statement thus reproduced by Stanhope:

His Majesty allowed Earl Temple to say that whoever voted for the India Bill was not only not his friend, but would be considered by him as an enemy; and if these words were not strong enough, Earl Temple might use whatever words he might deem stronger and more to the purpose.

Precisely how the document was used does not concern us. At Westminster, rumour spreads, gossip becomes fact, assumptions harden into the unanswerable. In one way or another the King's friends learned that the King would not remain their friend if the India Bill were passed. Even the Prince of Wales had to withdraw his support.

A challenge to Lord Temple only made the matter more definite. When the Duke of Portland hinted, when the Duke of Richmond alleged, Lord Temple avowed. Yes, the conference had taken place, and did he apologize for it? Not at all. He said:

. . . It is the privilege of the Peers, as the hereditary counsellors of the Crown, either individually or collectively, to advise His Majesty. I did give my advice; what it was, I shall not now declare; it is lodged in His Majesty's breast. But though I will not declare what my advice to my Sovereign was, I will tell Lordships negatively what it was not: it was not friendly to the principle and object of the Bill.

Manifestly as the result of the King's initiative, the bill was rejected in the House of Lords by 95 votes to 76. The measure was dead.

It was not merely a collision between Lords and Commons, it was a collision between the Commons and the Lords, plus the crown. First, there was the question whether it had been proper for two peers, leaders of the Opposition, to approach the sovereign with advice contrary to the advice of his ministers. Secondly, there was the question whether the sovereign, so persuaded by others than his ministers, should have indicated his wishes to the House of Lords as a whole. In the House of Commons, Mr. Baker of Hertford, a personal friend of Burke, moved a resolution, of which the precise terms, though formal, are eloquent:

That it is now necessary to declare that to report any opinion or pretended opinion of His Majesty upon any Bill or other proceeding depending in either House of Parliament, with a view to influence the votes of the Members, is a high crime and misdemeanor, derogatory to the honour of the Crown, a breach of the fundamental privileges of Parliament, and subversive of the Constitution of this country.

Pitt at once rose and denounced the resolution as "one of the most unnecessary, the most frivolous and ill timed that ever insulted the attention of the national Senate." He denied that there was a specific occasion for such a debate.

But Lord North, for twelve years Prime Minister, supported the Resolution, and Fox was at his best. How, he asked, were ministers situated?

. . . They hold their several offices, not at the option of the Sovereign, but of the very reptiles who burrow under the Throne; they act the part of puppets, and are answerable for all the folly and the ignorance, and the temerity or timidity, of some unknown juggler behind the screen!

On Pitt the denunciation fell with full force:

. . . Boys without judgment, without experience of the sentiments suggested by the knowledge of the world, or the amiable decencies of a sound mind, may follow the headlong course of ambition thus precipitately, and vault into the seat while the reins of government are placed in other hands. But the Minister who can bear to act such a dishonourable part, and the country that suffers it, will be mutual plagues and curses to each other.

The resolution was carried by 153 votes to 80. A further resolution, moved by Erskine, was also carried. It announced that the House "would pursue the redress of the abuses which had prevailed in the Government of India and would regard as a probable enemy any person who should advise His Majesty to interrupt the discharge of this important duty."

★

The two Houses were thus in direct conflict, and so it is that we come to the second great day of Pitt's life, December 18, 1783. What the King expected, what he desired, was the resignation of the government. But, with Fox and North standing to their guns, no resignation was sent to him. When it was near midnight, then, the King himself dealt the blow. The Secretaries of State received orders to deliver up their seals of office, and since a personal interview would be disagreeable to His Majesty, they were to send the seals by their under secretaries.

They found it difficult to believe that the royal messengers had authority for this demand. But the credentials were indisputable. The Secretaries of State had been dismissed.

On the 19th the position was yet further defined. The seals were handed to Earl Temple, who took the oaths as Secretary of State and proceeded as his first duty to dismiss the remaining ministers of the Coalition. Whoever else was or was not responsible for "the transaction," Temple's complicity was proved up to the hilt.

Within an hour or two it was made not less plain that he had acted with and for Pitt. On the afternoon of the 19th the House of Commons met. It was crowded. Everywhere there was the excitement which accompanies a crisis of magnitude. There was no doubt that the government had disappeared. Fox and North were seen in the seats of the Opposition. But what was to take the place of the government? That might be suspected. But it had not been announced.

It will be recalled that there was a gentleman named Pepper whom, with Pitt, Wilberforce had lately "persuaded to Church." His full name was Richard Pepper Arden, and he was a young member of the House. He was seen to enter the chamber with a piece of paper. He rose in his place, caught the Speaker's eye, and moved for a new writ for the election of a new member for the Borough of Appleby "in the Room of the Right Honourable William Pitt who, since his election, has accepted the office of First Lord of the Treasury and Chancellor of the Exchequer." It meant that, in actual fact, William Pitt, at the age of twenty-four years, was Prime Minister.

OVER the Parliaments of the Pitts, resounding with Homeric conflict, there has been shed the abundant light of a revealing history. We are able actually to reconstruct those scenes, to hear the deep reverberations of the cheers and the protests, to breathe the awful air, to feel the weariness of the long and sleepless nights, and even to sustain ourselves with the wines and soups and the sandwiches which were included in the political ration.

Yet history, despite itself, is deceptive. Not always do we bear in mind that the sittings of Lords and Commons, now so fully described, were held in the first instance behind closed doors. What the world now knows was unknown to the world as a whole when it happened. Discreetly veiled by a censorship over the press, as yet a century removed from its present rampage of irreverent publicity, Parliament was still the Holy Place of the political temple.

Within this Holy Place there had been developed slowly and silently a sanctuary, still more mysterious, a Holy of Holies, the Cabinet itself, into which cupboard of all the skeletons it was the grossest impiety for an inquisitive person to intrude an eavesdropping eye. At Downing Street, the room with its Georgian pillars, its open fire, and its dignified dinner table is the selfsame room where, to this day, Prime Ministers preside in safe seclusion over colleagues, rebellious with their own importance.

As an institution, the Cabinet of Pitt's day, whatever it be now, was peculiar to England; indeed, as Europe thought, very peculiar. Like oaks in the forest, the institution had been a long time growing, and it was to antiquity, therefore, that it owed at once its toughness and its anomalous irregularity. From time immemorial the sovereign had been advised by his Privy or Private Council, consisting of men nominated by himself. It was the Privy Council over which Queen Elizabeth ruled supreme for nearly half a century, and to this day a privy councillor is addressed as Right Honourable, also wearing one of those uniforms which are neither naval, military, nor diplomatic but a little of everything combined, including even a touch of the final finery of the flunkey.

As years passed an ever-increasing number of eminent subjects of His Majesty were admitted to his Privy Council, including in our day the statesmen of the Dominions, in which multitude of counsellors there was found to be less safety than loquacity. Hence, there grew up the practice of summoning to the presence of the sovereign no more than a selected few from the larger body, preferably those who, at the moment, did not happen to be, like Essex, meditating rebellion. For instance, King Charles II so formed an inner executive consisting of Clifford, Arlington, Buckingham, Ashley, and Lauderdale, the initials of whose names are still

honoured by our dictionaries as the word "cabal." It was
thus as a kind of conspiracy within the sovereignty that the
Cabinet was first developed.

The earliest Hanoverian monarchs enjoyed what they
themselves considered to be the immense advantage of speaking and understanding but little English, for which reason
their ministers gratefully reconciled themselves to the absence of the sovereign from their deliberations. It followed
that the King, already excluded from the House of Commons, became an absentee from the Cabinet also, and in
Pitt's day the appearance of His Majesty at Downing Street
would have been regarded as an unpardonable intrusion,
probably warranting some kind of inexpensive revolution. The
Cabinet was thus the one place in the British Empire where
neither the sovereign nor the nation enjoyed a *locus standi.*

While it so happened that the Prime Minister was responsible for the government of the British Empire, he had
not as yet achieved his own existence. Indeed, it was not until
the Twentieth Century that the persistent rumour of such
an office led to its recognition, and in recent years a pre-
cedence has been granted to the personage who holds it. The
Prime Minister was thus addressed as the First Lord of the
Treasury: a title singularly descriptive of his status, since
in the first place he might be like Ramsay MacDonald not a
Lord but a Commoner, and in the second place, like Ramsay
MacDonald, might have nothing personally to do with the
national finances. It was merely an accident that Pitt was at
once First Lord of the Treasury and Chancellor of the Exchequer. He knew arithmetic and lived in days when a knowl-

edge of arithmetic, being not only rare but hardly respectable, was something of a monopoly.

The Cabinet was thus quintessentially English, and for this reason it was but natural that the word itself should have been French. "The little Cabin" had been, of course, one of the King's small rooms where originally he met his ministers, and the name, with the ministers, was transferred to Downing Street, to which resort the ministers were still invited as "the King's confidential servants."

The term that Pitt and his contemporaries applied to such an administration was "the system." It was as to-day we talk about a committee. It was, however, the lack of system that impressed the student of the British constitution. About the meetings of the Cabinet there was a certain ostentatious informality. No minutes were kept and no notes might be taken, except by the Prime Minister himself, whose duty it would be to report the proceedings to His Majesty.

★

When it dawned upon a crowded House of Commons that William Pitt, as Prime Minister, had actually undertaken the task of forming an administration, there arose an outburst of loud and prolonged laughter. Fox and North were not less hilarious than the rest of them. Up to that moment the crisis had seemed to be serious. Now it was reduced to the merely ridiculous. If the King had been driven to seek the aid of a mere youth against the two historic parties in the state, the crown was already beaten. To quote the *Rolliad*, here was

A sight to make surrounding nations stare
A kingdom trusted to a schoolboy's care.

"Depend upon it," said Gibbon, "Billy's painted galley must soon sink under Charles's black collier."

No one—not even Pitt himself—dreamed that, eighteen years later, the administration now to be formed would still be governing the British Empire. Pitt in office—so it was assumed—would be merely an incident. He would find his position untenable, the King would have to surrender, and the Coalition would come back.

For this skepticism there was, after all, an ample reason. To kiss hands as Prime Minister is one thing; to form a stable administration is quite another. The moment that Pitt began to look for partners, ready to share his risks, he found that statesmen senior to himself were inclined to make excuse.

If there was one man on whom he thought he could depend, it was Earl Temple. Not only was Temple his cousin, but it was Temple who had, as it were, accepted office on Pitt's behalf. Imagine, then, Pitt's feelings when, in the very throes of his cabinet making, Temple resigned! During the long course of his government there were many occasions when Pitt, as Prime Minister, was awakened to hear news of moment—bad news—news of defeat in battle. As a rule, he was able to go back to bed and to sleep. But there were two occasions when sleep forsook him. One was the night when he heard of the Battle of Trafalgar and the death of Nelson. The other was this night when he heard of Temple's defection.

Fox was exultant. He wrote:

What will follow is not yet known, but I think there can be very little doubt but our administration will again be established. The confusion of the enemy is beyond description and the triumph of our friends proportionate.

Even the King became alarmed. He wrote:

December 23, 1783, 10.46 A.M.

To one on the edge of a precipice every ray of hope must be pleasing. I therefore place confidence in the Duke of Richmond, Lord Gower, Lord Thurlow, and Mr. Pitt bringing forward some names to fill up an arrangement; which if they cannot, they already know my determination. One will be an hour perfectly agreeable to me.

It was at this moment of supreme uncertainty that Wilberforce wrote in his diary:

Morning. Pitt's. Pitt nobly firm. Cabinet formed.

The men who thus met under Pitt were only six, and here are the names:

William Pitt—First Lord of the Treasury and
    Chancellor of the Exchequer
Earl Gower—Lord President
Marquis of Carmarthen }
Lord Sydney   } —Secretaries of State
Duke of Richmond—Ordnance
Lord Thurlow—Lord Chancellor
Henry Dundas—Treasurer of the Navy

Of those seven men the Prime Minister himself was by far the youngest. When Pitt was a boy of eleven Earl Gower was joining the Cabinet of Lord North, and in 1783 Gower might have been himself the head of a government. Yet here we find him, a volunteer in service under one who might have been his son.

Of experience, as usually defined, Pitt had none. Save for a month or two, he had never held office at all. Yet he was now not only Prime Minister but Chancellor of the Exchequer, and was destined to be more than usually active in both offices. Not for nothing had Chatham trained his son to be a statesman. There was never a suggestion that Pitt was inadequate to fill his station as that station was then understood. With an infallible propriety he was able to pick his way amid the pitfalls of etiquette, of political intrigue, of royal susceptibility and of diplomatic controversy; and strength in debate was associated with sweetness in council.

Indeed, it is appropriate enough that, at the centre of the mantelpiece of that room in Downing Street where Pitt spent so much of his life there should be placed, its only ornament, a simple bust of that man who, for eighteen years, was the only man in that room with a name worth mentioning. It is a bust of marble, set precisely on its classical pedestal, symbolic of Pitt in his chill, gleaming correctitude.

★

For Pitt to have formed a ministry at all was thus a personal triumph. But the success did not mean that Pitt had

won the battle. All that he had achieved was the chance of
fighting it.

It was a battle that had to be fought and won in the House
of Commons and what the House of Commons considered
to be the "country." Yet of Pitt's Cabinet, five ministers
out of seven were peers, and so debarred from rendering him
any help in either arena of conflict. Facing Fox and Burke and
Sheridan and North, Pitt had no one on whom he could depend except himself, with Dundas, a shameless turncoat, as
his armour bearer.

Out of office, Pitt could throw his head back, stand alone,
and proudly declare that he at any rate was not as other men
are, entangled with parties. But he had now to accept the
fact that he was in harness, no longer a critic of everybody
else but one whom everybody else had a right to criticize.

A man ostensibly without a party, he had leagued against
him, in name at any rate, not one of the two historic parties
but both. Fox was on the other side with his Whigs; so was
North with his Tories. All that Pitt could depend upon was
the group of Whig dissentients who, persisting in the tradition of Chatham, preferred a son of Chatham as leader to
Chatham's recognized successor, the Earl of Shelburne.

But in estimating Pitt's chances we must not omit other
facts in the case. In the Eighteenth Century, with scores of
members holding seats by nomination, parties were less
highly organized than they are to-day. There were many
men free to follow a new leader whom they approved—more
of them than usual.

Also, there was this further to be considered. Experts in

ecclesiastical reunion tell us that you cannot consolidate two
churches, however amicably, without creating a third. So is
it with a coalition. It splits the parties which it unites. In
1783 there were Whigs who did not want to work with Tories
in the Coalition, and there were Tories who did not want
to work with Whigs. They turned to Pitt. Like a youthful
David in the Cave of Adullam, he gathered unto him all who
were discontented.

Indeed, as the personnel of the Cabinet showed, one
coalition—to use a term familiar to the electrician—had
"induced" another. For years Gower and Dundas had acted
as Lord North's right-hand men. Examine the case on the
evidence, and it is not easy to discover any great distinction
in political ethics between Pitt's Coalition and the Coalition
of Fox, save that Fox did it first and so left Pitt without
much choice. Also, Fox and North were the principals in the
play of party. The men organized by Pitt were dissentients.

In the transatlantic phrase, not descriptive perhaps of his
physique, Pitt was thus the Bull Moose who bolted nor was
there a political machine to stop him. On the contrary, the
King, who alone had elaborated such a machine, was on his
side. Within a week, then, the Prime Minister found that he
was supported, even in the House of Commons, by a body of
adherents almost as numerous as the Coalition itself. Also,
he had the House of Lords in his pocket and an even chance
of carrying the country.

On the evening of December 23d—the day when the Cabinet was completed—there was bustle in Downing Street.
Through the wintry weather hundreds of members might be

seen making their way to the residence of the Prime Minister. They entered the house as units. Within its doors there was a long discussion, and the units emerged as a party. It was a party as miscellaneous in its elements as the Coalition itself. But it was the party, none the less, that governed Great Britain for fifty years. To that party, rallying around William Pitt, there were to belong Lord Liverpool, Canning, Castlereagh, Peel, and Gladstone himself.

The strength of the party lay in the belief that, high politics apart, it stood for a return to the simple decencies of public life. "Pitt must take care," said Wilberforce, as he and his friends sat in their hackney coach, "whom he makes the Secretary of the Treasury. It is rather a roguish office." Tom Steele answered, "Mind what you say—for I am Secretary of the Treasury."

★

As constituted, the House of Commons was against William Pitt and able, at any moment, to put him in a minority. Hence there arose the question whether or not the Prime Minister would make an immediate appeal to the country. The King himself contemplated such a dissolution. "I own," he wrote on December 24th, with his usual command of grammar, "I cannot see any reason, if the thing is practicable, that a dissolution should not be effected; if not, I fear that the Constitution of this country cannot subsist."

To the Coalition, the crisis was thus simple. King George III was acting like King Charles I, and William Pitt was his Strafford. Because the King did not like the House of Commons, he would destroy the House of Commons, as the Czar destroyed his first Duma, by means of what Burke called "a penal dissolution." "No one would say"—this was the statement of Fox—"that such a prerogative ought to be exercised merely to suit the convenience of an ambitious young man."

Hence the surprise when, following a rule, ministers, having accepted offices of profit under the crown, sought reelection to the Parliament then existing. Fox, sure that he knew, exposed the trick as he regarded it. "Though a new writ has been moved for Appleby," he said, "I am not to be deceived by such a device. I believe that there is not a man in the House who is not sure that a dissolution is at hand."

Jumping to the conclusion, therefore, that a dissolution was intended, Fox, on December 22d, made his first of many false moves. Pitt, having still to regain his seat on reëlection, was still absent. Over the House of Commons, therefore, Fox, though leader of the Opposition, was thus in undisputed control, and under his guidance the Commons went into committee on "the state of the nation." In committee, Erskine moved an Address to the Crown, condemning either a prorogation which ends the session or a dissolution which ends the Parliament.

Great was the surprise when Pitt's friend, Bankes—he whose partridges had been shot that summer—rose and, on Pitt's authority, declared blandly that the Prime Minister had no intention whatever of advising a dissolution. The address was carried but the furore over it was reduced to a fiasco. Fox found that he was fighting the air.

Two days later the fiasco was repeated. In the Twentieth Century, an address to the King is usually presented to His

Majesty by some minister who, honoured by a private audience, brings back the reply. But in the Eighteenth Century, what has become a form was still a spectacle. With Fox at their head, the Commons carried their address to the steps of the throne on which His Majesty had taken his seat.

In the reply, the voice was the voice of the King, but the words were the words of William Pitt. They were entirely respectful and conciliatory. The King promised that he would not interrupt the meeting of Parliament, either by a prorogation or by a dissolution. There would be no more than "such an adjournment as the present circumstances might seem to require." The talk about Parliament refusing, as in 1641, to be dissolved or prorogued without its own consent was reduced to irrelevance.

★

It was the Christmas of an olden time. In the kitchen, cooks were still careful to stir the pudding the right way, and it was served on a platter, sizzling above the blue flames of flickering brandy. Every town and village was musical with the waits, singing carols and playing them on instruments of brass. Holly around the pictures on the walls and mistletoe hanging from the chandeliers were among the decorations. For such a Christmas the House of Commons had to adjourn; even Fox could not prevent it; and an adjournment for Christmas is apt to take the edge off a crisis. It did not look like civil war.

Having demanded that the House be not dissolved, Fox was compelled likewise to agree that the House should not

be asked to meet until the new ministers had been reëlected.
Hence the adjournment over Christmas was extended until
January 12th. In conceding this arrangement, Fox declared
that he would not "dismiss one servant" during the vaca-
tion, while one of his friends, Mrs. Crewe, talking to Wilberforce, said, "Mr. Pitt may do what he likes during the
holidays, but depend upon it, it will be only a mince-pie
administration."

Even so, the mince-pie administration had at least gained
three weeks of invaluable time in which to consolidate its
position. Indeed, what Fox had failed wholly to realize was
that Pitt had his own reasons for desiring to postpone the
dissolution. The Prime Minister believed, doubtless, that he
could win an election. But he was convinced that, if he could
hold office for a few weeks with the existing Parliament, he
would win the election much more easily. In resisting a dissolution, Fox was thus forcing on Pitt the very Fabian
tactics which Pitt was anxious to pursue.

About the confidence of Pitt there was political genius.
Here he was—the nominee of a King who had wrecked the
very fabric of political parties. Yet he dared to hope that he
could achieve a popular victory at the polls, and events were
to prove that he was right.

It was Pitt's instinct that enabled him to divine the subconscious movement of opinion, and by his instinct, not by
his impulses, was he guided. His parents, calling him "eager
Mr. William" and "impetuous William," had talked of his
"ardour." But when, one day, the mature Pitt was asked
what quality was most required in a Prime Minister—was it

eloquence?—was it knowledge?—he answered, "No, patience."

Still the decision to fight Fox in the House of Commons—his own ground—was courageous. In that House the Coalition held a majority. On any test vote Pitt must be defeated, and such defeats, if pressed home, must bring his government to an end. Even King George III could not attempt to govern in defiance of the House. All he could do—all he had done—was to govern by corrupting and controlling the House.

Hence, at the meeting of his supporters Pitt put a vital question. "What am I to do," he asked, "if they stop the supplies?" Without money the government could not be carried on.

At a public meeting allowance should be made for "the voice." As a rule there is present some man, not of the front rank, whose mind leaps to the occasion with a pertinent interruption or retort. It was "the voice" that, at Downing Street, disposed of Pitt's misgivings.

To Pitt, no voice was more familiar. Lord Mahon, who answered him, was his brother-in-law—better known to posterity as the third Earl of Stanhope. He may best be described as the man with "a hunch." As a relief from the tedium of aristocracy, he dabbled in science, invented a printing press, and sympathized with the French Revolution. In William Pitt's thrilling incursion into high office the "Citizen Stanhope" of the future, still in his early thirties, discovered a welcome sensation. When Pitt had put his question about stopping supplies, his kinsman answered bluntly:

"They will not stop them. It is the very last thing which they will venture to do."

Pitt believed him and decided to call the bluff of Charles James Fox.

★

The event proved that Lord Mahon was right. Fox was willing enough to wound but afraid to strike. In the House, the Coalition which he led was like an army in the trenches which is affected by a loss of morale among the civilian population behind the lines. It was all very well for Burke to contend that here was a struggle between King and Parliament. There were many who, with Dr. Johnson, insisted that the issue was personal as well as constitutional. The question, argued Johnson, was whether the country was to be ruled by the sceptre of George III or by the tongue of Fox.

In the game of chess there is a maxim that a good player avoids useless checks. Charles James Fox forgot it. He adopted tactics which did nothing to injure the government but were calculated greatly to annoy members of moderate opinion in the House.

At half-past two of the afternoon of January 12, 1784, the Commons reassembled after the adjournment. The ministers had been reëlected but had yet to take their seats, and with the government bench empty, they stood, Pitt among them, below the bar. Fox was thus still in command of the situation.

Determined to make the most of his brief authority, he rose and moved the order of the day. As he was speaking he was interrupted—the elected ministers had to be admitted

—but when Pitt, having been sworn, rose with a paper in his hand, Fox also rose, and as the Speaker ruled that Fox was already in possession of the House, Pitt's business was obstructed.

All that afternoon, all that evening, and through the night until half-past seven in the morning, the battle raged—seventeen solid hours of futility. The strain of it, the bad blood, the worse air, are not easy to be realized, except by victims and at the time.

When at last Pitt was allowed to deal with what had been written on the sheet of notepaper, it proved to be no more than a wholly formal message from His Majesty, possibly of a curious interest even to-day. At that period the monarchy was still dual. George III was not only King of Great Britain, but of Hanover. Any use of continental troops in Great Britain without the permission of Parliament was held to be, therefore, highly unconstitutional.

But in the American war such troops had been employed, and with peace declared they were now to be brought home. Hence the message from the King, stating that the river Weser had been frozen, that two divisions of Hessian troops, returning from America, had been landed, therefore, in England, and that as soon as the river Weser should be open they would be sent forward to Germany. For this gracious message a weary House at once voted an address of thanks to His Majesty; and the struggle with the crown, declared by Fox, was dissolved for the moment in an outburst of technical gratitude.

How were those seventeen hours spent? Twelve were

devoted to the operation of going into committee. But this was a mere preliminary to five hostile resolutions. All these resolutions were carried against the government; two were hotly debated.

The general aim of the resolutions was to enforce the authority of the House of Commons. Of that authority there are two recognized safeguards: first, control of finance, second, control of the army. Both these safeguards began to be applied.

The first resolution was financial. Any person issuing money for the public service without the sanction of the Appropriation Act would be guilty of a high crime and misdemeanour, and secondly, an account of all such sums of money, issued since the 19th of December (when Pitt took office) but not yet appropriated, should be rendered. Pitt was limited to expenditure already authorized.

The third resolution dealt with the army. The Mutiny Bill is a measure containing the regulations which govern the military forces of the crown. It is passed annually, and unless it is passed the authority over the army ceases. Fox persuaded the House to postpone the second reading of the Mutiny Bill until February 23d. He calculated that, until the measure was renewed in the statute book, Pitt could not dissolve Parliament.

If Fox had limited himself to these first three resolutions and, at a later date, had stood firm on them, he might—perhaps must—have beaten Pitt. But he proceeded to two further motions of a different character. By the first it was declared to be necessary that there be an administration enjoying the confidence of the House and the public. By the second it was stated that during the change of government there had been reported an unconstitutional abuse of His Majesty's sacred name.

It was these later resolutions that disturbed the public mind. It is quite true that, on a test division, recorded in a House thinned by the long night sitting, Pitt was beaten by 196 votes to 54, an adverse majority of 142. But Fox had raised issues affecting the throne and the dynasty. He was no longer merely defending Parliament; he was criticizing the crown.

To give King George III his due, he was not one who, in the hour of danger, failed to support his man. As the news of the adverse divisions reached Windsor, His Majesty ordered his carriage and drove to town. Arriving there, he displayed a mood as firm as the mood of Pitt himself. Neither King nor Prime Minister accepted the verdict of the House as final.

★

At a moment of crisis there is always one necessity which should be borne in mind. The King's government must be carried on. The fact that the India Bill of Fox had been defeated meant that Pitt himself must devise an alternative to it.

Of Pitt's proposals it is fair to say that they represented a compromise which, after ultimate authorization by Parliament, lasted without substantial modification until the year 1858, when the career of the company was brought to an end after the mutiny and Queen Victoria's direct sovereignty was proclaimed. If, then, it be the virtue of a compromise that it works, Pitt's bills were justified.

But they were drafted doubtless with a friendly eye to the susceptibilities of the company itself, and care was taken to avoid an infringement of chartered rights. There was to be set up a Board of Control, without new salaries, which was to share with the directors of the company the task of administering the dependency. Patronage, however, was left severely alone. What Pitt desired was, in his own words, "a Board of political control, and not as the former was, a Board of political influence."

For Fox and his friends, the question was whether Pitt's bill should be accepted, and here was, to say the least, an awkward dilemma. It was not a case of half a loaf being better than no bread. Rather it was one man's bread that would be another man's poison. Acceptance of the measure would have been political surrender. At such a moment, and amid such emotions, the new bill had to be anathematized, and when Pitt had concluded his masterly exposition Fox rose at once and elaborated the damnation.

But the House of Commons was by no means happy over the position thus created. The bill introduced by Pitt was on merits a bill that might have been introduced by Fox; it remedied the evils which Fox had exposed; it avoided the evils which Fox had invited; above all, it was a settlement of a question that had continued unsettled far too long. The back-bench mind, indifferently concerned with the personal animosities of leaders, regretted the *impasse*, and when on the second reading of the bill Fox invoked his cohorts to deliver the death blow, his majority over Pitt fell to no more than eight.

Such a division meant, of course, that for the moment Pitt's India Bill was defeated, and that the bill of Fox was still before the country. But if ever a victory was pyrrhic it was this. On the contentious issue of the moment, a House that had been favourable to Fox and North and hostile to Pitt was now evenly divided. The majority, adverse to the government, had been wiped out.

The House seethed with excitement. Fox and North demanded of Pitt a statement of his intentions. Wild invective was hurled at the ministerial bench. Pitt sat still. The shouts increased in volume. His opponents ordered him to rise and speak. But Pitt sat still. And the tumult continued.

There was an occasion when a member, hitherto insignificant, suddenly vented on Gladstone the vials of a wholly unsuspected wrath. To his neighbour Gladstone turned and remarked grimly, "Do you know, I have heard it said that there is no animal so ferocious as a mad sheep." A certain General Conway, formerly a colleague of Pitt in the Shelburne ministry, proceeded to play this fascinating part. He accused Pitt of maintaining "a sulky silence," of pursuing a policy that was "dark and intricate," and then flung across the floor of the House a more serious allegation. "They exist only by corruption," he cried, glaring at the government, "and they are now about to dissolve Parliament after sending their agents round the country to bribe men." At this suggestion Pitt did rise and his self-control was overpowering. He asked for particulars of the alleged bribery and, as for his own honour, he did not stoop to defend it. He merely adorned it, as it were, with an apt quotation from the twenty-eighth book of Livy. On the dissolution he uttered not a syllable.

★

Among the private members of the House there was a certain Thomas Powys, member for Northamptonshire, afterward created Baron Lilford, a peerage that still relieves a blameless political oblivion. A country gentleman of influence and respectability, Powys was one of those middle-of-the-road politicians who are to be found in every Parliament —the architects of compromises and coalitions, not all of which stand the strain of gravity. Over the confusion of the country, Powys, next day, wept genuine tears. It was Saturday, and he impressed on Pitt's mind his distress over the uncertainty whether or not the House would meet on Monday. Pitt was so far moved by the anxieties of the appellant that he undertook not to prevent the Monday sitting.

It was on January 23, 1784, that Pitt's India Bill was defeated by so small a margin of votes, and on the 26th there assembled at St. Albans Tavern the "independents," many of whom had deserted Fox and North. They were fifty-three in number, and it was their opinion as sensible persons that Fox and Pitt should now shake hands, begin to love one another, and so form a new government. Pitt was duly approached.

He was candour itself. He would be quite prepared, he said, to meet the Duke of Portland, as leader of the official Whigs, and so far, at any rate, the negotiations seemed to prosper.

But the Duke of Portland consulted Fox, and Fox, also professing a sole regard for the public interest, insisted that, before the interview, Pitt should resign office! To this suggestion Pitt politely demurred, but the independents, nothing daunted, introduced into the House a resolution declaring that the state of the country called for an extended and united ministry. Again it seemed as if the dove of peace might flutter across that hall of debate, recently so tempestuous.

But no sooner had everybody fraternized over the one motion than everybody began to be fractious over another. On behalf of Fox, it was moved that the continuance of the present ministers in office was an obstacle in the way of forming another administration. Once more, and this time in public, Pitt was called on to resign. Once more, and with indignation, Pitt would have none of it. He refused—as he put it—to march out of the fortress of the constitution with a halter around his neck, change his armour, and meanly beg to be readmitted as a volunteer in the army of the enemy. The majority against Pitt was only nineteen. He still held nearly half the House.

The Coalition, opposed to Pitt, conscious of losing ground, now proceeded to make use of Mr. Powys and his independents. Lord North knew that Pitt would never consent to serve with him in a Cabinet and he offered, therefore, to stand aside. Fox agreed to eliminate the unpopular provisions from his India Bill. Mr. Powys, thus encouraged, proposed and carried through the House a resolution in favour of a united and efficient administration. On this resolution Fox immediately founded an Address to the King.

On February 25th, then, we may see the Speaker in his wig and robes, with a great body of members behind him, entering the royal presence, when His Majesty held in his hand a reply written by the Prime Minister. In tone, what the King read was conciliatory enough; but in fact it was a challenge. "I trust," said His Majesty, "my faithful Commons will not wish that the essential offices of Executive Government should be vacated until I see a prospect that such a plan of union as I have called for, and they have pointed out, may be carried into effect." Both the rivals were thus ready to negotiate. But each insisted that the other should be the fly who trustfully enters the parlour of the spider.

★

Both men were, indeed, looking not at a rival but at the country. Both were assured that, at a dissolution, the electors themselves would decide the personal issue. Each was confident that the decision could only be in his own favour.

To Fox and his "friends of the people" there could be no doubt as to the response of the nation. Even a limited franchise could not result in an endorsement of the royal *coup d'état* by which Pitt had been enabled to usurp office. The logic of the situation was indisputable.

But was it logic that would prevail? Over the personality of William Pitt there was beginning to be aroused an instinctive enthusiasm with which it was useless to argue. He was trusted; he was admired; and it happened that at the very climax of the crisis, his growing prestige was enhanced by what, in politics as in diplomacy, is called "an incident."

In itself, the incident may seem to have been trifling. It was its significance that impressed the nation, and in order to appreciate that significance we need to subject the affair to comparison and contrast.

Why was it that Earl Temple had resigned from the government? Various pretexts were offered—that he favoured a dissolution which Pitt insisted on delaying, and that he wished to be free to answer the charge of unduly influencing the King. The excuses were neither convincing nor even plausible. Pitt knew the truth. During his very first day of office he was receiving a lesson on the seamy side of politics and his kinsman was the teacher.

The place that Pitt offered to Temple was the Lord Presidency of the Council. It was a place of great dignity but, under the circumstances, the tenure seemed to be uncertain. What Temple wanted was something permanent, and Pitt's necessity, so he thought, was his opportunity. In a letter to the Prime Minister, dated December 29, 1783, he expressed his demand as a "mark of the King's approbation," and in the discussions various "marks of favour" had been mentioned. Pitt, hard-pressed, offered a peerage for Temple's son. But such a peerage was below what Temple considered to be his price. Hence his resignation.

If, at the risk of a digression, we deal with the sequel, it is because this also is instructive. In the year 1784 it was noticed that not one marquis remained in England! That

was an anomalous situation which Pitt was only too delighted to remedy. There were, in fact, two men whom he
wished to reward. Let them be asked to complete an imperfect aristocracy.

The first of Pitt's beneficiaries was—need we say it?—
Lord Temple. He was duly created Marquis of Buckingham.
Was he satisfied? He begged to be made a duke, and Pitt
also did some begging on his behalf. But even to Pitt, when
it came to dukedoms, King George III could say No. The
King held that the highest rank in the peerage should be reserved for his own sons. However—to complete the story—
in 1822, a son of the Marquis of Buckingham was actually
awarded the strawberry leaves and a century of ambition
was thus fulfilled.

Whether the prolonged scheming had been worth while is
doubtful. The second Duke of Buckingham was the last of
them, and he went bankrupt for a million pounds. Indeed,
his case was more desperate than that. He was driven to
write books. In 1923, just a century after the dukedom had
been conferred, Stowe House in Buckinghamshire was handed
over to a private school, and where a Temple pored over the
memorandum of a Thurlow, the hopeful youth of a country
that has survived both have had to pore over the history in
which Temple and Thurlow played so strange a part.

If Pitt's first marquis was a Temple, his second was—
whom? Somehow Lord Shelburne, once the centre of conflict,
had slipped beyond the circumference. He did not join
Pitt's government. But in 1784 the Duke of Rutland dropped
a hint to his young friend, the Prime Minister. Lord Shel-

burne had "entirely relinquished all views of business and office, yet some mark of distinction such as a step in the peerage would be peculiarly gratifying to him." Pitt, who a year or two before had been glad of a brief with a guinea marked on it, made a few magic marks with his pen, spoke a few words into the royal ear, and the Earl of Shelburne strode forth as the Marquis of Lansdowne.

The sedatives applied to Temple and Shelburne were typical. If Pitt was to avoid corruption he must find an alternative—what may be described as an inoculation against this disease in the body politic. Hence it was he who elaborated the modern Honours' List. It was he who created a thoroughly recent and up-to-date nobility.

When George III came to the throne there were 224 peers, temporal and spiritual, in the House of Lords. When George III died there were 372 such peers, and the increase was largely due to Pitt's devotion to a benevolent activity. In one month of 1784 he created seven peerages, and incidentally his patron James Lowther became the Earl of Lonsdale. In 1796 there were sixteen peerages conferred; in 1797 the number was fourteen. Pitt had paid his tribute to "the wand of the magician" wielded by Fox. He also was a magician whose wand was powerful. At his gesture, earls and viscounts, barons and baronets leaped into existence, and if his creative exploits hardly equalled the triumphs of his successors, especially in the Twentieth Century, it must be remembered that he was only a pioneer in a great political industry.

★

It is with this introduction that we may approach the incident that so suddenly affected Pitt's prospects. It may be that in fact he was no more disinterested than Temple. But between the two men there was a difference. Temple wanted place with a price. Pitt only wanted place with power. Give him power and he asked for no other reward. It was in no uncertain manner that his attitude was revealed.

On January 11th, the day before Parliament had assembled after the Christmas recess, Sir Edward Walpole died. He was a younger son of the Prime Minister, Sir Robert Walpole, and by his decease a sinecure, called the Clerkship of the Pells, worth £3,000 a year and tenable for life, fell vacant. The appointment was in the gift of the Prime Minister. According to precedent there was no reason why, as a statesman without private means, he should not have conferred the income on himself. Certain of his friends were, as Lord Thurlow confessed, "shabby enough" to urge Pitt so to do. Pitt refused.

The manner of his refusal was, moreover, a body blow at the orthodox Whigs led by Fox. Their leader, Lord Rockingham, had, as Prime Minister, given his sanction to a Bill for Economical Reform drawn up by Burke. That measure limited all pensions, granted by the crown, to a sum of not more than £300 a year. Yet, with the measure actually before Parliament, Lord Rockingham had granted a pension of no less than £3,200 a year, ten times the amount to be authorized, to a certain Colonel Barré. It was this indefensible excess of corrupt jobbery that Pitt wiped out by substituting the Clerkship of the Pells for the Rockingham pension.

Politicians of the old school rubbed their eyes with amazement. But it was an act that the entire country could appreciate. The Corporation of London passed a vote of thanks to the Prime Minister for his public conduct, and conferred on him the freedom of the city, inscribed in a box of gold, valued at a hundred guineas. In solemn procession, the city fathers proceeded to Berkeley Square where Pitt was residing with his brother, Lord Chatham. An immense crowd had assembled, and amid shouts of approbation Pitt was conducted to the Grocers' Hall in the Poultry where, amid the utmost enthusiasm, he took the oath as freeman. There was too the usual elaborate laudation.

Strange indeed was the scene—Pitt, standing erect and proud, the City Chamberlain, robed and furred, addressing him. The face of the City Chamberlain—where have we seen it before? Is it not a face familiar to the grim guardians of the Tower of London? Did not Paris become acquainted with a face, not unlike this, when she offered a refuge for an exile from justice? Above all, is not this the face that aroused the electors of Middlesex to defiance of the House of Commons and the courts? We cannot be mistaken. The panegyrist of William Pitt is none other than John Wilkes!

At last, even a banquet in the City of London comes to an end. Once more Pitt, his brother Chatham, and his brother-in-law Mahon find themselves returning home in the coach. They need no horses. The artisans of London are drawing the vehicle in triumph through the darkened streets; and their route lay past that stronghold of Fox and his devotees—Brooks's Club.

Presumably of the club Pitt was still a member. Indeed, ironical as the statement may seem to be, he had been proposed, as we have seen, by none other than Fox himself. But of quarrels, none are so bitter as quarrels among friends. As the coach reached Brooks's, men armed with bludgeons and broken chair poles attacked it, forced open the door, and aimed blows at the Prime Minister which were averted with difficulty by his brother, Lord Chatham. The servants were badly bruised, the carriage was shattered, and Pitt was fortunate to escape uninjured into White's Club, not far distant. Such was "the sad sequel of the grocers' treat."

But the applause of the merchants of London proved to be infectious. Their addresses, thanking the King for the rejection of the India Bill and the dismissal of its author, Mr. Fox, were reiterated by other towns. Fox tried to dismiss these manifestations as the "shifts and impositions" whereby ministers were "driven to prop up their tottering fabric." But the House of Commons took a more serious account of the movement. A second appeal to the King to get rid of Pitt was calmly rejected and could not be pressed home. "Not a century ago," said Thomas Powys, in his lachrymose manner, "a vote of the Commons could bestow a crown; now it cannot even procure the dismissal of a minister." Any idea of holding up supplies or refusing the Mutiny Bill had become unthinkable; and a long Representation to the King, written by Burke and supported by Fox, was only carried by a single vote, 191 to 190! No wonder that Pitt wrote to the Duke of Rutland that "the enemy seem indeed to be on their backs." He was "tired to death, even with victory."

On March 23d every preparation for an announcement to dissolve Parliament had been completed. "We shall now soon have a little more leisure," wrote Pitt, "and be better able to attend to real business in a regular way, instead of the occurrences of the day." But on the morning of the 24th there was brought to Pitt a singularly surprising piece of news.

The Lord Chancellor Thurlow had his house in Great Ormond Street. It was a house which at that time lay near the open fields. During the night, so it seems, certain thieves had broken into the back part of the house, found their way upstairs into a room adjoining the Lord Chancellor's study, and stolen a small sum of money, two silver-hilted swords, and, last but not least, the Great Seal of England. All of these treasures had disappeared. Despite the offer of a reward, none was ever traced or recovered.

That the "curious manœuvre," as Pitt called it, was political could not be and cannot be doubted. To Lord Stanhope, as Pitt's biographer, it recalled the action of King James II who, in 1688, tried to embarrass his successor by dropping his Great Seal into the river Thames. To dissolution the Great Seal was an essential formality, and at once Pitt summoned the Privy Council to meet at St. James's Palace, where an order for a new seal, dated 1784, was given. The workmen laboured on it all night; and next day the seal was completed.

The King was thus able to proceed, as arranged, to the House of Lords. There, in a brief speech, he dissolved the

Parliament which had been the arena of a strife so embittered. "I trust," said His Majesty, "that the various important objects which will require consideration will be afterwards proceeded upon with less interruption and with happier effect." It was a bland request that a certain disturber of the peace called Charles James Fox should be obliterated by the electors.

IN ITS triumphs and its tragedies the General Election of April, 1784, surpassed all the expectations of the most audacious prophets. "This I know," Disraeli was to say seventy years later, "that England does not love coalitions." It was on the precedent of which Pitt was the beneficiary that he based the famous dictum.

Of the supporters of the Coalition, no fewer than 160 lost their seats, and in accordance with the title of a still familiar work on the Reformation these defeated hybrids were described by the wits as Fox's Martyrs. It meant that there was here something more than a political victory for Pitt, something more than a political defeat for Fox. Amid those frantic hurrahs around the hustings, those fluttering favours on the horses—and, it should be added, on the gowns of the ladies—those occasional missiles, and those heated orations which invited them, an old era had died and a new era had been born. All the bewildering cross currents that had swayed the various groups—the Rockingham Whigs, the Chathamites, and the Tories—were obliterated, and what emerged was a solid majority for Pitt and the government, faced by a broken minority for Fox and the Opposition. On a test division the voting was 283 to 136, a margin of 147 votes, or roughly a superiority of two to one in a full House.

To Pitt such a division brought with it a complete and a final indemnity. Whatever may have been the constitutional irregularity attending his acceptance of office and persistent retention of it in face of frequent defeats in the House of Commons was thereby forever condoned by the country. "A youth of five and twenty," wrote Gibbon, "who raises himself to the government of an empire by the power of genius and the reputation of virtue, is a circumstance unparalleled in history, and in a general view, is not less glorious to the country than to himself." According to Lord Macaulay, Pitt had become "the greatest subject that England had seen during many generations. His father had never been so powerful, nor Walpole, nor Marlborough." His apotheosis terminated the serious career of Lord North. Until the year 1790 he lingered on the scene, then he succeeded to the Earldom of Guilford and so he vanished.

The elections, now held on one day, were then extended over many weeks. Hence, at the outset, Pitt would have been chosen by show of hands to represent the City of London, had he not withdrawn his name. Other cities claimed him, including Bath, which his father had represented, but to the King's annoyance he would have none of them. For years his heart had been set upon representing the University of Cambridge, which only four years before had been the scene of his only electoral defeat. Both of the sitting members of the university, Townshend and Mansfield, had held office in the Coalition, and Pitt's candidature thus meant a contest.

With Lord Euston, eldest son of his father's friend, the Duke of Grafton, he fought and won, himself being at the head of the poll, which success left him member for his university until he died. Paley, the theologian, whose "evidences" of Christianity have fortified the faith of successive students from one generation to another, suggested that a suitable text for a university sermon would be: "There is a lad here which hath five barley loaves and two small fishes; but what are they among many?" On one occasion Pitt is reported to have said that Paley seemed to him an excellent writer. Certainly his wit was apt. Of Pitt's tutors, Wilson was appointed a Canon of Windsor and Pretyman, a Canon of Westminster, with bishoprics in view.

"Tear the enemy to pieces"—this had been Pitt's genial war whoop to his friend, Wilberforce, and Wilberforce, fighting the whole of Yorkshire as one constituency, proceeded to collect and to spend a sum of £18,662 on this surgical operation. Even in 1780 the Freeholders had been aroused. "Hitherto," said Sir George Savile, "I have been elected in Lord Rockingham's dining room. Now I am returned by my constituents." In 1784 the Freeholders were not only aroused but rebellious. Against the combined resistance of the great Whig houses of Cavendish, Howard, and Wentworth, the banker's son thus tried his luck, and there was a terrific contest. To Pitt's enthusiastic delight Wilberforce was returned.

The part played by Fox in the fight was desperate indeed. As his personal battleground, he chose his old constituency of Westminster. Once more the ladies of fashion appeared to canvas for "the Man of the People." Georgiana, Duchess of

Devonshire, stepped out of her canvases by Reynolds and Gainsborough and, radiant in her condescension, dazzled the tradesmen and kissed a butcher in return for his vote. As a verse had it:

> *Sure Heaven approves of Fox's cause*
> *(Though slaves at Court abhor him),*
> *To vote for Fox, then, who can pause*
> *Since* Angels *canvass for him?*

At a banquet in honour of Fox, the Duchess entertained the Prince of Wales himself as a guest. Nor did the Prince stop even at this excess of impropriety. After attending the King at a review, he rode through the streets of Westminster wearing the colours of Charles James Fox, the protagonist against royal influence in politics!

For seven weeks the polling continued. Covent Garden, where had been erected the hustings, was transformed into a bear garden itself. Placards on the walls, drink in the taverns, riots along the streets continued in one long orgy of disorder, and when the figures were finally declared, it seemed that Fox was returned, second on the poll, and therefore as junior member. At the very moment when the King was drawn in procession to the opening of Parliament, the Prince of Wales celebrated the success of Fox in an open-air party at Carlton House on the route.

★

But there had arisen a hitch. The total number of votes recorded was found to be considerably in excess of the total number of voters on the register, and on this inconvenient discovery a scrutiny was demanded. The High Bailiff of Westminster conceded it and it followed that Fox would have been debarred from entering the new Parliament if one of his friends, Sir Thomas Dundas, had not provided him with a seat—the close borough of Kirkwall. It was in this humiliating fashion, then, that the Man of the People scrambled back to the House of Commons.

It may be that Fox did not appreciate to the full the magnitude of the disaster which had overtaken his career. Not for twenty years was he again to hold office, and even then, it would be after death had removed Pitt. Still the blow, when it fell, was sufficiently severe and it was as a sportsman that Fox bore the reverse. "Misfortunes," said he, "have the effect rather of rousing my spirits than sinking them."

The scrutiny was an aggravated humiliation. Fox denied that it was legal. He pointed out that the cost of it would be at least £18,000. He aroused sympathy by adding that he would spend his last shilling on the fight to defend his electoral honour, and everybody was well aware of the extreme importance which had to be attached to a last shilling, on the rare occasions when Fox was so fortunate as to have it in his pocket.

By the fury of his electioneering, Fox had landed himself, therefore, in an unpleasant predicament. But the predicament of Fox was the opportunity of Pitt, and it is not too much to say that if Pitt had seized the opportunity the history of Europe might have taken a different turn.

For Pitt was now no longer the spokesman merely of a party. As Prime Minister of the nation, and of the whole House of Commons, in matters affecting the House as a whole, he was the acknowledged leader. It was from this standpoint that he should have regarded the new relation in which he stood to Charles James Fox.

The Parliamentary system was not based on a government alone. It consisted of "His Majesty's Opposition" also, and every opposition must have a leader. Nothing that Pitt could do, short of assassination, would prevent Fox from sitting on the other side of the table.

The question was whether the High Bailiff had or had not the right to order a scrutiny. At the bar of the House, the gentleman appeared in person and a word from Pitt would have quashed the proceedings. The word that Pitt said was, however, in the contrary sense, and the House ordered the scrutiny to be held. It meant that Pitt had broken not only with Fox but with those liberal forces of which Fox was, however strangely, the spokesman. From that day onward the Prime Minister had to depend to an ever-increasing extent on what became the later Toryism of Great Britain. It was, indeed, the party of Pitt that, after his day, received from Croker the new name of "Conservative" by which it has been known ever since.

That the election at Westminster was a flagrant scandal cannot be denied. But grave as had been the follies of Fox and the malpractices of the Prince of Wales, the scrutiny, now authorized by Parliament, proved to be no kind of a corrective. For eight months the farce continued. Over doubtful votes counsel interminably argued and wrangled. At least two years more would have been required to complete the inquiry. Yet Pitt stood to his decision. At length two motions were made demanding an immediate return of the election—or in other words the acceptance of Fox. They were resisted by Pitt, and on the first his majority fell to 39; on the second it was no more than 9. A third motion of the kind was actually carried against the government and Pitt had no choice but to surrender. As member for Westminster, Fox was again recognized.

With the General Election of 1784 the prelude to Pitt's career as Prime Minister is brought to an end. It is on the drama itself that the curtain rises, a drama that was to embrace not England alone but the world.

★

As the young hero of the piece stepped into his appointed part, not a shadow was to be seen on that brilliant stage. True, he had to reckon with an implacable opposition. But that only added to the zest of the game. On vital issues his was a safe majority, both in the Lords and in the Commons. At every cut and thrust of debate the House rang with plaudits.

Over his personal habits "the boy statesman," as he was still called, imposed an iron discipline. Breakfasting at nine, he anticipated the custom of David Lloyd George by sharing that meal with any guest whose business might be urgent, and when Parliament was in session he was seldom able to find a few minutes for his ride in the park. During the recess it could hardly be said that he allowed himself a holiday. To the business of the prospective session—which, under Pitt, opened in January, not November—his energies were devoted. As light reading, he would still find relief in the Greek and Latin classics, and that he did not neglect the literature of his own country is no doubt probable. But he took few steps to become acquainted personally with the authors and artists of his day.

He was an Englishman, rooted in English soil. In 1785 he purchased a mansion in Kent, near his birthplace at Hayes, called Holwood, a name which he always spelled Hollwood, and there, for a time, he indulged what he called "a passion for gallantry." It cost him a sum of £8,950, of which he raised £4,000 by mortgage, paying the balance in ten annual instalments. It was not a large house, but the grounds included a Roman camp and offered a view of that ridge at Sydenham which to-day is adorned by the Crystal Palace. He would visit Brighthelmston, or, as we call it, Brighton, and there enjoy the sea. Also, he would get himself wet through, not too often, during a long day of shooting with a friend like Bankes. Of his private life there is, indeed, little to record. It was public life that absorbed him.

★

When the new Parliament met there was an item of "unfinished business" that had to be cleared up. That business was India, and promptly Pitt set about it. There was no reason why he should delay. All that he had to do was to introduce again his own defeated measure, with suitable modifications, and force it through the House. Here was an issue that had been decided by the General Election.

The debates on the bill were again stormy. Not only did Fox and Sheridan attack it but, in his most polite vein, Burke summoned to his assistance the trained reserves of an ample vocabulary. This "rawhead and bloody bones Bill," said he, was an abortion of tyranny. Pitt's earlier measure, like an imperfect fœtus in a bottle, had been only intended to be handed about as a show. But it was now nursed by hypocrisy into a full-grown monster. Such were the delicacies of discussion in those cultured days when no Labour member had as yet intruded his pronunciation into the House of Commons. Despite the bluster, the irreconcilables, voting on the principle of the bill, could only muster sixty in the lobbies.

Thus was a compromise enacted which, so it was assumed, would settle the government of India for years to come. The expectation was justified by history. But measures, however valuable, are less interesting to nations than men, and in India it has always been the man who has mattered. It was with a man that William Pitt had now to deal. Across his own stage there strode a figure, equal to Pitt in stature, his rival in pride of demeanour, sinister yet majestic, a man whom half the world applauded as the hero of the piece, while the other half hissed him as the villain. In June, 1785, the people of Plymouth were interested by the arrival of Warren Hastings, back from Bengal.

Of the men who have made the British Empire, there have been four of the most illustrious that have owed their upbringing to the rectories and the vicarages of the Established Church of England. Such a man was Nelson; such a man was Cecil Rhodes. Such men were Pitt's great-grandfather, the Governor of Madras, and Warren Hastings, the Governor General of Bengal. In the East India Company, Warren Hastings and William Pitt thus shared the same background of mingled romance and rapacity. The distinction between Governor Pitt and Warren Hastings was less ethical than accidental. Governor Pitt's aim was to found a family. His gaze was on the future. But the family of Warren Hastings, however impoverished it might have become, had arrived on English shores with the Danes. For a thousand years it had maintained its eminence in the courts, the camps, and the councils of the realm. It was not to found a family but to restore a family that had been the aim of the penniless youth who emulated the career of a Clive.

In the case of all these empire builders there arose a certain dilemma. Each added to the British Empire. But none could be wholly applauded. Governor Pitt was frankly a smuggler. Cecil Rhodes dabbled in the Jameson Raid. On the eve of Trafalgar Nelson wrote his farewell to Lady Hamilton. Even Gibbon Wakefield, who helped to save Canada and to found New Zealand, was imprisoned for abducting a schoolgirl. So with Warren Hastings. During the perilous days of the war with America he had saved British influence in southern Asia. But his methods were scarcely distinguishable from misdeeds, while his mistress, the "elegant Marian," as he called her, had been in effect purchased from her husband, the complacent Baron Imhoff, prior to the Franconian divorce which permitted marriage.

It was her health that terminated the career of Hastings in India. Like Lady Curzon as Vicereine she had succumbed to the climate. Her indulgent lover fitted out an Indiaman for her comfort with a suite of elaborate staterooms and she was sent home. If, then, Hastings followed her it was due to no censure on his conduct by a mere House of Commons. That censure, as Governor General, he had defied. Neither rebuked nor dismissed, he gave up his position of his own free will.

India's farewell to him was not only friendly but affectionate. He had played England's game for all it was worth. True, he had become rich. On January 31, 1786, his fortune was stated to be £65,313 and he had settled £12,000 on the "elegant Marian." But he had found India disturbed and he had left India tranquil. His decisions may have been despotic but his manners were mild. His tastes tended to culture not cruelty, and if he transgressed the line of equity, it was always for a reason. In Leadenhall Street his grateful directors presented him with an address of welcome and at Court his reception was most significant. At the levee, their Majesties were notably gracious and that trustee of correctitude, Queen Charlotte, displayed the utmost affability to the "elegant Marian." Indeed, the wits made merry over an ivory bedstead which the Queen accepted as a gift from the wife of the retiring Governor General. Such presents from proconsular personages are tactful.

To Lord Thurlow, the merits of Hastings were obvious. Whatever had happened in India, here was the public benefactor who had upset the Coalition. He had, as Thurlow expressed it, "put an end to the late ministers as completely as if he had taken a pistol and shot them through the head, one after another." Even Dundas, who in 1783 had moved the vote of censure on Hastings, was now complacent. There was reason for the confidence of Hastings himself, when, in a letter, he wrote, "I possess the good opinion of my country."

★

But there was one little fly in all that ointment. In the House of Commons a member rose and, in broad vague terms, gave notice of a motion affecting a gentleman lately returned from India. No motion was laid on the table. But the name of the member was Edmund Burke. It was a warning to William Pitt.

The case of Warren Hastings was not one that Pitt could avoid. True, Hastings was now a private citizen. But a retired officer of his eminence would receive, bar accidents, a peerage, and to the grant of peerages Pitt had no conscientious objection. To refuse such a peerage to Hastings would be, then, an adverse judgment of the issue.

The mind of Pitt, like the mind of Asquith, to which we have compared it, was judicial. It was his hobby to be impartial. He realized that here was a matter that transcended the usual play of politics. "I am," he said, "neither a determined friend nor foe to Mr. Hastings, but I am resolved to support the principles of justice and equity. Mr. Hastings, notwithstanding all assertions to the contrary, may be as innocent as the child unborn; but he is now under the eye and suspicion of Parliament, and his innocence or guilt must be proved by incontestable evidence."

Quite correct; but did it relieve Pitt of his judicial function? Not at all. If Parliament was to decide, whose influence over Parliament approached the influence of the Prime Minister? Pitt had indicated the Court of Appeal. But he was still the judge.

It was, indeed, an amazing situation. Here was the haughtiest of proconsuls, fifty-two years old, submitting his entire reputation and career to the haughtiest of Prime Ministers, just half his age. Both men were scholars. Both of them were born rulers. Above all, both of them were gentlemen, quiet and courteous in conversation. It is recorded that they had an interview. The meeting was private. But what a meeting it must have been!

They parted in strict neutrality. To any idea of a peerage for Hastings, Pitt did, indeed, demur. But only on Parliamentary grounds. He could not "with propriety" advise His Majesty to confer a distinction on Hastings as long as "the sting" of censure by the Commons continued on the records against him.

To remove "the sting" was thus the aim of Warren Hastings. Like Governor Pitt before him, therefore, he invested some of his rupees in a rotten borough—it was West Looe—which he conferred on a certain major of the Bengal Army called John Scott. History shows that few Indian officials and few officers in the army, on retirement, achieve a Parliamentary success. By a dual disability, therefore, Major John Scott was handicapped.

Obviously, he should have ignored Burke's notice of motion. It was no more than a threat. No notion had been tabled. But he could see in Burke nothing save "that reptile." He challenged him to bring his charges to the test, and the fat was in the fire.

In the House of Commons Warren Hastings had to deal with critics accustomed to debate and not courtiers accustomed to obeisance. It was not only that the critics were led by Burke. For Burke had now the assistance of a recent and singularly well-equipped ally. Among all the pamphleteers of that prolific period, there are two alone, perhaps, whose controversial writings are still worth reading for their own sake. Burke's *Reflections on the French Revolution* is literature. So is the *Letters of Junius*, and Junius, it is believed, was an Indian official and politician called Philip Francis. In the council chamber of the Governor General at Calcutta, Philip Francis had been for years the persistent enemy of Warren Hastings. The whole of his inside information, coloured by an intense animus, was placed at the disposal of the Whig leaders opposed to Pitt.

In the indictment advanced by Burke, there were at first eleven counts; they were multiplied to twenty-two; and Burke demanded the production of papers. Pitt's only important stipulation at this point was that, in the public interest, papers manifestly of a confidential nature would have to be withheld. It was an answer not unusual under such circumstances. According to precedent, it did not lie open to criticism.

Warren Hastings submitted a petition, praying that he be

heard in reply, and with Pitt's entire acquiescence was invited to the bar of the House. In that unfamiliar environment he found himself to be utterly at sea. If he had said a few words, accepting responsibility for his proceedings, pointing out the element of exaggeration in the charges against him, emphasizing the difficulties with which he had been confronted, and finally reminding the House that, while he was ready himself to accept any blame which might rightly attach to him, he left to Great Britain an established influence in southern Asia, it is, to say the least, very doubtful whether the case against him could have been pressed much further. Unfortunately he read from an interminable document until he could read no longer. When his voice failed the clerks at the table took up the monotonous tale and members stealthily slipped away from the doleful scene. Not only had Hastings defied the Commons, but in his defiance he had been merely dull.

Strange to say, he left the bar of the House convinced that he had there appeared "in a happy hour and by a blessed inspiration." True, he had been "stinted ... most dreadfully as to time," but despite this disadvantage, extended over so many hours of recitation, his defence, as he put it, "instantly turned all minds to my own way."

At first it seemed as if the optimism of Hastings would be justified. On June 1st Burke did indeed renew the attack but with no great success. True, the story that he told is one at which, to this day, the blood still boils. The directors of the East India Company persistently pressed their officials for money and Hastings had been no exception. In order to satisfy the company, he had resorted, therefore, to various artifices, and on one occasion had received no less a sum than £400,000 as hire for the use of the company's troops under his control. These soldiers were thus sold as mercenaries to an Indian potentate, the Nabob Vizier of Oude, Sujah Dowlah, who employed the force upon an expedition against a hardy, and to some extent even a cultured, tribe—Afghan in origin—called the Rohillas, and wholly innocent, it was asserted, of any offence against British interests. A British brigade broke the gallant resistance of Sujah Dowlah's victims. Their valley, hitherto peaceful and prosperous, was then handed over to the tender mercies of the Nabob Vizier's forces, utterly ineffective in battle but utterly merciless in banditry. A population of one hundred thousand people fled from their homes to the jungles. Their women were dishonoured. Their property was destroyed. Their goods were plundered. Their territory was reduced to destitution. The very directors of the company, whose extortion had been the cause of the crime, were shocked by the infamy when it happened. They took all the money that they could get, but they censured Hastings for his way of collecting it.

This, then, was the story unfolded to the House, not for the first time, by Edmund Burke. Pitt listened but remained silent. Dundas, however, raised what lawyers called a demurrer. He did not defend Hastings. How could he? He was the very critic who, in 1781, had moved a vote of censure on the Governor General. But he pointed out that since the Rohilla War there had been passed Lord North's Regulation Act of 1773, that in this act Warren Hastings had been appointed Governor General of Bengal by name, that, by a further act, he had been reappointed, and that his offence, however serious in the first instance, had been condoned.

The debate was one in which, to use our own phrase, the government did not attempt to apply the whips. Ministers and members alike were free to vote according to their consciences. The Prime Minister voted with Dundas. "The sting" of censure, so he had maintained, must prevent the award of a peerage to Hastings. Yet the censure was sufficiently condoned to obviate an impeachment.

★

If any man had now a reason to believe that he was safe, it was Hastings. According to Macaulay, the gossips of the coffee houses were again awarding him his peerage with the Star of the Bath, the oath of the Privy Council, and a seat on the India board. Had not Burke brought forward the most flagrant of all the allegations and had not Burke suffered a defeat? Any further attacks on Hastings would be, then, mere formalities, ending the same way. By Pitt's tactics, the accused man would be saved.

But it did not happen. The next charge was handled not by Burke with his vehemence but by Fox with an oratory that, for the audience and the occasion, was incomparably more effective. Cheyt Singh was the Zamindar of Benares and a potentate of considerable affluence within the recognized authority of the East India Company. Confronted by the costs of war, Hastings had required successive and not unreasonable payments of £50,000 a year from this vassal ruler. All of the payments were made and Hastings himself received a present of £20,000 which he concealed for a time and then thought it wise to hand over to the company. But because the Zamindar delayed somewhat his final disbursement, Hastings imposed on him a fine of £500,000 and proceeded to Benares with soldiers, his admitted intention being to seize whatever could be seized of the Zamindar's property. The Zamindar laid his turban on the knees of Hastings in token of absolute submission. But, unable to disclaim the wealth which was his only crime, he was arrested and imprisoned.

A sacred city, not devoid of fanaticism, rose in its wrath and overwhelmed the companies of sepoys, and in that hostile region the Governor General was left with slender defence. During the confusion the Zamindar discovered an opening from his place of detention which led to the high banks of the Ganges. A boat was procured into which he was lowered by means of the knotted turbans of his attendants. He escaped to the opposite shore of the river and began to organize revolt.

On Hastings the tables were now turned. But he managed to send for help and by a curious means of transmission. On a journey it was the custom of the natives to lay aside their golden earrings and replace them by a quill or roll of paper. It was on such a paper, thus rolled up, that Hastings despatched his appeals for reinforcements. The troops arrived. The Zamindar was crushed. His dominions were annexed. The company got the money.

As Pitt listened to the story he beckoned to Wilberforce, and the two friends met behind the Speaker's chair. "Does not this look very ill to you?" asked Pitt. "Very bad indeed," was the reply of Wilberforce; and Pitt returned to his seat. In due course he rose, and throughout the House the assumption was that, following his previous decision, he would side with Hastings. To the astonishment of all parties, the Prime Minister, who had remained silent over the tragedy that had dispossessed one hundred thousand Rohillas, innocent of the least offence that could have deserved such retribution, took the view that an excessive fine on the Zamindar of Benares justified a vote of which impeachment would be the corollary. The resolution against Hastings was carried by 119 to 79.

The meaning of Pitt's decision has interested and will always interest the historian. The simplest explanation suggested by a remark of Fox himself is that Pitt was governed by the dictates of Parliamentary correctitude. He was not comparing the intrinsic criminality involved in the massacre of the Rohillas and the spoliation of the Zamindar. He was arguing to himself that one offence had been condoned by Parliament while the other had been committed after the condonation.

But to expect that the lobbies could take this view would have been to ask too much of political intelligence. What the plain man saw was a clever man's somersault. Malice attributed it to an instinctive dread on the part of Pitt lest a man like Hastings, proud as himself, as illustrious as himself, should shine too near that throne of King George III which had become Pitt's monopoly.

Thirty years later Hastings, in a letter, declared that, according to his information at the time, Pitt's decision had been preceded by a nocturnal conversation with Dundas extending over three hours. It may have been so. But in any event the statement proves nothing. The affair was one, after all, on which the Prime Minister had a right to consult his colleague and the account of Dundas himself is at least plausible:

The only unpleasant circumstance (in our public situation) is the impeachment of Mr. Hastings. . . . But the truth is, when we examined the various articles of Charges against him, with his defences, they were so strong, and the defences so perfectly unsupported, it was impossible not to concur; and some of the Charges will unquestionably go to the House of Lords.

Little did Dundas imagine that, at a later date, these very words would be applicable to the writer himself.

In the indictment against Hastings there were not a few details, if details they can be called, which evoked acrimony and, in many minds, a genuine horror. The shameless robbery of the Princesses of Oude was described by Sheridan in what has been regarded as the most overpowering philippic of modern times. Not only did the banditry of the Governor General include the violation of the palace of these royal ladies at Fyzabad, but their later resistance was overcome by the simple method of semi-starvation. Most execrable of all was the seizure of two aged and trusted eunuchs who were consigned to a dungeon and subjected by written orders of the company to what was described as "corporal punishment." In the East of that day it was but a short step from extortion to torture.

Silent and scornful, Pitt again listened. Again he voted against Hastings, and after further preliminaries the famous impeachment was ordered. The proceedings lasted for eight years. In defending himself Hastings spent £71,000. Ultimately he was acquitted.

★

In 1813 it so happened that the House of Commons needed the evidence of Warren Hastings on a proposal to renew the charter of the East India Company. Once more he appeared, now an old man, at the bar where he had read his statement in answer to Burke, nearly thirty years before. It seemed as if he had been raised from the dead. He was received this time with acclamation. A chair was ordered for him. When he took his departure members rose and uncovered. Pitt was dead, Fox was dead, Sheridan was dead, and last but not least, Burke was dead. Philip Francis survived. Of the members who had been thanked by the House for arranging the impeachment of Hastings, one or two remained. As a compliment, the House had allotted to them special seats, and in those seats they sat during the ovation with their hats pulled over their eyes.

WE WHO look back on those Seventeen Eighties in which Pitt rose so suddenly to power are able to perceive that here was the calm before the storm which was to sweep out of existence the Christendom of a post-mediæval period. It is not easy for us to see these events as they unfolded themselves, year by year, before his own veiled eyes. The very term French Revolution is misleading. It was in July, 1789, that the Bastille was stormed; it was only after six years that Bonaparte, with his whiff of grapeshot, established the authority of the Directorate. This is the period of six years that we have foreshortened into a phrase.

It is thus as a pair of spectacles—blinkers, if you like—that we must, as it were, impose the vision of Pitt on our own vision. Not only was he as royalist as the rest of Europe, adding peers to the House of Lords and otherwise maintaining the hereditary principle, but he believed in the dignified quietude of orderly statesmanship. Sitting at his official desk, he did his day's work, not only remote from the indecent uproars of Paris, but with an ear unassailed by the modern roar of a democratized London. No telephone suddenly tinkled. No auto traffic raged along the still narrow and silent streets. Secretaries and servants were trained to tread softly and to speak *sotto voce*. To say that high politics were transacted in a padded room would be an under statement, for the padding that protected the nerves was velvet. Pitt was a busy man, but even public life was a form of leisure. An hour or two—indeed, a month or two—seldom seemed at the time to make a difference. News itself trickled in slowly; it was told discreetly; the tone of voice was muffled.

Not one person in a million anticipated even a possibility of the convulsion. In France there were those encyclopædists, doubtless, whose compendium of knowledge and imagination, especially the latter, only appealed to King Louis the Well Beloved when, at the Petit Trianon, he happened to be in doubt as to the manufacture of silk stockings. A quaint prophet called Rousseau also wrote about a mankind in chains and preached emancipation. But what of England? In England the leading radical was Wilkes and Wilkes was Chamberlain of the City, Wilkes had praised Pitt, Wilkes had even dined with Johnson. Across the Atlantic there had been rebels who, with inexplicable perversity, had established a "republic"—a word only respectable when applied to Greece and Rome—but even these Colonists had proved to be otherwise cautious in the framing of what they had the insolence to describe as their constitution.

Yet the royalism of Europe was crumbling. Within each state it imposed a kind of order. But between states it fomented wars which were more expensive than anarchy itself. Not only did royalism fail to keep the peace. It did not permit prosperity. In the fashion of Dresden china, it allowed itself to be painted by artists and praised by poets and it dabbled in a kind of culture. But despite an occasional king who was really the canny man of his realm—the Gustavus of Sweden, the Peter of Russia, the Frederick of Prussia, and the unauthorized Wallenstein who, perhaps, was the ablest of them all—these old dynasties existed as a preventive of progress. By a significant coincidence of dates, it was in the year 1786, just before the crash came, that Frederick the Great of Prussia died.

The only question was at what point the system would begin to collapse, and according to the symptoms there was no obvious reason to suppose that the break would come in France. Her people doubtless were poor. Her taxes were oppressive. The privileges of her aristocrats were infamous. But that could have been said of every country to the east of her and even of Great Britain herself.

Between the Great Britain and France of 1784 there was not the difference in social conditions which we are apt to assume. In both countries the structure of society looked as solid as that House of Usher of which the fall was imagined with such eerie realism by Edgar Allan Poe. In both countries the nation professed an unshakable allegiance to an immemorial throne. Both of these institutions were of a venerable antiquity. Both had survived a succession of ancestral vicissitudes. Both were surrounded by a landed aristocracy and allied to an established church. Buckingham Palace corresponded to the Tuileries; Windsor Castle to the Palace of Versailles.

We are accustomed to suppose that the Bourbons were

autocratic sovereigns, ruling by divine right, while the Hanoverians were constitutional sovereigns, reigning by a Parliamentary title. There is substance in the distinction. But in the year 1784 the difference between the authority exercised by King George III and the authority exercised by King Louis XVI consisted of tendency rather than fact. The etiquette of the British Court may not have been as complicated as the ceremonial at Versailles but it was certainly as compelling. It was in a standing posture that the King met his ministers and, during one audience, the King and Pitt thus stood for three whole hours and forty minutes.

Of the two courts, it could be said at once that both the kings were blameless in their domestic life. Both were sincere in the profession of religion, the one being as insistent on a Catholic as the other was insistent on a Protestant succession. But, if a comparison is to be pressed home, all the advantages of charm lay with the French Court. The Bourbon was infinitely less exacting than the Hanoverian monarch. If you gave to Louis XVI his lathe and his locks he would be entirely content with life. But George was discontented unless you submitted to him the names of bishops, the details of uniforms, the clauses of bills, and the votes of the Opposition. As a competitor in the game of tyranny, George would give to Louis long odds and beat him any hour whether of the day or the night.

Between the queens the advantages seemed to be wholly with Her Majesty of France. With her shepherdesses at the Trianon, Marie Antoinette, the loveliest of all the Hapsburgs, daughter of Maria Theresa, remained to the end of her life

among the acknowledged divinities of her sex. But of Queen
Charlotte it was possible for Colonel Disbrowe to express
the hope that the bloom of her ugliness was wearing off.
Her economies, however virtuous, aroused mere ridicule.
The King's civil list was £800,000 a year; he did not live
within it; and it seemed absurd that, under these circumstances, the Queen should stamp the unused butter on her
table with her signet ring in order to ensure its reappearance
at a subsequent meal and use up her crusts by inventing
what, to speak the truth, has become the most tolerable of
all puddings, namely apple charlotte. Suppose that historians
do, in their inquisitive way, suggest that charlotte russe
may have been the real origin of the Queen's alleged dish.
The importance of an anecdote depends not on its accuracy
but on its circulation.

If it was so with the French and British sovereigns, what
of the heirs to the throne? The Dauphin in Paris was still
an infant, scarce out of his cradle. But the Prince of Wales,
roystering in Carlton House, with his debts, his drink, and
his debauches, was everything that the least attentive
parent would wish that his son should avoid. Who could
have supposed that, in an excess of her irony, Fate should
have reserved ten years of regency and ten years of a reign
for the man and a mysterious and still unverified doom for
the babe?

★

Why was it, then, that a throne with a sane king collapsed
in France, while a throne with a mad king was established in
England on yet firmer foundations? In one word, the reason

was finance. It was arithmetic that saved Great Britain from revolution. It was arithmetic that condemned her neighbour.

In both countries it was the budget that was the barometer pointing to storm. Both budgets were unbalanced, and no civilization, be it domestic, municipal, national, or continental, can be accepted as secure in which expenditure is greater than revenue. In both countries, impoverished by recent war, there were repeated and ominous deficits. In both countries the debt had accumulated and was still accumulating. In both countries the highest financial office was held by a statesman worthy to hold it. Pitt was the Necker of Britain. Necker was the Pitt of France. The two men tackled similar tasks. If Pitt had failed, if Necker had succeeded, the scene of revolution, it is at least arguable to maintain, would have been not Paris but London.

The debts of the two countries were, it is curious to note, approximately equal. In sterling, the figure was £215,000,000, and in Great Britain the entire revenue for all purposes was no more than £25,000,000. It was no wonder that consols stood no higher than 57, that the unfunded debt, borrowed to meet expenditure, had accumulated to a sum of £14,000,000, and that outstanding bills had fallen to a discount of anything up to 20 per cent. The immediate excess of expenditure over taxation stood at £800,000 for the current financial year.

In the collection of revenue the leakages were notorious. It was estimated that no fewer than forty thousand persons made a livelihood out of smuggling and they were financed by men of rank and position. Rum Row, despite all its fame, has not presented a spectacle more interesting to the advocates of law enforcement. Ships of as large a burden as 300 tons stood off the coast and discharged their contraband into barges which consigned the cargoes to gunmen ashore, to whom the farmers supplied horses. The citizens of Boston themselves did not handle tea with quite so reckless an indifference to the customs. Out of a consumption estimated to be 13,000,000 lbs., not more than 5,500,000 lbs. were delivered by the East India Company through the legal channels. In the case of spirits distilled in London from molasses, the revenue had declined from £32,000 in 1778 to £1,098 in 1783. Of 12,000,000 lbs. of tobacco imported annually, no less than 5,000,000 lbs. was smuggled.

Pitt's first business was thus to save the nation from imminent bankruptcy, and in one respect, at any rate, he was more fortunate than Necker. Unprotected by a parliament, that statesman had encountered the hostility of Marie Antoinette and had suffered dismissal. But with one foot in the Court and another foot in the Commons, Pitt, a colossus of the constitution, was in a position to act.

First he dealt with the smuggling, and here it was the ingenuity of Lord Mahon, the Citizen Stanhope of the future and Pitt's brother-in-law, that emphasized the remedy. The duty on tea was reduced to a figure at which it was difficult for smuggling to be carried on at a profit. Within a year the reform began to be effective, and in due course Pitt could comment on the paradox that the smaller the duty, the larger was its yield.

Not less courageous was Pitt's resolve to impose new taxes.

"I confide," said he, "in the good sense and patriotism of the people of England," and it was this confidence, not misplaced, that saved the throne and the social system of the country. Reviewing the taxation in the light of subsequent experience, it is easy to criticize its numerous items. In theory, Pitt had become a free trader. With Adam Smith, he held that the prosperity of one nation is conducive to the prosperity of all. But in 1784 he had not appreciated, or at any rate he did not apply the principle, that one simple tax, say on income, the whole proceeds of which reach the treasury, with no more than a small deduction for the cost of collection, is better economics than a host of small and comparatively unproductive levies. Of his first budget, the mere introduction led to 133 resolutions on which in due course numerous bills were founded. During the debate other resolutions had to be added.

On ribands and gauzes, worn by women, this young yet confirmed bachelor laid his unchivalrous hand. Men had to pay two shillings per hat, or six pence if the hat was made of felt. On candles the tax was one halfpenny a pound. On printed linens and calicoes, hackney coaches, bricks and tiles, horses used for pleasure, licenses to shoot and to trade in excisable goods, and, last but not least, paper—the raw material of literature and the news—the hand of the tax gatherer was also laid, if lightly yet definitely. The extension of the duty on domestic coal was so fiercely opposed that it had to be withdrawn.

There was one increase of duty which has been notorious. In English houses of Pitt's period there may still be seen sometimes a curious and unsightly feature. A window has been blocked up and, in certain cases, painted black with squares of white lines, imitative of glass. These blind windows are memorials of Pitt's finance. A house of seven windows had had to pay four shillings. The tax was raised to seven shillings. But a house with more than ten windows paid half a crown per window.

For every reason the duty was abhorrent. True, it did graduate the impost roughly according to the size of a man's dwelling. But it acted as a penalty on light, on air, on health. It was indicative of a civilization on which the teaching of hygiene had yet to operate. It was by means of the window tax that Pitt made good his initial sacrifice of revenue on tea.

One retrenchment aroused immense enthusiasm. Peers and members of the Commons enjoyed the privilege of franking their letters. Merely by signing the name on an envelope, the sender, if in Parliament, was enabled to secure a free transmission. The privilege was valuable. As late as 1840 the rate on letters was not less than fourpence and rose according to a scale of distance to over a shilling. The custom of "crossing" letters is thus understandable. To save money, correspondents wrote to each other, not only in small, close lines but in lines that covered the page twice over—right and left, up and down.

It was thus no wonder that banks, for instance, kept boxes full of envelopes graciously signed in advance by some obliging politician at Westminster, or that letters were frequently addressed to a member at places where that member never resided. Pitt laid it down that, for the future, no member should be permitted to frank more than ten letters a day, which must be dated and addressed fully in his handwriting, while only at his own address might a member receive letters post free. The regulations continued until 1839 when the penny post was established. They stopped the worst of the former abuses, and could only be evaded by the unusually inventive mind. One counterfeiter used the name of Sir John Hope and defended himself by maintaining that he had merely written on his own letters the words "Free I hope." Another frugal peer, at his death, left behind him the franked announcements of his own decease.

In the next year there had to be still increased taxation. Gloves, pawnbrokers' licenses, salt carried coastwise, and maidservants came within the budget, and in 1786 Pitt applied an excise to wine.

So the budgets followed one another, and in 1792 Pitt could claim that, over a period of four years, his annual revenue had averaged £400,000 in excess of the expenditure. On the eve of the war he was able to take the taxes off female servants, carts, and wagons; also off candles and houses having fewer than seven windows.

Nor was it enough that the Chancellor of the Exchequer should deal with revenue and expenditure. He had also to reorganize the debt. That he invented the idea of a sinking fund may not be strictly the fact. For many years, doubtless, sinking funds, like other obvious devices, had been talked about in a vague and inconclusive manner. It is not, after all, the function of a statesman, of necessity, to originate such ideas; enough that he knows a good idea when it is suggested to him. The point is that Pitt did what economists had dreamed might be done.

★

In handling the sinking fund Pitt was captured by an idea which to-day is held to have been fallacious. It was an idea developed by a certain Dr. Price of whom we shall hear later. He pointed out, truly enough, that a sum of £200,000 set apart annually at compound interest would accumulate in eighty-six years to £258,000,000, or more than enough to wipe out the national debt with which Pitt had to deal. The magic of compound interest thus fascinated the financial imagination of the Chancellor of the Exchequer. But the scheme meant, of course, that somebody would have to pay the compound interest. That somebody was the state itself. It was thus obviously simpler that, year by year, the state should not only purchase its own paper, but cancel it out-right.

On the other hand, Pitt, whatever his error in method, had at least asserted the true principle on which all credit must be based. Since his day Great Britain and every responsible nation has applied—or at least knows that it should apply—a sinking fund of some kind to its obligations. Between the years 1784 and 1792, when war intervened, Pitt wrote off nearly eleven million sterling of obligations. It was when, during the war, his million sterling of sinking fund had to be borrowed at higher rates of interest in order to reduce a million of debt at low rates that the fallacy became an extravagance.

The magnitude of the task may be estimated from the simple fact that, taking the actual year 1784—a year of peace —Pitt was faced at the outset by the necessity of borrowing. He needed £6,000,000 for immediate deficits and he needed another £6,600,000 for the funding of some, at least, of the floating debt. The first of these loans was raised on terms which a third-rate Latin-American republic would consider to be ruinous. A subscriber who found £100 in gold received in exchange, (1) consols at 3 per cent. amounting to £100 face value, (2) consols at 4 per cent. amounting to £50 face value, (3) an annuity 5s 6d a year, and (4) three fifths of a lottery ticket in a lottery of 36,000 tickets. Yet the actual value of these varied benefits was computed to be only £103– 14s.– $4\frac{1}{2}$d. as the market then stood. As for the second loan, it was issued at 93 and bore interest at 5 per cent.

Such was the price that Great Britain had to pay for her financial redemption. Happily there was another aspect to these expensive operations. In issuing loans Lord North had arranged the price with his friends in the city and had then allotted scrip at a lower figure to his supporters at Westminster who pocketed the margin. Pitt's loan was thrown open to public tender; the bids were handled by the Bank of England and from that day onward even the slightest taint of jobbery was excluded from such financial operations.

In 1787 Pitt's financial resolutions actually numbered no fewer than 2,537, and even Burke had to admit that he was rendering a public service by his reforms. The next year, 1788, saw the budget balanced, with the exception of one item, the claims of the American loyalists. A sum of £1,228,000 was found for these families, with £113,000 for Florida. The money was raised by means of lotteries.

The net result of all these arrangements was that, amid an insolvent Europe, one country established her solvency. That country was Great Britain, and the achievement is due entirely to the rectitude and genius of William Pitt.

IT WAS in the autumn of 1788 that the tests of stability began to be applied to the rival thrones of France and England. In France the test seemed to be mild enough. His Most Christian Majesty was merely considering the summons of the Estates General. It was a Parliamentary legislature, consisting of peers, ecclesiastics, and the bourgeoisie, and no more revolutionary than the Parliament that met in the Palace of Westminster. It was in May, 1789, that the Estates General met at Versailles.

What had been happening in England? If ever a throne reeled under a staggering blow of fate, it was there.

About King George III there was a lovable quality which it was not easy even for his critics to resist. In August, 1786, he was stepping out of his coach at St. James's Palace when an excited woman, respectably dressed, handed him a petition with one hand and, with the other hand, tried to stab him with a knife. The King's behaviour was superb. "I am not hurt," he said quietly. "Take care of the poor woman; do not hurt her." Examined by the Privy Council, she proved to be a seamstress who believed herself to be the rightful Queen of England. For forty years she was detained in the Bethlehem Hospital.

If the King was sympathetic there may have been a reason. In the year 1765 he had suffered a mental malady sufficiently serious to warrant the preparation of a Regency Bill. The cloud lifted, however, and nothing more was thought of it. During the troublous period of the American Secession, when the King played so prominent a part, nobody ventured seriously to suggest that he was other than sane in the usual sense of that word. Whatever may have been his political errors, they were after all shared by the main body of the governing aristocracy, both in Parliament and in the country as a whole.

But in the summer of 1788 there was no doubt that His Majesty was tired out. He became bilious and, writing to Pitt, confessed that he was "a cup too low." His habit of taking long walks had to be discontinued. "My dear Effy," he said to one of the Queen's ladies, the Dowager Countess of Effingham, "you see me all at once an old man."

On October 22d Sir George Baker, his physician, wondered whether his brain was affected. But on the 24th the King, anxious "to stop further lies and any fall in the stocks," attended the levee, but at an audience afterward aroused Pitt's concern by his "bodily stiffness." He asked the Prime Minister to postpone sending him papers until the next levee, but his letters were not incoherent. On November 3d His Majesty wrote:

Windsor, Nov. 3, 1788.
The King thinks it must give Mr. Pitt pleasure to receive a line from him. This will convince him the King can sign warrants without inconvenience: therefore he desires any that are ready

may be sent, and he has no objection to receive any large number, for he shall order the messenger to return to town and shall sign them at his leisure. He attempts reading the despatches daily, but as yet without success; but he eats well, sleeps well, and is not in the least now fatigued with riding, though he cannot yet stand long, and is fatigued if he walks. Having gained so much, the rest will soon follow. Mr. Pitt is desired to be at Kew at two or three o'clock, whichever suits him best.

G. R.

On that date, November 3d, Fanny Burney, then in the royal household, made this entry in her journal:

We are all here in a most uneasy state. The King is better and worse so frequently, and changes so daily backward and forward, that everything is to be apprehended if his nerves are not some way quieted. I dreadfully fear he is on the eve of some severe fever. The Queen is almost overpowered with some secret terror. I am affected beyond all expression in her presence to see what struggle she makes to support serenity. To-day she gave up the conflict when I was alone with her, and burst into a violent fit of tears. It was very, very terrible to see!

Two days later the King was "all smiling benignity, but gave so many orders to the postilions, and got in and out of the carriage twice with such agitation, that again my fear of a great fever hanging over him grew more and more powerful." At dinner, the King was in a delirium and there began to be distressing scenes. Stanhope wrote:

During the night which followed there were many anxious watchers in the apartment next to the Royal sufferer's. The

Prince of Wales, the Duke of York, the physicians, and the gentle-men of the Royal Household, sat on chairs and lay on sofas round the room. All were in dead silence, and amid the partial darkness the two Princes were still to be distinguished by their stars.

Into that room, which he had supposed empty, the King, fully dressed, suddenly walked. They whispered to Sir George Baker that, as the physician, he should conduct His Majesty back into his bedchamber. But Baker, whom the King called "an old woman," hesitated. To continue Stan-hope's account:

At length the Queen's Vice-Chamberlain, Colonel Stephen Digby, an old servant of their Majesties, resolved to act. He went boldly up, and taking the King by the arm, entreated him to go to bed; but finding entreaties in vain, began to draw His Majesty along, and to say he must go. "I will not," cried the King. "I will not! Who are you?" "I am Colonel Digby, Sir," he answered, "and your Majesty has been very good to me, and now I am going to be very good to you; for you must come to bed, Sir—it is neces-sary to your life." And then, continued the Prince of Wales in his narrative, the King was so surprised that he allowed himself to be drawn along as gently as a child, and thus was he brought back to his chamber.

To the Duke of York, the King, bursting into tears, had said, "I wish to God I might die for I am going to be mad."

★

In order that we may appreciate this crisis, it is permis-sible, so we submit, to contrast it with a more recent oc-currence. As these words are written there has been an anxiety, of a wholly different character, brooding over the British Court. A sovereign, greatly beloved, has been lying for weeks on the threshold of the unknown, and his duties have been discharged in part by a council of state. But what has been the attitude of peoples and parties toward the illness of King George V? In all lands where his sovereignty is acknowledged there has been prayer for his complete recovery. Not a whisper of faction has disturbed that unanimity, and if there had been a whisper, the last person to give ear to it would have been the heir to the throne, greatly honoured in our day as the Prince of Wales.

But in 1788 the tragic rumour that the King might be displaying symptoms of an incipient mania, a tragedy that evoked from so reserved a man as Pitt himself a profound personal emotion, was received by the Whigs at Brooks's Club with exulting glee. The madness of man was a gift from the gods. The Prince of Wales would be Regent, Pitt would be dismissed, Fox would be installed in his place, and there would be a payment of all the old scores, with interest added. The principals in the drama were under no illusions as to what would be their respective destinies. Fox, travelling in Italy with his mistress, Mrs. Armistead, hurried home post haste. Pitt prepared himself for a return to his career at the bar.

At Windsor, one day, there was a council. It was noticed that the grim ruffian, Lord Thurlow, had arrived before his colleagues. When the council was over Lord Thurlow's hat was nowhere to be found. But at length one of the pages ran up with the hat and, anticipating the thanks of the Lord

Chancellor, exclaimed, "My Lord, I found it in the closet of His Royal Highness, the Prince of Wales." For Lord Thurlow, as Keeper of the King's conscience, it was a bad moment. He had been found out. As the price of the grossest treachery to Pitt, he had been promised by the Whigs that, in their government, if it should be formed, he would be, once more, Lord Chancellor.

About the Woolsack, at this period, there seemed to be some mysterious influence that incapacitated those who sat on it for honest dealing. When the Whigs arranged matters with Thurlow they had to throw over their own man, Loughborough, and Fox, returning from Europe, confirmed the betrayal.

Loughborough was as unscrupulous in his intrigues as Thurlow. But he was more polite about it. Very able, he played, not the curmudgeon, but the courtier.

On this occasion, however, he was outwitted. For knowing nothing of Thurlow's approaches, he had proposed to the Whigs that the Prince of Wales seize the regency and ignore Parliament. He wrote out his *coup d'état* in pencil and ministers, hearing of it, agreed among themselves that if it went further they would arrest His Lordship, send him to the Tower, and impeach him for high treason. On his return to the scene Fox, however, quashed his henchman who, in the House of Lords, explicitly denied that he had ever held the heresy expressed in his then private memorandum!

On December 3d there was held a solemn meeting of the Privy Council. Fifty-four of the councillors attended, of whom it was estimated that twenty-four belonged to the

Opposition. Five physicians testified on oath that the King was incapable of business, adding that such a case might last for only six weeks, while, on the other hand, they had known the malady to continue for as long a period as two years. But Parliament did not always accept information from the Privy Council, and early in December Lords and Commons each appointed a committee to examine the medical facts. The result was that, after deliberations lasting one day, the King's incapacity was accepted, and Pitt proposed a further committee to search for precedents.

Waste of time—that was the verdict of Fox on this second inquiry, and there was much to support the contention. Suppose that regencies had been proposed for Edward II in 1326, for Richard II in 1377, and for Henry VI in 1422 and 1455? What of it? Great Britain was living in the Eighteenth, not the Fourteenth, Century. She had developed a Parliament. The only precedent that conceivably might be relevant was the Revolution of 1688.

When, however, Fox came to discuss what action should be taken, his impetuosity surpassed itself. He claimed that, as Heir Apparent, the Prince of Wales had a right, then and there, to exercise all the functions of sovereignty. There was no distinction to be drawn between the incapacity of the King and his death. All that Parliament had to do was to assign a date when the Prince of Wales should enter on his prerogatives.

Such an assertion of the divine right of kings from Fox, of all men, aroused astonishment. As his rival developed his thesis Pitt listened intently and, when the position was clear, he slapped his thigh in unconcealed delight, whispering to his neighbour on the Treasury Bench, "I'll *unwhig* the gentleman for the rest of his life." In his reply Pitt maintained that the doctrine of Fox was treason to the constitution and that, save by the decision of Parliament, the Prince of Wales had no more right—speaking of strict right—to assume the government than any other individual subject of the realm.

To such a discussion Edmund Burke might have been expected to contribute a philosophic impartiality. This strangely overrated man, however, proceeded to describe Pitt as "one of the Prince's competitors" and as "the Prince Opposite." For these expressions he was called to order, and Pitt, in his turn, inquired whether Somers had not insisted on the Parliamentary basis of the title to the Crown, and "would it have been fair or decent for any member of either House to have pronounced Mr. Somers a personal competitor of King William III?"

If this was not civil war, it was at least a war of incivility. Fox even went so far as to warn the House against "the danger of provoking the Prince to assert his right," and these words of menace were answered by an uproar of protest. In due course Fox had to explain that he spoke only for himself, with no other authority, and certainly without any authority from the heir to the throne.

The conduct of the Prince does not directly concern us. That he arrived at Windsor, assumed command of everything, domineered over his mother, and struck the ground with his stick in his displeasure suggests no pleasant picture.

Among his least tactful proceedings was the seizure and search of his father's private papers amongst which he found evidence that some paternal remonstrances which he had received had been drafted for King George III by William Pitt.

The quarrel between the parties was extended to the King's physicians. If Dr. Warren said the King was worse, Dr. Warren was for Fox. If Dr. Willis declared that His Majesty was better, Dr. Willis was for Pitt. Threatening letters poured in on the doctors, and on one occasion Sir George Baker was stopped in his carriage by the mob and asked roughly about the King's health. He replied that it was bad and the people answered in threatening terms, "The more shame for you!"

The treatment of the King by his doctors was hardly calculated to inspire confidence. They wanted to move him to Kew and he did not agree to be moved. They therefore sent his wife and daughters in advance, promising His Majesty that if he followed he should join them. On this condition the King willingly agreed to go, but at Kew the promise was broken and he was not allowed to see his family. The result, as might be expected, was to throw the sufferer into a fresh paroxysm of anguish.

Happily, there was found a clergyman, the Rev. Francis Willis, Rector of Wapping, who deserves a larger place in the history of mankind than he has yet received. He lived in days anterior to psychology, but, anticipating much of our later wisdom, he had alleviated the derangements of many unfortunates, of whom he had had charge of no fewer than nine hundred. On seeing the King, he said at once that, if he had been called in earlier, the illness would have been of short duration. "He laid aside," says Stanhope, "all false pretences, all petty vexations, all unnecessary restraints." The King had written a letter to the Queen but said sadly that he knew she would never get it. "I will take it myself," said Willis, and he brought back an affectionate reply. If the King did not want to go to bed, Willis asserted a commanding authority to which his illustrious patient surrendered. But, on the other hand, Willis restored to him his knife and fork and even his razor. As His Majesty removed a five-weeks' beard, his adviser credited him with too much sense of what he owed to God to make an ill use of the blade.

The King demurred at first to having a clergyman for his doctor. Willis reminded him that the Saviour healed the sick. "Yes," said His Majesty, "but I never heard that he had £700 a year for so doing," a retort which hardly suggested irretrievable insanity. In fact, he began to improve. He could see the Queen and hold her hand. He could allow the Princess Amelia, his favourite child, to sit on his lap.

★

The Opposition was thus confronted by the terrible possibility that, after all, the King might recover before Pitt had been dismissed. In the House of Lords, therefore, the Duke of York, in a maiden speech, disclaimed with dignity any desire on the part of the Prince of Wales to put forward a claim not derived from the will of the people as expressed in Parliament. The conspirator, Thurlow, therefore rose from the Woolsack, and in a voice choking with emotion cried, "When I forget my King, may God forget me!" the effect of which outburst was electric. Wilkes, standing near the throne, regarded the Lord Chancellor with an experienced eye and remarked, "Forget you! He will see you damned first!" Burke's comment was "the best thing that can happen to you!" Pitt rushed away, exclaiming several times, "Oh, what a rascal!"

But out of doors the words became a national anthem. They were embossed on snuff boxes. They were embroidered on pocketbooks. Around portraits and wreaths they were engraved. Of Pitt and the government they became what to-day we would call the political slogan.

The debates on the regency continued, and, if possible, with even more embittered rancour. We hear Fox accusing Pitt of being unworthy of the confidence of the Prince of Wales, and we also hear Pitt's crushing rejoinder: "As to my being conscious that I do not deserve the favour of the Prince, I can only say that I know but one way in which I or any man could deserve it—by having uniformly endeavoured in a public situation to do my duty to the King his father, and to the country at large." Finally we see Burke, hardly as sane at times as George III himself, declaring that Pitt's proposals were less "excusable" than "housebreaking" or "highway robbery." Pitt was "acting treason"; he was seeking "to degrade the Prince of Wales and to outlaw, ex-communicate, and attaint the whole House of Brunswick"; and the King had been "by the Almighty hurled from his throne and plunged into a condition which drew upon him the pity of the meanest peasant in his kingdom." Why should the Prince of Wales as Regent be debarred from granting honours to the Cavendishes? This being the wild rhetoric of Edmund Burke, is it any wonder that his friends tired to restrain him or that Mr. William Young should write, "Burke is Folly personified but shaking his cap and bells under the laurel of genius"?

Pitt was now in an unprecedented position. If the King recovered, he remained Prime Minister. If a regency was established, he fell from office. Yet, in the meantime, he was responsible for governing the country. Indeed, a new Speaker had to take the chair without the royal approval, usually signified at such appointments.

The Regency Bill passed the Commons. In the House of Lords it awaited a third reading. All things seemed to point to a return of Fox and his friends to power. When— alas—there was the slip between the cup and the lip. To the infinite chagrin of the Whigs there began to be circulated the terrible rumour that the King of England was on the highroad to recovery! At this distressing news the Opposition did not hesitate to spread the insinuation, which Pitt had to answer, that there had been "collusion" between the Queen and Dr. Willis for the misrepresentation of the King's state of mind. But the recovery was undeniable; no collusion could have accounted for it; and in a day or two the Regency Bill, with all the debates founded upon it, was blown into the air.

It meant that once more Fox had staked his career and

that once more he had lost. Not only did Pitt remain Prime Minister. It was as if he had carried a second election as triumphant as the election of 1784.

★

The rebound of the nation to the monarchy was overwhelming. What had seemed to be a calamitous struggle by factions over the throne resulted in a veritable festival of loyalty. "They will never kill me to make you King," said Charles II to his brother James; and whatever may have been the faults of George III, the country had no wish to see him supplanted by the future George IV. At the news of his restoration to health London was illuminated. The Thanksgiving of April 23d in St. Paul's Cathedral, with five thousand children from charity schools singing the Hundredth Psalm, sounded forth the devotion of a people never wholly out of touch with the deeper sources of reverence.

The King spent his summer at Weymouth, by the seaside. He could look over the sea and enjoy his rest cure. The view was, of course, toward France where they happened to be storming the Bastille.

As for Pitt, he had important matters to deal with. An ecclesiastic called "J. Lichfield and Coventry" was not only a bishop but brother of Earl Cornwallis, back from a village called Yorktown and now Governor General of India. The bishop was greatly upset. What he wanted was the Deanery of St. Paul's. But Pitt merely offered him the See of Salisbury. The bishop therefore accused the Prime Minister not only of "violation of repeated assurances, but of the strongest ties," at which Pitt retorted:

I am willing to hope that on further consideration, and on recollecting all the circumstances, there are parts of that letter which you would yourself wish never to have written.

My respect for your Lordship's situation and my regard for Lord Cornwallis prevent my saying more than that until that letter is recalled, your Lordship makes any further intercourse between you and me impossible.

The bishop apologized but apparently did not obtain the deanery. However, he was not sent to the guillotine, which was one comfort.

IT IS as an upholder of peace, as an apostle of prosperity, that we have been watching the career of William Pitt. We have now to recall the strange and tragic circumstance that he was the man of all men who was responsible for leading his country into a war worldwide in its range and extending over two whole decades.

If William Pitt had lived in the Twentieth Century we may rest assured that professors of universities and graduates intent upon their theses would have translated and collated many tons' weight of dispatches, of diaries, of memoranda, of biographies, and of other archives which might have been held to determine the precise depth of what would have been called his war guilt. But if you had talked to the men of the Eighteenth Century about war guilt they would have been puzzled over the meaning of the term. It was not the guilt of war but its glory that impressed men's minds. It was in terms of battles and sieges and conquests, of treaties and frontiers and alliances, that history was taught and that diplomacy was conducted. Of what war guilt was the great Chatham accused? Victory was his virtue, and the triumphs of Chatham were the only inheritance that devolved upon the younger Pitt.

The Napoleonic Wars, as conveniently they are named, lasted from 1793 to 1815, and contemplating such prolonged uproar and slaughter, the rhetorician may suggest that the Almighty has never laid on mankind an interdict so ruthless as the interdict which man lays by his folly on himself. But at the end of it all there was no suggestion that war as war should be outlawed.

It is true that, amid the silence of professors, a poet spoke. In the most savage cantos of *Don Juan* we read of musketry as "murder's rattles." But was Byron a pacifist? The very reverse. His complaint of the Greeks was that they failed "to make a new Thermopylæ," while, as he declared, Washington's "every battlefield was holy ground." What aroused Byron's scorn was not that the war had been fought but that it had been futile. Pitt

> had his pride
> And as a high-soul'd minister of state is
> Renowned for ruining Great Britain gratis.

Of William Pitt it is not untrue to say that, on occasion, he summoned the army and the navy to assist his diplomacy with a nonchalance not always displayed by householders when they sound the alarm for a fire brigade.

Another circumstance, sometimes overlooked, is the fact that, during his entire term of office, Pitt was trying to do the work of three men. He was no Earl of Liverpool with a Castlereagh for Foreign Secretary, no Melbourne with a Palmerston for Foreign Secretary, no Asquith with a Grey for Foreign Secretary; nor yet a Harding with a Hughes for Secretary of State. If ever there were a ministry of one man and only one man it was Pitt's ministry and, in all decisive affairs, it was he, he alone, who drafting many of the decisive dispatches with his own hand, conducted the international policy of the British Empire.

In times of comparative placidity, that is the Eighteen Nineties, it was possible for Lord Salisbury as Prime Minister to preside over the Foreign Office. But Pitt attempted a task infinitely more complex. Lord Salisbury's only personal contact with Parliament was a seat in a House of Lords at once somnolent and obedient to his will. But Pitt was leader of a still untamed House of Commons to which no closure was to be applied for a century. Moreover, he was the Chancellor of the Exchequer as well as Prime Minister, and as such he had undertaken a complete reorganization of the imperial finances. It is thus the important fact that while, for instance, he was watching the lunges and plunges of Gustavus of Sweden, he was studying also the eccentricities of King George III, the intrigues of Lord Chancellor Thurlow, the yield of the tax on maidservants, the discontents of Cousin Temple at the denial of a dukedom, and interminable proceedings against Warren Hastings. It may well be that the administration of public affairs was simpler than it has since become: sessions were shorter; there were fewer questions to be answered. But on the other hand, there were fewer people to answer them, and throughout the administration there was a more elaborate formality to be observed.

His Majesty King George III would have been much surprised if he had been informed one day that even a William Pitt had dared to ring him up on the telephone. A letter from Pitt to a duke required a supreme effort at once to write and to read.

As an executive minister Pitt was, by general consent, superb. But in what did his efficiency consist? If he was to get through the work of the day and, at the end of it, remain the most effective debater and even the greatest orator in the House of Commons, it could only be by an intense concentration on the immediate issue to be decided. To describe Pitt as "ignorant" would be ridiculous. He did not even cultivate what Woodrow Wilson called the single-track mind. On the contrary, he was a man who kept all his irons constantly in the fire. But to attribute to him the prophet's vision would be to mistake his method. He was a statesman who lived, as far as possible, a week at a time. To wait and see, this was his wisdom, and usually it sufficed.

★

We complain to-day that Europe is economically disintegrated by fiscal frontiers. That was Pitt's criticism of Europe in the Seventeen Eighties. Anticipating the negotiations undertaken in 1860 by Richard Cobden on behalf of Gladstone, he proposed, therefore, a commercial treaty with England's nearest neighbour and traditional enemy, namely, France. His aim, expressed in the King's Speech of January 23, 1787, was "the encouragement of industry and the extension of lawful commerce in both countries."

The Treaty of Commerce was successfully concluded, and in any estimate of moral responsibility must be counted unto Pitt, so far as it went, for righteousness. But how was it received by Fox and his friends? At the first mention of it in Parliament the Francophil of the years to follow was on his feet denouncing any idea of a concert or alliance with the French. Every effort was made by the Whigs to stir up the traders against the treaty and a petition for its postponement was presented. It has been said that it is the duty of an opposition to oppose. Over the Westminster Scrutiny, over the Prince of Wales, feeling ran high. But the fact remains that Fox and his friends, the trustees of what then was meant by liberalism, went on record as high protectionists and that a majority for the treaty of 236 to 116 votes was only obtained despite their eloquence.

The importance of the debates lay in the fact that they affected, not tariffs alone, but the peace of the world. In view of the sequel, it is essential to note precisely what Pitt said of France. On this significant occasion Pitt was, as usual, emphatic, but he was also conciliatory:

Considering the Treaty in its political view, I shall not hesitate to contend against the too frequently expressed opinion that France is and must be the unalterable enemy of England. My mind revolts from this position as monstrous and impossible. To suppose that any nation can be unalterably the enemy of another is weak and childish.

Fox, on the other hand, was deliberately bellicose:

Undoubtedly I will not go the length of asserting that France is and must remain the unalterable enemy of England, and that she might not secretly feel a wish to act amicably with respect to this kingdom. It is possible, but it is scarcely probable. That she, however, feels in that manner at present I not only doubt, but disbelieve. France is the natural political enemy of Great Britain. . . . I say again I contend that France is the natural foe of Great Britain, and that she wishes, by entering into a commercial treaty with us, to tie our hands and prevent us from engaging in any alliance with other Powers.

By an advocate of Charles James Fox so wholehearted as Mr. J. L. Hammond it is conceded as a matter of course that he was a statesman who regarded France as England's traditional opponent in Europe.

★

To those debates there were two important contributions. Gifted with a sonorous eloquence, Charles Grey, supporting Fox, delivered his maiden speech and so began that long career which, nearly fifty years later, culminated in the passage of the great Reform Bill. Then there was Philip Francis, the Junius of the East India Company, announcing on general principles that war is inevitable. "Nations," cried the colleague of Fox and Burke, "which border on each other never can agree; for this single reason, because they are neighbours." Displaying the sarcasm which adorns his letters, he proceeded to attack the Prime Minister thus:

But now it seems we are arrived at a new enlightened era of affection for our neighbours, and of liberality to our enemies, of which our uninstructed ancestors had no conception. The pomp of modern eloquence is employed to blast even the triumphs of Lord

Chatham's administration. The polemic laurels of the father must yield to the pacific myrtles which shadow the forehead of the son. Sir, the glory of Lord Chatham is founded on the resistance he made to the united power of the House of Bourbon. The present Minister has taken the opposite road to fame, and France, the object of every hostile principle in the policy of Lord Chatham, is the *gens amicissima* of his son.

Pitt was young. Pitt was proud. Pitt was human. It was thus, as he sought peace, that he was taunted with treachery to the martial fame of his father.

In truth, he was the very last man on this planet to need any such instigation. No one who studies the careers of old Governor Pitt, the interloper and smuggler, and of Lord Chatham, the father of William Pitt himself, can be under any illusion as to the gambling instinct which ran in the very blood of this unaccountable family. When Pitt as a young man first made his appearance in the clubs of London it was noticed at the card table—as we have seen—with what concentration he devoted himself to the game. Indeed, from a pastime thus absorbing to the mind and expensive to the pocket, he, like his friend Wilberforce, thought it a precaution to turn aside. To Fox and the Prince they surrendered their hands, all save the King. To forsake the casino and the race course was not, however, to eradicate a love of chance, so deeply inborn in the nature of the man as this. Pitt was praised for his prudence. He deserved the praise. But men are prudent for diverse reasons. Some prudence is merely lassitude; not so Pitt's. Never was any man, even in his prudence, more painfully intense than he. Not once did he allow himself to do a thing by halves, and it was to his strong impulses that he applied so strict a discipline of bit and bridle and bearing rein.

This, then, was the daring speculator to whom destiny assigned a game which, for thrilling uncertainty, outclassed every other excitement devised by the most reckless of societies. The old diplomacy conducted in the Eighteenth Century was, indeed, the sport of kings. Compared with the issues staked on these international hazards, the wagers of Fox and his friends at Brooks's were mere bagatelles. At every throw of the dice the issue was peace or war, and for no issues more stupendous than this did that forerunner of Pitt, the youthful Alexander the Great himself, career headlong over his conquests in the East.

Chatham, when he was asked for the secret of his success in the Seven Years' War, replied, "Obtaining accurate information respecting the places which I intended to attack." Pitt's confession was, however, that he "found it very difficult to acquire such information." His objectives were usually over the skyline, and, to recall a phrase of Wellington's, he could not always pretend to know what was happening on the other side of the hill. Even of a riot in Scotland, it was not easy to obtain the facts. If, then, Pitt guessed at facts—say in Russia—it was because only a guess was within his reach. Guided by his guesses, he dispatched what amounted to ultimata into the dim beyond and calmly awaited whatever might be the answering reverberations of the resultant earthquake.

Every move was a chance, and in a succession of such

chances the sportsman might win once, he might win twice, but sooner or later he was bound to awake on a day when the luck was against him. Pitt was matching his wits, not against this power or against that power, but against the uncertain. He was defying the inexorable laws of mathematics applied to probability.

To George Washington, it seemed to be the highest wisdom during this period to avoid entangling alliances with Europe, and especially to steer clear of her quarrels. But Pitt was not a statesman who could see anything "splendid" in "isolation." In finance he was active. But no less active was he in foreign affairs. From the first he practised as "spirited" a policy as his father before him, and as his diplomatic successors, Castlereagh and Canning and Palmerston, imitating him, were to practise in years to come. That policy was wide as the world itself. It embraced the sea and it embraced the land. Pitt's manner might be cold, cautious, and courteous. But his will was adamant.

In protesting that the Napoleonic Wars were not fought for liberty, Byron was right on the facts. What Pitt considered was neither autocracy, as such, nor democracy, as such, but British interests as he understood them. He did not live and move and have his being in the Fifteenth Century and the Italian Renaissance. He wore no poisoned gloves. He supplied no stilettos to hired assassins. But he was, none the less, the complete Machiavelli, entrenched in Downing Street. To him, surveying the chessboard, kings and peoples were no more than pieces to be moved from square to square.

★

About the guiding rules of his policy there was no secret. He wanted, and everyone knew that he wanted, three things —first, a balance of power in Europe as the essential condition of the equilibrium that we call peace; secondly, the *status quo* in Europe, as the only law that all nations could clearly understand and obey; and thirdly, an unrestricted elbow room outside Europe for what Seeley used to call "the expansion of England." In days long anterior to the League of Nations and the Hague Court these were Pitt's empirical theorems of diplomacy, as clear to his mind as the Monroe Doctrine was clear to the mind, let us say, of President Grover Cleveland.

In the year 1787 there had been no actual and overt outbreak of a revolution in France. But the influence of the revolution in the United States was permeating Europe, and among the indirect results of this new leaven was a struggle between the Prince of Orange, as Stadtholder, and the States of Holland. The Stadtholder was driven from The Hague, and his Princess appealed for help to her brother, the King of Prussia; also, there was an appeal to England.

What was the consideration that weighed with Pitt? The merits of the controversy in Holland? Not at all. If the British Ambassador at The Hague, Sir James Harris, afterward Lord Malmesbury, hurried over to London, if he advocated vehemently that at all costs the Stadtholder should be supported, if Pitt's colleagues, not less vehemently, supported the Ambassador's plea, it was for one reason only. The insurgent States of Holland had appealed to France for assistance and had not appealed in vain.

ment which heralded a message from the King. Lords and
Commons were politely informed that there was a prospect
of war and, there and then, the Commons accepted a vote of
credit amounting to £1,000,000. It was a vote that might be
compared with the initial appropriation of £100,000,000
which, as Prime Minister, Mr. Asquith obtained in August,
1914.

A press gang, suddenly rollicking through the deserted
streets and lanes of Deptford—but why? Was Pitt alone
responsible? The Eighteenth Century recedes from our vision
as we are carried back and back into the past, three hundred
years, to the Appartamente Borgia in the Vatican, somehow
adorned with frescoes, if not by the hand of Pinturicchio.
There Pope Alexander VI maintained a court as secular as it
was sacred, and had not a thought in his mind whether of
Pitt or the press gang. All that he did was to issue a somewhat famous bull, and all that the bull did was to divide the
New World, as discovered, between Spain and Portugal.
Thus did the diplomatic incident begin.

From that day onward Spain had the idea that British
seamen were mere privateers. Just fifty years before Pitt
issued his order a sea captain called Jenkins had appeared,
stating that the Spaniards had cut off his ear. Whether a
pillory nearer home could have told a different story has
always been a question, but, in any event, the ear, exhibited
at Westminster, was enough to drive even the peaceful
Walpole as Prime Minister into a war with the peninsular
power. On January 21, 1790, British seamen had arrived in
London with a somewhat similar tale.

It is true that, within Pitt's lifetime, Great Britain had lost a world to the United States. But she was already finding other worlds to take its place. There was a mariner whose voyages over uncharted seas recalled the heroism even of the merchant adventurers, Drake and Hawkins, the glory of Elizabeth's incomparable England. He was Captain Cook, killed in February, 1779, on the island of Hawaii. Cook had sailed northward over the Pacific Ocean and had reached a somewhat attractive harbour on the west coast of North America which the Indians called Nootka, and the Canadians, at the moment, describe as Vancouver. Cook was followed by Spanish vessels and also by certain British ships —the *Sea Otter*, the *Nootka*, the *Felice*, and the *Iphigenia* among them. A little settlement was established by the British who, with commendable initiative, began to import Canadian furs into China with a plant called ginseng, which the Chinese valued as a drug.

To the Spaniards in Mexico, the whole of this activity was a clear trespass on the region of influence allotted to themselves by Pope Alexander VI. A frigate, the *Princesa*, with a sloop appeared on the scene, seized the British shipping, put the sailors into irons, and, it was said, so maltreated them that, in one case, suicide was effected as a relief. It was the news of this occurrence that linked Pope Alexander VI with the British press gang by way of an island seven thousand miles distant, and only accessible in those days by means of a voyage either around Cape Horn or around the Cape of Good Hope. So far from apologizing for what seemed to be an outrage, Spain declared that the errant seadogs, released by the clemency of her King, should be duly chastised by Great Britain herself.

The issue was thus clearly enough stated, and the only question was what importance was to be attached to it. In the lobbies members asked each other where was this place called Nootka and how was the name to be pronounced? Also, of what value was the trade with China? Was not a whale caught in the Pacific Ocean worth only £90, whereas a whale caught off Greenland was worth £170? Not at all, said another—Alderman Curtis—from the city who knew about trade. He had himself sold Pacific whale oil for £50 a ton, whereas Greenland whale oil only fetched £19 a ton. But it was not according to the prattle of politicians that Pitt acted. If the Spanish claim held good, the whole Pacific seaboard up to latitude 60, that is Alaska, would be closed forever, at once to international shipping and to the expansion westward of the United States.

Rejecting all idea of arbitration, Pitt began at once to mobilize his forces, naval, military, and diplomatic. Britain had ninety-three warships at her disposal, Spain had fifty; so far, so good. Troops also were mustered and the allies of Great Britain, that is, Holland and Prussia, were promptly approached. They undertook to fulfil the obligations embodied in the recent partnership.

With Spain confronted by Britain, Holland, and Prussia, the attitude of France became, obviously, of a paramount importance. By decree, the National Assembly was fitting out fourteen sail of the line; but, said M. de Montmorin, the Foreign Minister, only as a precaution. The Tuileries had

become the scene of an excited drama. Within the edifice
there resounded the eloquence of Mirabeau. Without, an
immense multitude awaited echoes of the debate. For what
was the issue as it appeared to Paris? The right of Spain to
arrest British sailors on the Nootka Sound? Not at all.
What interested Paris was the question whether international diplomacy should still be included among the prerogatives of the King. Mirabeau insisted that diplomacy should
so continue as a secret art, he was accused of "treason,"
and finally a compromise was adopted which Camille Des-
moulins described with his usual humour. "The question was
decided," said he, "first, in favour of the nation; secondly,
in favour of the King; and thirdly, in favour of both."

That some of the royalists wanted to create a diversion
by means of a war with England was obvious. Mirabeau
himself was by no means friendly. What mattered to him as a
Frenchman, revolution or no revolution, was what mattered,
revolution or no revolution, to Pitt, and that was the balance
of power. There had been a family compact between the
Kings of France and Spain. Let there be, then, a national
compact between the peoples of France and Spain. That was
Mirabeau's appeal.

★

Here there entered into the situation an element which,
during the Great War of the Twentieth Century, became only
too familiar throughout the world. It was true that Pitt continued to display toward Spain the stiffest of stiff upper lips.
He would not hear of the French appearing "as Mediators,
still less as Arbitrators." If, however, Spain declined the

conflict, it was because she was faced, not only by Pitt's firmness, but by his finesse and his finance. Outwardly he appeared the very embodiment of a proud dignity. But behind the scenes, he was rivalling Zinovieff himself in the instigation of propaganda.

During the American war, Spain had joined France against England. Pitt contemplated a tit-for-tat. The grievances of the Thirteen Colonies had been serious. But not one of them could compare with the burden of the commercial system applied to Latin America which raised the price of iron, sold at Quito, to 4s. 6d. a lb. or at least £500 a ton. For the statesmen of Spain it was thus a grave matter indeed when Pitt graciously granted repeated interviews to Miranda, the revolutionary exile from territory now called Venezuela. It could only mean that the Prime Minister of Great Britain was ready, as an act of war, to foment revolution throughout the Spanish Empire.

The policy of propaganda was extended to France herself. It is true that, at this stage, Pitt insisted that formal negotiations should be conducted decently and properly with the French Foreign Office, speaking ostensibly in the name of King Louis XVI. But were these the only communications?

The historian does not think so. "Pitt is the most upright political character I ever knew or heard of," so Wilberforce might write to Bankes, and the tribute still rings true. But how was it that Johnson in his Dictionary happened at the moment to be defining the word "patriotism"? Did he not describe it as "the last refuge of a scoundrel"? For himself, Pitt asked nothing. He was not only honest, but honest with ostentation. When, however, it came to the interest of his country, that was different. He did not hesitate to send to Paris a pair of political agents, William Augustus Miles and Hugh Elliott, who were well supplied with money. Elliott addressed the Diplomatic Committee of the National Assembly, and Miles was actually elected a member of the Jacobin Club. Talleyrand, Lafayette, and Mirabeau were quietly approached and Elliott explained that his "more intimate conversations with individuals cannot be committed to paper." Also he referred to what he called "the secret springs of action." As for the letters between Miles and Pitt, we have the word of Dr. J. Holland Rose for it that they "have all been destroyed." If, then, Mirabeau secured forty-five battleships for Spain and then took steps that they should not be employed, it may have been that he had tangible reasons for both decisions.

Faced by Pitt, Spain did not carry her contentions further. The diplomatic victory was complete. The Pacific seaboard was secured. Pitt seemed to be, as Macaulay puts it, at "his zenith." But, like the rest, Pitt was beginning to be expert in the seamy side of politics.

CHAPTER TWELVE

CATHERINE

IN THE year 1790 the rise of William Pitt, wholly
without precedent in British politics, had been fully achieved.
It was, indeed, hard to believe that this veteran of Downing
Street, as he had become, was still no more than entering on
his thirties and had been but recently ridiculed as "the boy
statesman." He had saved the national finances. He had adjusted a solution to the problem of India. He had emerged
triumphant out of the regency crisis. In every direction his
foreign policy had been victorious. Indeed, it seemed as if
Pitt had surpassed the incredible. As the son of Chatham, he
had enhanced even his father's name.

In the House of Commons his position was admittedly
impregnable. But there now arose an opportunity of testing
public opinion in the country. Under the Septennial Act it
was usual for Parliament to be dissolved after six years of
continuance. In 1790, therefore, a general election was called.
The appeal to the country was regarded as a mere formality.
Its result was a foregone conclusion. Pitt's majority was
handed back to him, if anything increased.

It was at this moment, when the very stars in their courses
seemed to be fighting for him, that the most powerful of all

Prime Ministers encountered a check. It was all but a check-mate. If Pitt escaped, it was only with a loss of prestige, and the piece that checked him was a Queen.

British diplomacy was confronted by two problems. The nearer of these problems was the political decadence of western Europe which culminated in the French Revolution. The more remote of the problems was the expansion of Russia. What Pitt did was to stake his entire influence on that which, in fact, mattered least. With France in flames, he risked everything over Russia.

To the idea of colonization the mind of Europe was well accustomed. Men had seen how Phœnicians had established Carthage, how Anglo Saxons and Danes had made England, how Spaniards had landed in Latin America, how the British had settled in Maryland and Massachusetts, how the Dutch had founded a city at the Cape, and the French a Gibraltar at Quebec. But about the migrations of the Slavonic peoples into Muscovy there was a particular circumstance which, to this day, Europe as a whole has hardly appreciated.

The familiar colonist disembarks from his ship and settles on the shore. But the Slavonic peoples were inlanders and what they desired was access to the sea. Hence, their migrations were, if the phrase be permitted, not inward but out-ward. They did not want to leave the warm water for the shore. They wanted to leave the shore and take to the water.

Look at a map of Muscovy, dated, let us say, the year 1500. The country is as completely encircled by land, save for the Arctic regions, as is Switzerland. Over these harsh steppes the tribes overflowed; the fluid population then froze; and under the resistless pressure of this static expansion the entire circumference cracked and crumbled, like rocks in winter. Over the Baltic, Sweden began, slowly, but surely, to relax her hold. The great kingdom of Lithuania collapsed, Poland crumpled into fragments, and to the south, Turkey began steadily to disintegrate. Russia did not explode. During the summers she was water; during the winters she was ice; first hot, then cold, she acted on her neighbours as a battering ram with a very short stroke and a very big mass behind it.

When William Pitt ascended his Parliamentary throne it was this that had been going on intermittently for centuries. As early as the year 1719 Stanhope, as Secretary of State, attempted "to drive the Muscovites as far off as possible." On the other hand, Pitt's own father, Chatham, had written to Shelburne, "Your Lordship knows that I am quite a Russ." Over the expansion of Muscovy, British opinion had been quiescent. Lord North, for instance, was busy elsewhere. He had to think of his lost colonies in America.

At the outset of his official career Pitt regarded Russia as a possible friend. Like his father, he was "quite a Russ." He would have liked a commercial treaty with the czars and, in looking for the allies that he badly needed, he preferred St. Petersburg to Berlin. But his approaches were not received in that quarter with enthusiasm. He was rebuffed.

It is a strange fact that the greatest of Russian rulers, not excluding Peter the Great himself, should have been neither a man nor a Slav but a German and a woman. Sophia Augusta was a daughter of the Prince of Anhalt-Zerbst. Married to

the future Czar Peter III, this girl of sixteen was baptized
into the Greek Church as Catherine. Her bridegroom greeted
her with a countenance caricatured by the smallpox, and at
sight of him, so the story goes, she fainted. From that day
onward her mind achieved a complete mastery over her
morals. Fascinating as Cleopatra, vicious as Messalina, ruthless as Jezebel, devout as Mary, Queen of Scots, calculating
as her namesake, the Medici Queen of France, she was the
equal of Elizabeth in efficiency and ambition for her country.
On the one hand, Catherine was an unrepentant prostitute.
On the other hand, she was an incomparable patriot.

★

To William Pitt, with his prim potations and correct
cravat, Catherine of Russia was a person to be kept in her
place. She must be fitted into the *status quo* and adjusted to
the balance of power. Catherine was grimly amused. Pitt?
Who was this Mr. Pitt? She was fully old enough to be his
mother. When Pitt was scarcely out of his cradle, a puling and
muling and weakly infant, where was Catherine? She had
arrested her consort, the Czar himself; she had flung him into
prison; within a week she had seen to it that, a man too much
pitied, he was strangled; and with conscience unperturbed
she had then calmly issued the proclamation: ". . . we,
putting our trust in the Almighty and His divine justice,
have ascended the sovereign imperial throne of all the
Russias." It was one of those ascensions that coincided with
an assassination.

  Status quo? Balance of Power? Commercial Treaty? What

interested Catherine was that triumphal arch, erected for her welcome into the City of Kherson, on the Black Sea, and inscribed in reminiscent Greek, "the Way to Byzantium." Catherine treated "Mr. Pitt" as a man who took himself a little too seriously. If "Mr. Pitt" was not aware that Russia was remote from England, she knew well how remote was England from Russia. The British Fleet? Let it sail, if it could, overland to Moscow.

A curious memorandum has been found which Pitt must have read. Possibly it influenced his outlook over the problem. In this unsigned paper a distinction is drawn between Russian aggression, as it was regarded, in the Baltic and Russian aggression in the Black Sea. To encourage Russia in the Baltic, so it was argued, would be to increase her trade with England's allies, namely, Prussia and Holland. But if Russia were to trade through the Dardanelles she might establish commercial contacts with France and Spain, who were England's opponents. Once more, the balance of power delicately trembled as this or that was added to one or the other scale. Even Russia was reckoned to be a duality. Russia to the north was balanced against Russia to the south.

It was toward the Black Sea that, at the moment, Russia was advancing, and Pitt did not like it. But for Pitt's scruples, Catherine cared nothing. Spain had turned the Moors out of western Europe. Why should not Russia turn the Turk out of eastern Europe? In one case as in the other, it was the mission of Catholic armies, Roman or Orthodox, to bring to an end the unhallowed intrusion of the Moslem onto Christian soil. The reconquest was not politics; it was piety, and the smoke of battle rose to heaven, mingled with the incense at the altar.

When the great Chatham was summoned in 1757 to save England, the fleets and the armies were already at war. Nothing mattered during that emergency except to win. But Pitt was still at peace. Faced by Catherine, he knew that he had met his match. Knowing it, he was determined that Catherine, on her side, should meet her match also. But he did not want to fight. He hoped that, without fighting, he would get his way.

★

Europe was a chessboard crowded with pawns, and pawns sometimes were used to check the kings and the queens. Such a pawn, at the moment, was Sweden. For many years the country had been rent by the dissensions of the "caps" *versus* the "hats," that is, the democracy against the aristocracy; indeed, to Pitt, it was the Dutch situation over again. As France supported the States of Holland against the Prince of Orange, so did Catherine of Russia support the popular party among the Swedes against the party of privilege. As a matter of course it followed that Great Britain, when friendly with Russia, exhibited a similar sympathy with the "caps." But when her feeling toward Russia was altered, so was her attitude toward the "caps" and "hats" in Stockholm.

Over Sweden there reigned that "king with two faces," Gustavus III, whose strange life was to be ended at a ball by a bullet from Ackerstrom's pistol. By a *coup d'état* Gustavus overwhelmed the "caps" and made himself an absolute monarch. Not only was he absolute as monarch;

he was also an absolute mercenary. To quote Carmarthen, he had "a most voracious appetite for subsidies." Russia had financed his opponents, the "caps." He would be himself financed by Russia's enemies, the Turks. His stipend from the Sultan was no less than one million piastres a year.

So remunerated, Gustavus flung himself at Russia, and finding Catherine with only six thousand troops at her side, he pressed his way to the very gates of her capital. Catherine shed floods of tears, but the violence of her emotions did not deflect the aim of her counter stroke. She also had her treaties, duly financed, including one with Denmark. By that treaty Denmark was to aid her, if need be, against Sweden. That aid was given. Suddenly, Gustavus found that his troops, nearing St. Petersburg, would advance no further. He had to hurry home, and in effect his throne was lost. If it was restored to him the reason was a vigorous action on the part of England, supported by her allies, Prussia and Holland. "Sire," said the British envoy to the distressed monarch, "give me your crown; I will return it to you with lustre."

To Pitt, the salvation of Sweden was another feather in his cap. Once more the balance of power had been subjected to violent oscillations. Once more it had trembled back to some kind of equilibrium. But Catherine was even better satisfied. To her, a balance of power along the Baltic meant the liberty to upset that balance of power on the Black Sea. Not without a plausible reason, she suspected that Great Britain—even if she had been too frugal to grant a subsidy—had instigated the attack on her by the Swedes, and with a chilling sarcasm she remarked, "As Mr. Pitt wishes to chase me from St. Petersburg, I hope he will allow me to take refuge in Constantinople." "The way to Byzantium"—more than ever did it lure the Empress to risk all on an advance.

★

Seventy years later Great Britain and France were to resist that approach of Russia to Constantinople by fighting the Crimean War. The gallant six hundred of the Light Brigade were to charge to their death on the plains of Balaclava and the battles of the Alma and Inkerman were to be fought less by the generals than the soldiers. The prize was then Sevastopol, the great fortress of the Crimea. But the Sevastopol of Pitt's day was a city, the very name of which is scarcely known outside Russia. It was Ocksakow that, in the Seventeen Eighties, was the symbol of Russian encroachment. It was Ocksakow, on the disposal of which, so men thought, depended the future of mankind—Ocksakow which commanded the area between the rivers Bug and Dneister, with an outlet on the Black Sea.

The story of Ocksakow was grim indeed. In the winter of 1788 Catherine's favourite, Potemkin, discarded as a lover but promoted as a general, was investing Ocksakow. Amid snow and ice, red-hot shot were fired into the city, and one of these ignited the powder magazine. There was an upheaval that killed five thousand people, and part of the wall of the city was demolished. On the 17th of December, 1788, Ocksakow was surrendered by the Turks to the Russians.

Just two years later there was a second and even more terrible success. "You will take Ismail at whatever cost"—

so ran the orders of Prince Potemkin, and Suwarrow obeyed. On December 22, 1790, Ismail on the Danube was stormed. In the siege and the sack, the Turks—men, women, and children—lost more than thirty thousand lives.

For William Pitt there arose the simple question whether Ocksakow was or was not his business. With French châteaux in flames, with the Bastille in ruins, with Europe shaken to her foundations, was he or was he not to stake his entire position and his country's future on such an item of distant geography? The gambler within him gained the day. On the whirlwinds of the Near East as his Pegasus, he rode forth, in a famous phrase of Lord Milner, damning the consequences.

Catherine had lost many men. Catherine had spent many millions of rubles. But, on the other hand, Catherine had won great victories and captured strong cities. There was thus a certain audacity in Pitt's calm injunction, the edict from an armchair, that, in effect, there should be one rule for Great Britain occupying the Nootka Sound, and quite another rule for Russia retaining possession of Ocksakow. Finding herself inside that place, Catherine did not look as if she would be inclined to be turned out.

Once more the balance of power began violently to oscillate. That Pitt would be able to depend on his allies, Prussia and Holland, was, of course, taken for granted. It would have been a gross insult to Great Britain's loyal and trusted friends in Europe to have assumed anything else. Pitt had been able to coerce Spain over the Pacific. He had coerced Denmark over Sweden. He would coerce Russia over Ocksakow. Of course he would!

With all the wizardry of a Mona Lisa, Catherine watched her youthful rival. In due course he would learn about allies. She would be glad to give him his first lessons. For, while Pitt knew all that was said to his face, Catherine also knew what was said behind Pitt's back, and such knowledge is power.

It was true enough that, on paper, Prussia was committed to support the *status quo*. Indeed, for this reason, Prussia had joined England in persuading Austria to abandon Russia and her war against Turkey. But did Prussia, did Austria, care enough about Ocksakow to declare war on Russia? Catherine scouted the idea. The cynical old schemer remembered only too well that long and intimate journey by coach in which she and the Emperor Joseph of Austria, brother of Marie Antoinette, had so much enjoyed their chats over the coming partition of Turkey. She also knew that the France of Marie Antoinette had been greatly interested—as Napoleon was to be—in the archæological mysteries of Egypt. Most important of all, she was aware that Prussia's notion of a *status quo* was to complete the division of Poland between herself, Russia, and Austria. It meant that over Ocksakow, Pitt, apparently secure of allies, in reality stood alone. There was not another responsible statesman in Europe who was so foolish as to join him, as Lord Salisbury expressed it at a later date, in "putting his money on the wrong horse."

★

As the negotiations were proceeding there occurred an incident that aroused no little irritation in Downing Street. Allies or no allies, it was essential to William Pitt that he should appear to Catherine to be speaking at least for a resolute and united England, that the language of Pitt should be the only language heard just then at St. Petersburg.

Among the friends of Fox there happened to be one of those members of the House of Commons whose whole lives are spent in what we may describe as an anecdotage. Robert Adair was an excellent fellow; everyone liked his company, and in the superabundance of his friendship for the world at large he set out for St. Petersburg, there to promote good feeling. At once it was alleged that Fox had sent him to Russia with the express purpose of defeating Pitt's diplomacy. The charge, as stated, is untrue. All that can be said against Fox is that he knew in advance of Adair's pilgrimage and took no steps to prevent it. "Well," Fox had said, "if you are determined to go, send us all the news."

By the adroit Catherine, Adair was received with open arms. To all that he had to say of England's friendship she listened eagerly. Of the great Charles James Fox, of whom she had heard so much, she sang the praises. Nay, more, she gave orders that the bust of the famous Whig orator should be installed at her palace, where it occupied a place between the pedestals of Demosthenes and Cicero.

It was on the very brink of the precipice that Pitt now stood. There were certain ominous preparations, known at the time as "the Russian armament," which cost money. Under a parliamentary system of government, the preparations could not be kept secret. On March 27, 1791, Pitt met his Cabinet. Resolute youth overcame reluctant experience. The Cabinet agreed to leave the quarrel in his hands. But when "the King's confidential servants" went their several ways, the Duke of Richmond, "ever most truly and sincerely yours," sent to his Prime Minister a letter of grave remonstrance. "Unless," he wrote "we have Holland, in some ostensible shape at least, with us, and the Swedish ports open to our fleet, with an accession of Poland to an alliance, we risk too much in pledging this country to Prussia to make war against Russia in order to compel her to make peace with the Porte upon the *status quo*."

But by this time the Prime Minister, unaccustomed to contradiction, had the bit in his teeth. On March 28th the faithful Commons were asked to find the money for an increase in the navy. To Russia, a messenger had already started with an ultimatum and the time limit was ten days.

It was at this crisis, decisive of the entire future, that Fox spoke. Not only did he speak, but, as Pitt was quick to realize, he held the House. The majority for the government fell first to 93, and then, in a further House, to no more than 80. All the signals began to point to danger.

Pitt knew that if he persisted in his folly his power would be at an end. On the very brink of disaster he drew back. A second messenger was dispatched after the first, with instructions to overtake the ultimatum and prevent its delivery. Happily, he won the race for safety. Peace was preserved.

★

But the blow inflicted on the Prime Minister made him wince. Joseph Ewart, the British Ambassador at Berlin, who happened to be visiting London, found Pitt as none had ever seen him. There were "tears in his eyes." The Prime Minister confessed that "it was the greatest mortification he had ever experienced." His power continued, but his spell was broken. He was still a man who could rule. But he had become a man who could blunder. "We are none of us infallible," said a famous master of his college, "not even the youngest." The King had found it out; so had the Commons.

Ewart returned to Berlin charged with trustful apologies to the King of Prussia, who received the explanations with admirable philosophy. In due course Catherine also comforted him with another slice of Poland. She kept her Ocksakow, and Pitt, with rueful countenance, proceeded along his allotted road to Austerlitz.

OR A generation that lives in the Twentieth Century it should be possible to appreciate the emotions aroused by the French Revolution. It may be that the Muse of History is less confident than she used to be that she is able to repeat herself. She has Criticism as her chaperon. Yet criticism itself must admit that, about revolutions, there may be the similarity that doctors discover in cases of typhoid or measles. Diagnosis identifies the premonitory symptoms. There develops the same high fever. It is followed by a crisis and a long and restless convalescence after which life is resumed on a new basis.

Between the French Revolution in the Eighteenth Century and the Russian Revolution in the Twentieth, the correspondence is indeed accurate. If Russia had her Tolstoy, France had her Rousseau and Voltaire. In a benevolent ineptitude, the Czar Nicholas was the King Louis XVI of Russia and the King Louis XVI was the Czar Nicholas of France. In superstition, motherhood, and unpopularity, Alexandrovna and Marie Antoinette, proud, beautiful, and imprudent, were sisters in sorrow. That glint of green eyes which was hypnotic in the ruffianly Rasputin recalls the chicanery of Cagliostro and the scandal of the Diamond Necklace. Like successive avalanches thundering over precipices of a mountain, the revolutions themselves tore their way through a similar path of destruction. In both countries and both centuries an aristocracy had become at once selfish and effete. In both cases the economic structure of society had been undermined by futile wars. In both cases a parliament was summoned, and when in being was refused the power to act. In both cases the parliament was superseded in its authority by a municipal commune. In both cases the currency collapsed and the people were driven into fury by hunger. If Russia had her Bolshevists in the cities, France had her Jacobins, and in both cases it was the cities, especially Moscow, especially Paris, that imposed their will on a peasantry less politically conscious than themselves. In both cases Europe dreaded the contagion of the revolution and tried by force to stamp out the plague. In both cases Europe failed. In Russia and in France alike the intervention of Europe provoked a reign of terror in which royalty, religion, and civilization itself were involved for a time in an end of all things. Between the revolutions there is, perhaps, one distinction of importance to be emphasized. Both the upheavals were social; one only was socialist. When France challenged Christendom modern industry was still combating feudalism and Karl Marx had still to write on Capital.

In estimating Pitt's view of the Revolution we must realize, first, that his was not the private opinion of an individual. He was Prime Minister, and of this as of other matters he could not speak without speaking for the government.

What was opinion in other men was in him the policy of an empire. A century after the date we are considering Queen Victoria was still protesting against her ministers' practice of airing their ideas on the public platform.

Surveying the scenes in France, Pitt followed his usual rule. What mattered to him, and all that mattered, was British interests. France in chaos was no different in this respect from the milder upheavals of Holland, of Sweden, and of Latin America, with which already Pitt had been brought into diplomatic relation.

British interests as he conceived them being Pitt's compass, he had been ready and indeed anxious to go to war with Russia over a city remote as what was spelt, when it was not misspelt, Ocksakow. Yet when ancient mansions, much nearer than Russia, flamed to heaven as bonfires, when polite viscounts dangled dead from *La lanterne*, when daughters of marquises, as pretty as they were penniless, stepped ashore and, on English soil, were grateful to earn their living as governesses, when ladies and gentlemen of breeding and substance were bound, back to back, and "married" by submersion in the river Loire, and when the fair head of the Princesse de Lamballe was paraded through Paris on the point of a pike, Pitt, with his chill correctitude, continued to count his surpluses and select his peers.

His estimate of what he called "the present convulsions of France" was, like all his views, simple and direct. He did not minimize the happenings. It seemed to him that "the restoration of tranquillity" would be "distant," but he pointed out that the disturbances "must sooner or later

comrades Burke, Sheridan, and Wyndham had gone tiger hunting together, especially in the Indian debates, with all the gaiety of the Three Musketeers. A question of moment was thus what views of the Revolution were adopted by the only men who could take the place of Pitt as an alternative government.

It was fifty years almost before a shaggy Scotsman called Thomas Carlyle, writing English as a jargon of genius, was to startle the world with the first epoch-making interpretation of what the paroxysms of France really meant. What Carlyle brought to bear on the phenomenon was hindsight. It was foresight that was displayed by Charles James Fox. He did not hesitate in his judgment, not for a day. When he heard that the Bastille had fallen he cried, "How much it is the greatest event that ever happened in the world! and how much the best!" His die was cast, never did he waver from his conviction, and that conviction was shared by Sheridan.

In our own day the skill of the medical profession and the practise of hygiene have extended the span of human life by several decades. At sixty a man may still be in his prime. But at sixty Edmund Burke was an old man. That magnificent mind which he had lavished over the grievances of the American Colonies and the wrongs inflicted on the peoples and princes of India had reached the limit of its constructive sagacity.

Yet it was at this closing period of his life that Edmund Burke was to play his most decisive part. About his astonishing influence there was an element of paradox. Like arteries, his ideas had hardened. He could only think those thoughts which had been his thinking hitherto. But if his political sense was overcast by senility, his literary style shone forth the more resplendent. His meaning might be not only rubbish but disastrous rubbish. Yet in its gorgeous flamboyance his language achieved the sublime. He was like a musician whose ear cannot escape from the fascination of a favourite theme which he renders, therefore, with variations of his own, each more brilliant than the last in the ingenious glory of its harmonies.

Burke had come to believe that Great Britain was a fabric based on the sure foundations of the rotten boroughs. To expect him to approve of the somewhat sanguinary reforms proceeding in France was out of the question. From the first, his attitude was as decisive as the attitude of Fox himself. He wrote:

You hope, Sir, that I think the French deserving of liberty. I certainly do. I certainly think that all men who desire it, deserve it. It is not the reward of our merit, or the acquisition of our industry. It is our inheritance. It is the birth-right of our species. But whenever a separation is made between liberty and justice, neither is in my opinion safe.

What did he mean by simple yet swelling words like "justice" and "liberty"? He erected those abstractions as a lofty statue at which men were to gaze and was wholly unconcerned with the lives of the humble whose fetid hovels were clustered around a pitiless pedestal. Even Pitt was able to look ahead so far as to catch a glimpse of the more splendid France that was to arise.

Burke, however, announced a national suicide. "The French," he cried in strident tones, "have shown themselves the ablest architects of ruin that had [has] hitherto existed in the world."

★

Under the wear and tear of debate the well-tried comradeship began to weaken. Whatever might be the topic under discussion, it was of France that Burke on one side and Fox on the other were thinking. In 1791 a bill for the better government of Canada tempted Fox to allude to the better government of a country nearer home. Burke was overcome with anger, and on rising to put his point of view was interrupted by the friends of his nominal leader. That Fox wished to see him thus subjected to disrespect is unthinkable. At a later date he confessed that it would have been far wiser to allow Burke to say his say. But the incident happened.

Genial and admiring, Fox made amends by calling on Burke, and for the last time the friends were seen to enter the House together, arm in arm. It was a short-lived reconciliation. Burke insisted on answering Fox, and on May 6th he rose in a House crowded and expectant. The business was still not France but Canada, and Fox was now most anxious that only Canada should be discussed. As Burke proceeded there arose, then, what, in his own phrase, has been called "a most disorderly rage for order." Under the gusts of interruption Burke's anger was inflamed to a white heat. Fox, hitherto his "friend," became "the right honourable gentleman," and when he whispered to Burke that there was no loss surely of friendship, the Irishman, now beyond all control, retorted,

"Yes—yes—there is a loss of friends. I know the price of my conduct. I have done my duty at the price of my friend. Our friendship is at an end." Fox rose. It seemed as if his huge bulk was shaking with his sobs. For a time he could say nothing. Then he confessed that he had learned more from Burke than from all other men put together, and that the pain of their severance would only end with his life.

To Pitt's attitude toward the Revolution, therefore, Burke and Fox opposed a schism. It was more than a difference over politics. It was a feud that involved a faith. To Burke the Revolution was a wrong; to Fox the Revolution was a change of wrongs into rights; and between these views there could be no compromise. The bitterness of the Liberal Imperialists against the pro-Boers during the South African War, the bitterness within the Labour Party over the European War suggest what bitterness there had to be between the Old Whigs led by Burke and the New Whigs led by Fox.

To a Prime Minister dependent on the support of the House of Commons such a quarrel between his leading opponents must always appear to be a gift from the gods. Twice had Pitt triumphed over all his adversaries at the polls. But here was a victory in the House of Commons itself—a victory the more crushing because it was unsought. The Opposition to Pitt, though defeated, had been at least united. But the enemy was now scattered and the day was rapidly approaching when Fox, eloquently upholding the new France that was enduring a birth, would think himself fortunate if he could lead fifty members into the lobby.

More than ever did it seem as if the most solitary of Prime Ministers were alone in his dictatorship. The King's health was still doubtful. He could digest a letter more easily than attempt "a desultory way of speaking." Pitt was thus comparable with a President of the United States. Indeed, he wielded what appeared to be a power to act, especially in foreign affairs, which Congress has never permitted in time of peace to any President. It was a power that, in the nature of things, cannot be again conceded under the British Crown. To-day a Prime Minister of Great Britain is no more than *primus inter pares*. But as chief adviser to the sovereign, Pitt stood alone. Over his decisions no colony thought of asking to be consulted. What Pitt said, what Pitt did, was accepted at home and abroad as the definitive policy of that far-flung monarchy over which King George III reigned, and the nominee of King George III was authorized by Parliament to rule.

★

But it was at this precise instant of renewed autocracy that the real power of William Pitt began to wane. A famous ode of William Wordsworth's, we admit, was never intended to be put to the use here following. Yet it may be said of Pitt as "the boy statesman" that during the Seventeen Eighties he had abundantly revealed his "intimations of immortality." In the Seventeen Nineties, however, there had begun to gather around him "the shadows of the prison house."

In a sense Pitt had been endowed by circumstances with prerogatives as absolute as Mussolini's. But absolute authority may be associated with personal impotence. The prerogatives of the czars kept them prisoners in their palaces. The infallibility of the Pope means that he can only speak the infallible word *ex cathedra*. Pitt's very prestige at Westminster made him the prisoner of Parliament. No man can control the House of Commons as he did unless he has been absorbed by the House. By that of which he is the master, he is himself mastered. Pitt was captain of the ship of state. His hand and his alone was laid on the wheel. But it was his crew who insisted on setting the sails.

Macaulay expresses it by saying that the tide turned. It suggests no more than the half truth. It was not the turn of any tide that began to upset the Prime Minister. What he had to face was the embarrassment of a tide at its flood. It was on the crest of his own wave that he was carried splendidly aloft but helpless amid the froth and foam of the enthusiasm of his admirers. He who wanted to lead was pushed. The dispersal of the Opposition was one of those strokes of luck which, like a too vigorous slap on the back, leaves a man staggering.

It was impossible for Burke to drift away from Fox without drifting toward Pitt. What Burke supported was authority, and of authority Pitt was trustee. During that year 1790, when forces were rapidly consolidating, Pitt happened to speak in the House on Warren Hastings. Wilberforce was lost in admiration. "He put things by as he proceeded," so wrote the reformer, "and then returned to the very point from which he had started with the most astonishing clearness." Only "a mathematician" could have made that speech.

chairman, they proceeded from the London Tavern to a
chapel in Old Jewry where a preacher of the Unitarian per-
suasion incidentally denounced "all supporters of slavish
governments and slavish hierarchies." An address of congratulation to the National Assembly in Paris was then
duly carried and signed by the chairman. It was sent to
France and received by the National Assembly. The signature was noted, and immense was the exultation of the
revolutionaries. It was no wonder. This was the incident in
which Burke discerned his opportunity. Forthwith there appeared certain "Reflections on the French Revolution"
which were, in direct terms, a challenge to the address carried by the Revolution Society.

As a "stunt," the success of the Reflections was and con-
tinues to be overwhelming. For every hundred persons who
have heard the name of Burke, it is doubtful whether one
could identify either the preacher of that sermon or the
signatory on that address. Yet, of the three men, the one so
illustrious, the other two consigned to comparative oblivion,
it has to be said that Burke's fame, in so far as it depends on
this passage in his life, consists in the magnitude of the dis-
service which he rendered to mankind. Dr. Richard Price,
who occupied that pulpit, far surpassed Burke in the wisdom
of his practical statesmanship. What he had realized throughout a long and useful life was the fact that the future of
Great Britain depended on the solidity of her credit. Precisely to what extent Pitt owed to Price his ideas of a sinking
fund has been a question hotly controverted by historians. It
is one of those questions, so often controverted, which lead

nowhere. The fact remains that Dr. Price was the man whose eminence as an authority on economics induced the Congress of the United States by resolution to offer him an honorary citizenship in order that he might assist the republic in the organization of her finances. It was not the Burkes who prevented a revolution in Great Britain. It was the Prices.

Whose was the signature on that address of congratulation? The memory harks back to that first meeting of Pitt's supporters when "a voice" declared that Fox and North would never dare to stop supplies. Pitt's brother-in-law, Lord Mahon, had succeeded by now to the Earldom of Stanhope. He was one of those men who are never at ease unless the crowd is against them. For Pitt fighting uphill against the Coalition, Mahon was enthusiastic. But in Pitt, when secure of power, he lost interest. Mahon did not like the tax on bricks and tiles, and Pitt retorted with irony. So began their estrangement. In the House of Lords the Earl of Stanhope came to be known as the "Minority of One." It was he who presided over the Revolution Society.

Burke had little difficulty in pointing out that the Revolution of 1688 which substituted a William III for a James II was a wholly different affair from the reorganization which had to be undertaken in France. But it was not the argument that mattered; it was the invective appeal to the prejudices of the period. Published at five shillings, Burke's pamphlet sold none the less by the tens of thousands, and those tens of thousands were, at that period, the only people who influenced the government of the country. Burke had put into words what they had only been able to feel. His sneers at "sophisters, economists, and calculators" were their sneers. His gush over "the age of chivalry" was their gush. His insults to "the swinish multitude" were their insults. Also, Burke had romance on his side. Queens in distress always have stirred and always will stir at any rate a masculine sympathy. It was no reply to Burke's panegyric on Marie Antoinette to ask, as Philip Francis asked, "Are you such a determined champion of beauty as to draw your sword in defence of any jade upon earth, provided that she be handsome?" The true and final answer was that Burke had in effect suggested that there should be one standard of honour for a woman who was a Queen and a very different standard for a woman who belonged to the peasantry and was subject to the infamous customs of the seigniory.

Among the emigrants in their exile Burke's philippics aroused an immense enthusiasm. Years later Etienne Dumont expressed the view "that the Essay of Burke may have been the salvation of Europe." As the Revolution disclosed its delirium, it seemed as if Burke's most ominous prognostications had been justified. In the courts of Europe, not excluding the Court of Great Britain herself, the essay supplied precisely that focus on which resentment against France could be concentrated. It is, perhaps, not too much to say that for the first time in the history of the world a great writer, merely by the greatness of his writing, recruited armies, launched navies, and summoned the cohorts of a dozen nations to join in the most costly and the most futile of all the crusades.

CHAPTER FOURTEEN
REVOLUTION

I T WAS in the old diplomacy, as we call it, that William Pitt had been brought up. According to the rules of that diplomacy, a map was divided by frontiers into countries, each distinct in itself, and the relations between countries were determined by treaties and adjusted by negotiation or war. Foreign politics were as clearly defined as the chronology of Scripture by Archbishop Usher or the propositions of geometry by Euclid.

It was a game played according to rules, and moves of the game included conquest, chicanery, custom-houses, and other respectable artifices. But there was one amusement that the game did not include and this was revolution. It could not be objected to revolution that it was any more costly or cruel than war. Guns killed a hundred times as many people as guillotines, and in killing, guns gave a thousand times more pain. No, what was condemned in a revolution was a breach of etiquette.

By their revolution, so it was thought, the French, like the Russians in our own day, were stopping the game by upsetting the board. All the elements of the game which had been set out decently on the tables of aristocracy were

scattered higgledy-piggledy on the ground floor of democracy, and instead of playing the usual chess, the canaille
were treating kings and queens as pawns, and pawns as kings
and queens. At the reverberations of the prolonged earthquake in France, there was not a country in Europe that did
not tremble. The fate of the French throne affected every
throne. Every aristocracy wished to make common cause
with the French aristocracy.

Usually we assume that an internationale means Socialism
and only Socialism. The assumption is based on a fallacy.
Of all the internationales, the earliest was the Christian
Church, within which was born the Holy Roman Empire.
Art is an internationale, science is an internationale, and in the
Seventeen Nineties the most obvious of all the internationales
was monarchy. It was the kings, not the peoples, who de-
clared the class war.

★

At his summer palace of Pilnitz, the Elector of Saxony
entertained the Emperor Leopold and Frederick William,
King of Prussia. There, in August, 1791, they arrived at "a
declaration." They would be ready to employ "the most
efficient means in proportion to their resources, to place the
King of France in a position to establish with the most absolute freedom the foundations of a monarchical form of
government, which shall be in harmony with the rights of
sovereigns and promote the welfare of the French nation."

Here was a new model for a Magna Carta. "The most
absolute freedom" was claimed not for citizens but for their
rulers. "The rights of sovereigns"—*they* were what had to

come before everything else. "The welfare of the nation"—
it was only an afterthought.

In July, 1792, monarchy marched its troops on France.
The anointed captain of the royalist crusaders was the Duke
of Brunswick. He issued a manifesto, denying belligerent
rights to the National Guards and threatening that resistance
would be punished by the burning of houses. The answer of
Europe to the French Revolution was thus "no quarter."
At a later date Pitt would not have it that the Declaration of
Pilnitz contained a secret clause providing for the dismem-
berment of France. But Poland was suffering this surgery
and the French had every reason to suppose that they would
receive similar treatment.

When the White Armies of our own day encircled Russia
the result was a reign of terror. The aggression against France
provoked the same calamity, and it was amid the roll of
drums around the guillotine that Pitt strove for peace. He
regretted that the King of Prussia, as ally of England, had
put his name to the Declaration of Pilnitz. He refused to join
in any armed advance on Paris.

To the French *émigrés*, gathering at Coblenz and Dresden
and wherever they could obtain hospitality, the Declaration
of Pilnitz was a passport to power and to property. To win
Pitt became their objective, and Burke was their envoy. Of
the system of caste then pervading England it is illustrative
to note that apparently the Prime Minister had never met a
philosopher so distinguished as Burke on a private and social
occasion. However, a dinner was arranged and there were
some hours of talk.

It was one man against two. There was Burke, eager, informed, fighting for privilege, but himself socially an outsider. There was Pitt, sober even over his wine, and with him William Wyndham, recently created Lord Grenville, Pitt's Foreign Secretary and spokesman in the House of Lords. Grenville was Pitt's cousin by birth, and through his wife, Anne Pitt, daughter of Lord Camelford, he became cousin also by marriage. In character, too, there was a kinship between these colleagues. It was to his Grenville blood that Pitt owed his pride of manner. Assiduous in his duties, grave in his rhetoric, jealous in his patriotism, Grenville, who was to be a successor to Pitt as Prime Minister, had become already his *alter ego*.

"I am not competent to the management of men," so Grenville confessed; certainly, there was no success, that evening, in the management of Edmund Burke. What he wanted was intervention by England to save the French monarchy. To any such idea, however, Burke discovered that Pitt and Grenville were "cold and dead." The *status quo* still stood the strain. However unstable, there was equilibrium.

Like President Wilson when he was confronted by an old world in collapse, Pitt was eager to keep his country out of war. But as President Wilson realized, to be neutral in policy is not enough. If policy is to be neutral, a nation must be neutral also in mind, and it was this deeper neutrality that Great Britain failed to achieve. Over the issue that had arisen, men, with blood throbbing in their veins, could not withhold their views. To them, the idea of liberty, leaping all frontiers, was as dangerous or as delicious as the idea, whatever it be, which we call Bolshevism, is to us. To some, here was a life-giving breeze. To others, it was poison gas. The only hope was that the contradictions would cancel one another.

There were many who expressed a sympathy with France. Among them was Pitt's brother-in-law, Stanhope, whose "voice," already quoted, influenced Pitt at the meeting in Downing Street. "Good God! my dear Lord," wrote he to Grenville on the very eve of war, "you have no conception of the misfortunes you may bring upon *England* by going to war with France. For as to *France*, I believe all Europe cannot subdue them, whatever efforts may be made. It will only rouse them more." Grenville's endorsement was "to be circulated." It was a letter that Pitt and his colleagues must have seen.

When the Prussians were driven by the French from Verdun and Longwy, Fox wrote with enthusiasm, "No! no public event, not excepting Saratoga and Yorktown, ever happened that gave me such delight." It was the attitude of a man who supports the other country when it is right against his own, when he believes it to be wrong.

Pitt was in a perplexity. He could not defend the French Revolution. That acceptance of the sacrilege would have been directly to challenge the monarchy under which he held office. On the other hand, he did not wish to have trouble with France. While others were talking so loud, what was to be his talking point? He began to develop the theory that, whatever happened in Europe, England was different. She had no need of revolutions. She had no need to be upset by revolutions elsewhere.

Writing as Pitt's biographer, Stanhope declared that the nine years of peace, 1784–93, were "the most prosperous and happy, perhaps, that England had ever known." Was not the public credit restored? Were not the finances thriving? Did not exports and imports indicate a growing commerce? Look at the canals that were carved across the country! Listen to the horns of the coaches which, as a means of traffic, were at last organized on a business basis! During the reign of King George III the population which had been seven and a half millions rose to fourteen millions. Plagues and fevers were abated, and cotton shirts, now cheap, were also clean. There were reasons—certainly there were reasons —why a Prime Minister should declare to the House of Commons that Adam Smith had been the "author . . . whose extensive knowledge of detail and depth of philosophical research [would] furnish the best solution to every question connected with the history of commerce or with the systems of political economy."

The theory of a different England was, then, the theory that Pitt held as an antidote to anxiety over a revolutionary France. He used every opportunity. On January 31, 1792, Parliament was opened as usual by the King in person. Immediately Pitt introduced his budget and once more the occasion was a field day. The army was to be reduced, the navy was to be reduced, the taxes were to be reduced, and if he did not also reduce the four per cents. to three-and-a-half per cents., it was because he hoped next year to make a reduction to three per cent. It was the climax of neutrality.

In a tone of triumph he reviewed not the past alone but the future, and the gambler within him indulged in a prophecy which, from that day to this, has been an argument for reticences. "Although," said Pitt, "we must not count with certainty on the continuance of our present prosperity during such an interval, yet unquestionably there never was a time in the history of this country when from the situation of Europe we might more reasonably expect fifteen years of peace than we may at the present moment."

About this famous prophecy much rubbish has been written. Because Pitt foretold fifteen years of peace when Great Britain was on the eve of twenty years of war, it is assumed sometimes that he was blind to the possibilities of the moment. No man should interpret a parliamentary appeal unless he understands what is the meaning of parliament. Pitt's prophecy was a part of his strategy. He wanted peace and he knew that prophecies sometimes fulfil themselves. What chance of peace would there have been if he had foretold twenty years of war?

The theory of a prosperous England remote from a distressed France pleased neither party. It was true that Pitt had balanced the budget and so saved the national finances. But the England of the later Eighteenth Century was still that inscrutable country of which George Herbert had written, "Half the world knows not how the other half lives." The purpose of that system of caste into which Pitt had been born was to keep the Many at a respectful distance from the Few. What Pitt saw of England was neither more nor less than what could be seen from a window with a rectangular Georgian frame across an intervening park bounded by a sunken wall. From the rest of England the mind of Pitt was as far removed as the Manchus in their citadels were distant from the rest of China.

To Shakespeare's John of Gaunt, England was the "other Eden." It was the language of a poetic dawn and what Pitt did was to translate it into the prosaic light of day. Yet even John of Gaunt, challenging death with a rhapsody, only dared to extol "the precious stone set in a silver sea" as a "demi-paradise." What men were realizing in the Seventeen Nineties was that the demi-paradise implied a demi-purgatory. To declare, as Pitt declared, that "no man is so poor or inconsiderable" as to be denied the protection of the laws was mere rhetoric. Many of the laws, so far from protecting the poor and the inconsiderable, oppressed them. Under those mild and equal statutes the debtor could be seized by the bailiff, the infant pauper could be sold as a serf, women and children, slaves in fact if not in name, could be chained in the mines as beasts of burden, girls could be hanged for theft, transported to a life of shame, or flogged through the streets naked, while the dissenter was loaded with disabilities and the Catholic was registered as less a citizen than a criminal. It was no wonder that Shakespeare had not only sung of England but sighed over her:

> *What might'st thou do, that honour would thee do,*
> *Were all thy children kind and natural!*

★

In this prosperous England there were thus grounds for social discontent. True, it was half a century before the menace of Chartism drove the government of the day to call on Wellington to mobilize the army as a garrison for London. It was nearly a century and a half before organized labour was to capture control of the House of Commons and subject the nation to a general strike. But these were the harvests of which the seeds had been sown far and wide long before those early Eighteen Nineties.

To meet the discontents of a nation, the statesman may pursue two methods. He may concede or he may coerce. In the early flush of his enthusiasm as Prime Minister there is no doubt that Pitt stood for constitutional progress.

In his first session as Prime Minister, 1784, one of those Liberals who then emerged from the cities, Alderman Saw-bridge, took up Pitt's own task as private member, and proposed a motion for reform. Pitt begged him to desist, but only because the motion was "greatly out of season at this juncture." He had "the measure much at heart," and he added, "I pledge myself in the strongest language to bring it forward the very first opportunity next session." The alderman's motion was rejected by 199 votes to 125. But Pitt voted in the minority.

In the following year Pitt fulfilled his pledge. On behalf of reform, he did his utmost, in his own words, to "exert his whole power and credit, as a man and a minister." He proposed to disfranchise thirty-six rotten boroughs, each returning two members, and the representation of the counties and of London would be increased. As a sop to the reactionaries, he actually offered—and the precedent proved to be important, as we shall see—a million sterling as compensation to the "proprietors" of these constituencies.

Yet Pitt, though popular, though supported on the issue by Fox, was defeated. He had 174 members on his side. But he had 248 members against him. It meant that the road to reform was blocked. The House would allow Pitt to reorganize finance. The House would not allow him to change its own legislative statutes. In the years preceding the French War the attitude of Parliament toward an extension of the franchise and a redistribution of seats was the same as the attitude of the Prussian Diet before the Great War that broke out in 1914.

In another direction Pitt's impulse was defeated. Under what came to be called Wilberforce's Oak in his grounds at Holwood, he had been convinced that the time had come to abolish negro slavery, and on May 9, 1788, he gave notice to the House that in the next session he would propose a motion "to take into consideration the circumstances" of this traffic.

If ever there was a case of legislation it was here. There, in the river Thames, you could see the slave ship as it was fitted for its voyage—narrow quarters into which the victims were to be crowded and the shackles with which they were to be loaded. The story as told to the House by Wilberforce was overwhelming. It convinced Pitt. It convinced Fox.

Of Pitt's appeal for the suppression of the traffic, it is enough to say that it was probably his greatest oration. Let us imagine ourselves in a crowded legislature, every man watching the central figure. Let us hear again the quiet, clear voice of youth uttering the words with no hesitation save the pauses of eloquence itself. So let us surrender ourselves to the following:

There was a time, Sir, when the very practice of the slave, trade prevailed among us. Slaves, as we may read in Henry's *History of Great Britain*, were formerly an established article in our exports. "Great numbers," he says, "were exported like cattle from the British coast, and were to be seen exposed for sale in the Roman market." But it is the slavery in Africa which is now called on to furnish the alleged proofs that Africa labours under a natural incapacity for civilization; that Providence never intended her to rise above a state of barbarism; that Providence has irrecoverably doomed her to be only a nursery for slaves for us free and civilized Europeans. Allow of this principle as applied to Africa, and I should be glad to know why it might not also have been applied to ancient and uncivilized Britain? Why might not some Roman Senator, reasoning on the principles of some Hon. gentlemen, and pointing to British barbarians, have predicted with equal boldness, "There is a people destined never to be free"? We, Sir, have long since emerged from barbarism; we have almost forgotten that we were once barbarians. There is, indeed, one thing wanting to complete the contrast and to clear us altogether from the imputation of acting even to this hour as barbarians; for we continue even to this hour a barbarous traffic in slaves.

Sir, I trust we shall no longer continue this commerce, to the destruction of every improvement on that wide continent; and shall not consider ourselves as conferring too great a boon in restoring its inhabitants to the rank of human beings. I trust we shall not think ourselves too liberal, if, by abolishing the slave trade, we give them the same common chance of civilization with other parts of the world; and that we shall now allow to Africa the opportunity—the hope—the prospect of attaining to the same blessings which we ourselves, through the favourable dispensations of Divine Providence, have been permitted, at a much more early period, to enjoy. If we listen to the voice of reason and duty, and pursue this night the line of conduct which they prescribe, some of us may live to see a reverse of that picture from which we now turn our eyes with shame and regret. We may live to behold the natives of Africa engaged in the calm occupations of industry, in the pursuits of a just and legitimate commerce. We may behold the beams of science and philosophy breaking in upon their land, which, at some happy period in still later times, may blaze with full lustre; and joining their influence to that of pure religion, may illuminate and invigorate the most distant extremities of that immense continent. Then may we hope that even Africa, though last of all the quarters of the globe, shall enjoy at length, in the evening of her days, those blessings which have descended so plentifully upon us in a much earlier period of the world. Then also will Europe, participating in her improvement and prosperity, receive an ample recompense for the tardy kindness, if kindness it can be called, of no longer hindering that continent from extricating herself out of the darkness which, in other more fortunate regions, has been so much more speedily dispelled.

> *Nos . . . primus equis Oriens afflavit anhelis;*
> *Illic sera rubens accendit lumina Vesper.*

Understand the Latin or not, there it is, the completion of what Coleridge, referring to Pitt, has called "the proud architectural pile of his sentences," and as the lines were uttered the rising sun of the early morning—for the debate had continued all night—did indeed shine through the windows and greet the orator as he stood inspired by the wonder of his thought.

But what was the result of it all? A dilatory motion. The selfish interests of Liverpool and the Indies prevented action. As there was to be no effective suffrage at home, so there was to be no emancipation abroad. The franchise of the citizen and the freedom of the slave were alike vetoed.

It meant that the liberalism which was to change the face of Great Britain during the Nineteenth Century, already forming under the surface of society, was denied its logical outlet. This was the liberalism that, anticipating the verdict of mankind, supported the French Revolution. The Friends of the People, clamouring for reform, included twenty-eight members of Parliament who followed Fox, and the schism within the Whig Party thus reflected a debate spreading from end to end of the country. On the one hand, Burke thundered forth "An Appeal from the New to the Old Whigs." On the other hand, there arose a veritable reincarnation of Rousseau, notorious as Thomas Paine, who flung back an essay on "The Rights of Man." France and the United States between them had forced on England a discussion of Royalty *versus* Radicalism.

It was a whole century before Great Britain was to become generally literate. Not many people, judged by percentage of population, read either Paine or Burke. But here was an issue which could be stated in slogans and broadly appreciated in its essentials by multitudes who had no books and no newspapers. On the one hand, there were "Republicans and Levellers" and people who were so seditious as to tell "tyrants to beware." On the other hand, there were the Church and King Club and defensive societies of that kind.

It may be said that the mob, having no vote, did not matter. But men without a vote may still use the voice, and, excluded from the register, certain cities substituted the riot. The opinions of the Whig Party itself were not more mixed than the emotions of these excited multitudes. In Birmingham, a scientist and Unitarian like Dr. Priestley, with his friends, had their houses raided and their property destroyed. On the other hand, at Dundee, the cry, arising over the high price of meal was, "No excise! No King," and there was planted, as in France, a Tree of Liberty; while at Sheffield an ox was eaten whole and the French tricolour was flown.

That British institutions were endangered by these controversies Pitt did not believe. In 1789 he had been an eye-witness of the nation's rejoicing over the King's recovery. Moreover, there was apparent also a romantic sympathy among the masses of the people with King Louis XVI and his Queen, and a very genuine determination that no such calamity as theirs should befall King George III.

But whenever there are riots or a use of language calculated to provoke them, a government is compelled to consider not merely the merits of controversy, but the maintenance of public order. That principle has applied to Ramsay MacDonald in his attitude toward the Nationalists in India and Egypt. Faced by the happenings in Birmingham, Sheffield, and Dundee, Pitt began to depend on the militia. He was driven from the left to the right, from faiths to forces.

To the governing classes, a Tree of Liberty in Dundee and the tricolour flown at Yarmouth appeared to be much more dangerous to society than the destruction of Dr. Priestley's scientific instruments at Birmingham. The very idea of suggesting that kings were tyrants, that statesmen were corrupt, that priests were hypocrites, and that the enforcement of law was slavery! That the London Corresponding Society and the Society for Constitutional Information should encourage such notions, especially in the navy and army, could not be tolerated. In May, 1792, there was issued a royal proclamation "solemnly warning all loving subjects" against "diverse wicked and seditious writings." Fox denounced the proclamation. But in the House of Lords the Prince of Wales, preferring the prospect of a crown to his partiality for his "dear Charles," condemned the offending pamphlets and supported the edict against them.

Slowly but surely the balance of opinion supporting Pitt's neutrality was upset. Burke was now opposed even to so simple a measure of justice as the repeal of the act imposing religious tests, of which, in earlier life, he had been an advocate. As a protest against the rights of man, the disciples of Edmund Burke insisted that slavery itself must continue, and on April 18, 1791, despite the efforts of Pitt and Fox, a bill to prevent the further importation of negroes into the West Indies was defeated by 168 votes to 88. It was impossible for the Prime Minister to be unaffected by the reaction. On a motion for reform, advanced in April, 1792, Pitt, though recognizing its theoretical "propriety," raised the cry of "mischief or danger" and of "anarchy and confusion." Said he, "I see nothing but discouragement." Paine was an exile in

France. Priestley, wronged yet discredited, could make nothing of the situation and migrated to the United States. But Burke went on from strength to strength.

★

It is said that it takes two to make a quarrel. But in diplomacy it takes two to keep the peace. What England thought of France was, doubtless, important. Not less important was what France thought of England.

At the outset, it was in France as it was to be in Russia: the Revolution was actually pro-British. They who promoted it looked upon the British constitution as the exemplar of ordered liberty. It is thus by a strange irony that, in one case as in the other, British statesmanship was unable to retain so obvious an advantage.

There was a high authority who enunciated the saying, *If thine enemy hunger, feed him.* They were words that William Pitt had heard a thousand times. In the year 1789 the traditional enemy of England offered him a supreme opportunity of displaying that wisdom. A starving Paris begged for 20,000 sacks of British wheat.

Wilberforce urged that the food be sent. Pitt demurred. Undoubtedly there were arguments against the export. For England also was short of supplies, and it was shown that a comparatively slight diversion of the necessities of life was followed by a sharp rise in prices. But what a request to decline! The day was soon to dawn when in England also the cry would be, "Bread, bread!" and they would find it not.

With the imprisonment of King Louis XVI another opportunity presented itself to William Pitt. Monarchies other than the British, even if neutral to France, had withdrawn their ministers from Paris. The French Republic, again anticipating the experience of the Russian Soviet, must not be "recognized." In the House of Commons, it is true, Fox moved a resolution that a liberated France should be acknowledged and that a minister continue to be accredited to Paris. But the leader of the Opposition had now no more than fifty supporters at Westminster; in the words of Lord Malmesbury, "The cry against him out of doors was excessive, and his friends were hurt beyond measure; several left London." The result was a compromise that again satisfied nobody. Chauvelin, the French Ambassador, was allowed to remain in London, but only in an unofficial capacity. With Chauvelin there was a secretary called Talleyrand.

"Delicate and critical"—that was how Pitt described the situation in the autumn of 1792, and little incidents, here and there, were significant. It was noticed that the fortifications of the Tower of London were under repair and that the guard at the Bank of England was strengthened. On December 1st a proclamation summoned a part of the militia to the colours. Moreover, an Alien Bill laid certain restrictions on foreigners. Other measures prohibited the export of arms to France and—note again—they forbade export of food.

In Paris there were reactions. "Pitt and Coburg" and "that monster Pitt" were denounced even by the less violent Girondists. "War with kings and peace with nations!" cried Merlin de Thionville; it was to be *La Fraternité* or *La Mort*. The Zinovieff letter which caused such inconvenience at a

WAR—so it had come once more. Royalty or revolution had made no difference to this chronic recurrence. Every dozen years or so an outbreak of conflict was as surely to be expected as the return of the sun spots.

To Burke, the war for which he had worked so hard appeared to be achieved, a final rapture. As his beatific vision, so the old man babbled of bloodshed. With miseries at home and abroad accumulating around him, he wrote in ecstasy to Pitt about "the prosperity and glory of His Majesty's reign," and he adjured the Prime Minister who was patronizing him with a pension that he should never be "led to think that this war is, in its principles or anything that belongs to it, the least resembling any other war." In his last great speech he cried, "Enflame a Jacobin! You may as well talk of setting fire to Hell! Impossible!"

Yet there were moments when even the completed egotist was conscious of the tragedy of it all. With the nation driven by the war to the verge of bankruptcy, he was not troubled only by his own debts. With millions of homes shadowed by actual or prospective sorrow, it was not only the loss of a son, Richard, that plunged him into a hot bath of self-pity.

Burke it was who spoke of "the disastrous events which have followed one another in a long unbroken funereal train, moving in a procession that seemed to have no end."

It was the old men in their armchairs who with Burke wanted the war. It was the young men with Pitt who did not want it, yet had to do the fighting. The lives of Nelson and Sir John Moore were not more surely cut off in battle than was he. In a couple of years he was writing to his mother about "a larger shoe" for his foot. The proud cidadel of his being, undermined by liquor, was beginning to be subject to the long siege of the ancestral gout. Two years later he was complaining of headaches. Also there was rheumatism, a swollen face, and other occasional ailments.

On the day that war was declared Pitt, as Prime Minister, was chained to the chariot wheel of a pagan god. Anyone who, like Wilberforce, wanted peace, and said so, was cut by the King when he attended the levee. For Pitt there was thus no escape. "My head would be off in six months were I to resign," said he grimly as he sat one day at supper.

At Burton Pynsent, Wilberforce called on Lady Chatham —"much interested in politics—seventy-five years old, and a very active mind." According to Sir Robert Peel, no woman since the days of Philip and Alexander of Macedon had ever such reason to be proud at once of her husband and her son as this old lady living eagerly on "the four and a half per cents." which Pitt thriftily allotted to her from certain West India duties. One day her little granddaughter, afterward Lady Griselda Tekell, put to the old lady a childish question: "Which do you think the cleverest, grandpapa or Mr.

Pitt?" The answer was immediate: "Your grandpapa, without doubt," and it was what any wife, so loyal as she, would have said.

At first sight it did look as if the elder Pitt were much cleverer than the younger. In that year of wonder, 1759, when Pitt himself was born, it was victory, victory for the father, all the way from India to America. The son had a dozen years of it, and on land, at any rate, they were years of defeat. Yet it is a question for argument whether the glamour of a brief moment is to surpass a prolonged and persistent greatness maintained over a prolonged period of supreme stress and strain. Any man can shout when he wins. Not many men can silently refuse to know when they are beaten. Such a man was the younger Pitt.

In Europe there were thus two persons who mattered. The one was a civilian in a black morning coat, who had never sailed a sea nor heard a gun fired, except as salute. In Downing Street, Wilberforce found him with "a great map spread out before him." He was the first of the modern generals, the man whose head is his headquarters.

The other was a young officer from Corsica directing artillery against Toulon. He was ever in the thick of the fray, storming a bridge at Lodi, stumbling over the snow and ice of an Alpine pass, and wreathing his own brows with the laurels of a military glory. He was the last of the ancient generals, and of them all the most gorgeous in his achievements. Which of these men would win?

What that great map suggested to Pitt was, at the outset, not discouraging. On the one side there lay France, dis-

tracted by her own torments; France, where the royalists of
La Vendée had been ruthlessly harried by the revolutionists
and the very name of Girondist Lyons had been erased;
France, without a friend in Europe. On the other side, there
was a coalition consisting of Great Britain, Spain, Sardinia,
Prussia, Holland, and Austria-Hungary, with Russia and
Sweden to be reckoned as benevolent neutrals. Balance of
power? Was there ever a preponderance more overwhelming?
Yet this was the map of Europe on which a Bonaparte was
to scrawl his forceful signature from the Mediterranean to
the Arctic Circle and from the Atlantic Ocean to a Moscow
in flames.

★

It was true that Pitt, meditating over his map, was pursu-
ing a more modern method than Bonaparte, handling the
musket of a somnolent sentry. But it so happened that
Bonaparte appeared at a moment when the ancient practice
of war had been brought to its perfection. To Frederick the
Great, a campaign was no mere ceremonial conducted as a
tournament by cousinly kings. A campaign had an objective.
So with that strange hard-bitten Russian zealot for success,
Suwarrow. He, storming Ismail, was the forerunner of
Napoleon Bonaparte.

Chatham had no such opponents to face. Where the son
had to face a France in resurrection, the father only faced
a France on the verge of collapse.

The difficulty that Pitt had to reckon with was that maps
are not enough. The success of a method depends on the
efficiency with which it is carried out. According to Macau-

lay, "the English army under Pitt was the laughing stock of Europe" and "his military administration was that of a driveller." They are phrases worth examining.

When war broke out Pitt's "contemptible little army," as a certain Kaiser would have called it, was no more than 18,000 men. Even the personnel of the navy had been cut from 18,000 to 16,000 men. Nor are these facts to be reckoned as a discredit to the Prime Minister. They are a conclusive proof that he refused, by military preparations, to provoke the conflict.

For it was not the size of the British Army that made it a laughing stock. After all, there were only 24,000 British troops at the Battle of Waterloo. It was the leadership. The great advantage enjoyed by Napoleon was that, as the result of the Revolution, he could promote a competent officer and dismiss the incompetent. Pitt did neither. With France a nation, Britain was still subject to her aristocracy. In one country the commander was addressed as citizen. In the other country he had to be addressed as My Lord, Your Grace, or even as Royal Highness.

In one of her vivacious indiscretions Pitt's lively niece, Lady Hester Stanhope, put the point with a womanly precision. Pitt's Foreign Secretary happened to be, at the moment, Lord Mulgrave, and at breakfast he was only able to discover a broken spoon. "How can Pitt have such a spoon as this?" he asked of Lady Hester. "Have you not discovered," so she retorted, "that Mr. Pitt sometimes uses very slight and weak instruments to effect his ends?"

"What officer have we to oppose to our domestic and ex-

ternal enemies?" asked Lord Grenville himself bitterly.
"Some old woman in a red riband." The old woman in a red
riband was Frederick, Duke of York, the favourite son of
King George III. In the year 1789 he had fought a duel with
Colonel Lennox, the shot from whose pistol had actually
grazed one of his curls. But of experience and the ability to
handle a campaign he had none. On one occasion he was
nearly surrounded and had to flee on horseback. But it was
hoped that a prince would please the troops. He landed at
Ostend.

The report of him was, in Pitt's words, "very unfavourable." Yet he was backed by the King. It was all very well
for the Duke to say, "when not on duty I wear a brown
coat." Despite that sartorial condescension, to supersede him
was difficult. As Pitt put the case, "it seems clear that if Lord
Cornwallis has the chief command, the Duke of York will
come away entirely." It was thus not until November, 1794,
that the Duke of York was dismissed. The King was "very
much hurt" and wrote, "Even a son of mine cannot with-
stand the torrent of abuse." It was this same Duke of York
who, a dozen years later, was much offended because the
peninsular command was conferred on one who was to be
the Duke of Wellington.

Manifestly the thing to do at the outset of the war was
to march straight on Paris. The Duke of York himself advised it. But the Prince of Coburg was of opinion that, according to "the best writers," the fortresses on the border
must be first reduced. This was the delay that enabled France
to recruit her armies and to promote Bonaparte. It was not

only the British Army that then became a laughing stock. Every army in Europe except the French Army was made to look ridiculous.

★

Hitherto many a war had been an amusement that kings could begin when they so felt inclined and that, as a rule, kings could bring to an end. But in stating that this war was different, Burke had been right. The war was a fact that began to absorb all other facts, an insatiable emergency that engulfed all hopes of prosperity and all safeguards of liberty. For Pitt the struggle involved a blunt denial of everything that he had ever desired, whether of sound finance, of reform, or of freedom itself.

For both the combatants, money became an anxiety. It was by plunder that, in large measure, Napoleon paid his expenses. Pitt had to depend on his purse. On taking office, the army only cost him about £4,000,000 a year, and the navy about £3,000,000. But he had now to meet not only the additional expenditure incurred by Great Britain. In a phrase familiar enough to the Downing Street of our own day, he had to finance the allies. One subsidy alone to Austria, dated 1794, was £6,000,000. When war broke out the national debt was £260,000,000, and the annual charge was £9,437,862. At the Peace of Amiens, about ten years later, the capital of the debt stood at £620,000,000 and the interest was nearly £20,000,000. In 1797 the three per cents. fell to 48, or far below the quotation at which Pitt, on taking office in 1784, had found them.

In February of that year there was actually a run on the

Bank of England. It was to Pitt that the directors appealed.
The King was brought to town. Though it was Sunday, a
council was held at St. James's Palace. By an Order in Council, the bank was forbidden to issue cash until the will of
Parliament should be known. Parliament met and Great
Britain adopted what was in effect a paper currency. There
appeared the epigram:

> *Of Augustus and Rome*
> *The poets still warble,*
> *How he found it of brick*
> *And left it of marble.*
>
> *So of Pitt and of England*
> *Men may say without vapour,*
> *That he found it of gold*
> *And left it of paper.*

At such a crisis everything depended on the prestige
of the minister. Fox declared that the country had been
brought "into the very same gulf" of bankruptcy where
France with her *assignats* was floundering. "Mark my prophecy, my Lords," said Lansdowne, "if you attempt to make
banknotes a legal tender, their credit will perish." Happily,
Pitt was not dependent on the financial judgment of the
aristocracy. In the city of London the merchants and bankers
met at the Mansion House and, to the number of three thousand, agreed to accept the new tender. Other bodies followed
their example and, at the rate of £6.17.0 per cent. on the
next loan, the situation was saved.

That there was debate on Pitt's proceedings cannot be

denied. When it was proposed to enlist French royalists in the British Army an irate officer ca led Tarleton declared that the measure would "destroy the privileges of Magna Carta, undermine the Bill of Rights, and finally annihilate the British constitution." But on the whole Pitt received from Parliament whatever he asked. When he put a tax on rum and spirits, bricks and tiles, plate glass and attorneys, it was noted that not even the attorneys complained. A guinea imposed on any person who used hairpowder was expected to yield a revenue of £210,000. Nor did dogs escape attention. As for borrowing, when the people hesitated to subscribe he called it a Loyalty Loan and got the money. Not only was an income tax instituted. Patriotic people began to send in their payments on a voluntary basis. Even the manufacturers, who said so loudly that they couldn't and wouldn't pay, could pay and did pay.

Among the people of Europe there began to be discontent. The harvest of 1795 had been poor. Along the Rhine and the Vistula some of it had been laid waste by war. In Birmingham the mob, demanding "a large loaf," broke open a bakehouse and mill. It was not the only incident of the kind. In St. George's Fields a mass meeting was held at which biscuits were distributed, embossed with the words "Freedom and Plenty, or Slavery and Want."

★

For the first time Pitt himself became nervous. Of Britain at peace he was sure. But of Britain at war he had his misgivings.

In 1792, coöperating with Fox, he had secured the passage of an act which is still regarded as a safeguard of the liberty of the press. The point may seem to be technical but it was important. If an alleged libel had been printed a jury had been allowed merely to decide on the question of fact—that is, the question whether or not the words had been actually published. The judge decided whether the words as published did or did not constitute a libel. But by the act of 1792 the jury was entitled to decide the whole of the question—not only publication but whether the publication was or was not libellous. This was what Macaulay called "the inestimable law which places the Liberty of the Press under the protection of juries."

With the outbreak of war the temper of Pitt himself changed. As early as 1794 he insisted on the suspension of the Habeas Corpus Act. New penalties were devised for a traitorous correspondence with the enemy. But giving information to the enemy was the least of the offences against which action was taken. To publish the works of Thomas Paine was treated as a crime. A yeoman, himself drunk, was told by the village constable, in the same condition, to keep the peace in the King's name. "Damn you and the King, too," retorted the yokel, and he went to prison for a year. Men who in their association called one another "citizen" were transported for fourteen years. Of arms, a few were discovered here and there. For instance, in Sheffield there was the notice:

Fellow citizens, the barefaced aristocracy of the present administration has made it necessary that we should be prepared to act on the defensive. A plan has been hit upon, and, if encouraged sufficiently, will, no doubt, have the effect of furnishing a quantity of pikes to the patriots. The blades are made of steel, tempered and polished after an approved form, and each, with the hoop, will be charged one shilling.

Also, it was alleged that there was a plan to kill the King by discharging a poisoned missile at him through an air tube. It was called "the pop-gun plot," and it is a fact that, in 1795, when the King was proceeding to open Parliament, the window of his coach was pierced by some small projectile. Once more the cries of the mob were "Bread!" "Peace!" "No War!" "No Famine!" and last but not least, "No Pitt!" For saying "Down with George!" Kyd Wake, a journeyman printer, was sentenced to an hour in the pillory and five years in prison.

★

The hero of these prosecutions was the Lord Chancellor. Not any longer Thurlow. From the Woolsack, Pitt had had the courage at last to oust that surly and disloyal colleague. His successor was Loughborough, later Lord Rosslyn, whose severities against sedition-mongers entitled him to the honours paid during an earlier crisis to Judge Jeffries.

In one case the future Lord Eldon, as Attorney General, addressed the jury for nine hours. A juryman confessed later that he could not convict a man of a crime when it took the Attorney General nine hours to tell what it was. One defendant, dissatisfied with Erskine who happened to be his counsel, sent him a note: "I'll be hanged if I don't plead my own cause." Erskine replied: "You'll be hanged if you do."

Men and women became apocalyptic. Robespierre had
accepted Catherine Théot as his prophetess. So in England
there appeared a "Nephew of God" and "Prince of the
Hebrews." Another of these enthusiasts published a tract
called "The Last Trumpet and Flying Angel." Others preferred annual Parliaments and universal suffrage.

Pitt replied in two ways. He brought in measures intended
to facilitate the supply of food. Also he strengthened the law
against treason, seditious meetings, and similar offences.
"Say at once," cried Fox, "that a fine constitution is not
suitable for us." He threw up his hands in dismay.

Taxes, hunger, sedition, riots, defeat—all these disturbed a
nation that was trying to fight a red-handed France with
kid gloves. One fact, however, was evident. Under Pitt as
Prime Minister, England might suffer and grumble. But after
twelve years of his government she trusted him. In finance
there might be deficits. The debt might be accumulating.
Reform might be arrested. Not a rotten borough might be
suppressed, not a citizen granted the vote, not a slave set
free; and the Habeas Corpus Act itself might be suspended.
But the foundations of Pitt's power were unshaken. When
he failed he inspired more confidence than other men inspire
when they succeed.

In the year 1796 he came to an end of what may be called
his second term of office. Under the Septennial Act there had
to be an election. Those few people who exercised the suffrage
returned him to power with as big a majority as ever. For
another six years he was safe.

In his administration there had been the usual changes.

Pitt had broadened the basis of his government. As early as 1792, with war a possibility, he had wished to take in the Whigs and so form—not a coalition, for that word was taboo! —but what he preferred to call "a strong and united ministry." But there had been difficulties. "You see how it is," said Burke; "Mr. Fox's coach stops the way." Fox "had gone too far" in his support of the Revolution. But in 1794, with the war in full swing, Fox was isolated. The Duke of Portland thus became Pitt's Home Secretary and brought to his support those Whigs who, with Burke, approved of the struggle.

Not for an instant had Pitt ceased to desire peace. "I feel it my duty," he would say, "as an English minister and a Christian, to use every effort to stop so bloody and wasting a war." Indeed, peace seemed again to be possible, and by an astonishing irony it was the whiff of grapeshot, administered to Paris by a young man called Bonaparte, that seemed to blast the path to tranquillity. For it was the end, both of the Revolution and the Counter Revolution. It meant that at last France had returned to a settled form of government.

In a message to Parliament, dated December 8, 1795, King George III, using the words of Pitt, expressed "an earnest desire to conclude a treaty for general peace," and negotiations with France were initiated. It was at Basle in Switzerland that the contending nations discovered what Lord Rosebery, in another connection, has called "a wayside inn." No settlement, however, was reached, and in the House of Commons Fox proceeded to denounce Pitt in a speech that lasted for four hours. Pitt replied and the great case, for and against the war, was fully stated.

What Pitt had reason to dread was the defection of his allies in Europe, for instance, Prussia. He decided, therefore, again to treat with France, and Lord Malmesbury was sent to Paris. Again the negotiations were fruitless. England demanded that France surrender Holland; France, having conquered Holland, refused to give up the country; as "a studied insult," so Pitt called it, France therefore ordered Lord Malmesbury and his suite to leave the country in forty-eight hours. The comment of Pitt was decisive:

The question is not how much you will give for peace, but how much disgrace you will suffer at the outset of your negotiations for it. In these circumstances, then, are we to persevere in the war with a spirit and energy worthy of the British name and the British character? Or are we, by sending couriers to Paris, to prostrate ourselves at the feet of a stubborn and supercilious Government?

To begin the war—how easy it had been; to end it—how difficult. All the perorations against the Jacobins that had seemed to be, when uttered, so loyal, so patriotic, so eloquent, had penetrated into the French mind as poisoned arrows and left an impression that England hated, not merely the principles of her Revolution but the people who professed those principles.

IN THE Twentieth Century war has been at once organized and outlawed. If it is now prohibited by diplomacy, the reason is simple. The world cannot afford a process which sweeps away civilization as a scythe cuts grass, destroying cities, manufactures, cathedrals, and all the amenities of human life.

To the world of William Pitt war was, as it always must be, sufficiently terrible. But it was not what war is to-day. With mankind jogging along at four miles an hour, the infliction of death, like the promotion of life, was a cumbrous business. Hostilites were subject to delays. Armies, which to-day are numbered by millions, were then numbered by scores of thousands. There was no poison gas. There was no high expiosive. There was no gun or rifle loaded at the breach. There was no airplane, dropping bombs and giving information. There was no power-driven battleship. There was no submarine. The sufferings of war were cruel. But they were not, as it were, inclusive. Amid the sufferings it was possible to survive.

The field of decisive conflict was Europe. But, dis-

tant from Europe, the struggle raged in remote areas,
east and west and south. Among "the sideshows," as
we should call them in our modern dialect, may be mentioned the seizure of the Cape, the fights in the Carib-
bean, and that warfare in India where a certain officer,
Arthur Wellesley, was building up a reputation and French
enthusiasts addressed the Maharajah of Mysore as "Citizen
Sultan."

Amid the confusion of a struggle that raged, hither and
thither, throughout the world, what we have to do is to keep
our eyes fixed on the familiar figure of William Pitt. There,
in Downing Street, he was the incarnation of order amid disorder.

Of his courtesy, the evidence is conclusive. His intimate
friend, George Rose, could say after twenty years of association with him that never had he seen him out of temper nor
had he ever to suffer an unpleasant sentence. Malmesbury
described him as "the most forgiving and easy-tempered of
men."

Lord Elgin, as ambassador, was setting out for Vienna.
Pitt asked him to dine and he found that they two were
alone. It is proof of Pitt's prestige that Elgin was nervous.
But Pitt set him at his ease and they talked for hours. "I
have no instructions," said Elgin, as they parted. "You shall
receive your instructions before you leave the house," was
the Prime Minister's reply, and he called for writing ma-
terials. "He wrote with wonderful rapidity," so runs the
record, "making at the time many erasures and alterations.
When he had finished writing he said: 'Here are your instruc-

tions; enclose them to Lord Carmarthen. He knows my handwriting, and will sign them at once.'"

England knew Pitt's handwriting.

★

While the war went on, both sides were still thinking of peace. Even to war, there was thus a limited liability. In July, 1797, Pitt again dispatched Lord Malmesbury as his emissary of conciliation, and this time the discussions were conducted at Lille. Over one of the French demands there was much irritation. Since the reign of Edward III, the King of England had borne the title of King of France. He had always been so described. The French requested that he drop it. It was very annoying.

The rise of Bonaparte was the big fact to be faced. In the year 1799, there he was, First Consul, forsooth. Regarding Pitt, the opinion of Bonaparte was respectful. In 1815, he was discussing the constitution that he had granted to France. How would he manage the Chambers? Said Napoleon:

Monsieur Fouché thinks that popular assemblies are to be controlled by gaining over some old jobbers, or flattering some young enthusiasts. That is only intrigue, and intrigue does not carry one far. In England such means are not altogether neglected; but there are greater and nobler ones. Remember Mr. Pitt, and look at Lord Castlereagh! . . . With a sign from his eyebrows, Mr. Pitt could control the House of Commons and so can Lord Castlereagh now. . . . Ah! if I had such instruments, I should not be afraid of the Chambers. But have I anything to resemble these?

Needing a parliamentarian Napoleon thus longed for a Pitt. But King George III had first call on the required services.

Pitt, on his side, had formed an opinion of Napoleon. It is written by his own hand:

I see various and opposite qualities—all the great and all the little passions unfavourable to public tranquillity—united in the breast of one man, and of that man, unhappily, whose personal caprice can scarce fluctuate for an hour without affecting the destiny of Europe. I see the inward workings of fear struggling with pride in an ardent, enterprising, and tumultuous mind. I see all the captious jealousy of conscious usurpation dreaded, detested, and obeyed—the giddiness and intoxication of splendid but un-merited success—the arrogance, the presumption, the self-will of unlimited and idolized power, and—more dreadful than all in the plenitude of authority—the restless and incessant activity of guilty but unsated ambition.

Pitt estimated, not the generalship of Napoleon, but his character, and it was thus a single combat between the military and the parliamentary mind, each supreme in its own sphere.

Yet there is evidence that, as First Consul, Bonaparte wanted peace. He wrote a letter to King George III direct, offering to negotiate. But it happened that, at the moment, Pitt was engrossed in what admirals and generals describe as "amateur strategy." He was arranging to land an ex-peditionary force on Belle Isle, so invading France. No army did land on Belle Isle. But, on the other hand, nothing came of Napoleon's pacific gesture.

Wilberforce was "strongly disposed to condemn the rejection of Bonaparte's offer to treat." He was "greatly shocked at it." But he saw Pitt, and of Pitt he said, "He shook me." Pitt still claimed to be "a sincere lover of peace," but, in ominous words, he added, "I cannot be content with its nominal attainment." He did not trust Bonaparte. Truces would be merely strategic.

Fox did not content himself with a desire for peace. He was an active partisan. He sympathized with France. We see him at the Crown and Anchor Tavern, banqueted by two thousand adherents on his birthday. The Duke of Norfolk, in the chair, compared him with "the illustrious George Washington" who also "had not more than two thousand men to rally round him when his country was attacked." Yet, said the duke, "America is now free." Later in an evening, when doubtless the exhilaration had been duly stimulated in the usual manner, the duke's exuberance was even more flamboyant. "Give me leave," he cried, "before I sit down to call on you to drink our sovereign's health—The Majesty of the People." There was talk of sending Fox to the Tower, but what happened was that he was struck off the Privy Council. His Majesty himself drew his pen across the offending name.

★

Fox was now no longer "the right honourable gentleman" but "the honourable member," and he was seen in the House of Commons less frequently than before. His understudy was the son of a merchant, born at Gibraltar, called George Tierney, and Tierney became Pitt's *bête noir*. On May 25, 1798, Pitt roundly accused him of "a desire to obstruct the defence of the country." Tierney appealed to the speaker but Pitt repeated his words; and as the contention developed, he added, "I will neither retract from nor further explain my former expressions." Next day Tierney challenged Pitt to a duel, and as a personal friend, Pitt informed the son of his physician, Speaker Addington. It meant that Addington, having heard of the affair in this way, was debarred from entering upon official interference.

At a moment when, if any man was regarded as indispensable it was the Prime Minister, we thus see his life submitted to the chance of a shot from the pistol of an angry opponent. On Sunday morning, May 26, 1798—Pitt—having made his will—walked from Downing Street along Birdcage Walk, by the park, and up the steps to Queen Street. There he entered a chaise for Wimbledon Common. At three in the afternoon the parties met on Putney Heath. Anxious over the affair, Speaker Addington also had ridden to the scene on horseback. He dismounted on a small hill, where had been erected a gibbet. Recently a felon had been hanged thereon. The gibbet and the Speaker of the House of Commons stood together, then, quietly watching what would happen to the Prime Minister.

The seconds did their utmost to stop the business but failed. Pistols were then discharged but without effect. A second pair of pistols was furnished to the opponents, and this time Pitt fired into the air. The seconds then decided that "perfect honour to both parties" had been satisfied, and Addington, joining the group, was greeted by Pitt with the words, "You must dine with me to-day."

To Wilberforce these proceedings, whether in fact they were serious or farcical, were horrible, and he threatened to

bring in a motion against duelling. Pitt wrote to him plainly
that such a motion would be, as he put it, "for my removal."
In any event, Wilberforce discovered that only five or six
members would support him. So he dropped his protest.
"Pitt told me," wrote Wilberforce, "the King approved of
his conduct." It was, indeed, in a duel that Pitt's cousin,
Camelford, was to lose his life.

It was Tierney, his opponent on Putney Heath, who, in
the absence of Fox, addressed to Pitt the plain question,
"What is the object of the war?" and he demanded an answer
in "one sentence." Pitt's rejoinder was even more laconic:

The Hon. gentleman defies me to state in a single sentence the
object of the war. Sir, I will do so in a single word. The object, I
tell him, is Security! Security against the greatest danger such as
never existed in any past period of the world society.

The Prime Minister proceeded to elaborate Tierney's
objection to "ifs and buts." He ended:

These are my ifs and buts. This is my plan and on no other do I
wish to be tried by God and my country.

Yet it was not quite so simple, after all, as that. The
Cabinet itself was not homogeneous in opinion; no Cabinet
ever is; and at Downing Street Pitt found that some of
his colleagues were against making peace except with the
Bourbons. Others considered that France was still a little too
revolutionary but would doubtless improve. While the war
was thus waged as if it were inevitable, there were thus
varying shades of bellicosity. Yet, it need not be said, during
the whole of this period the brutal fact that had to be faced—

the only fact—was that this war, on which real opinion was so divided, went on.

★

The question had long since ceased to be whether the allies could march on Paris. What alarmed the people was the possibility that the French might march on London.

If, then, Great Britain attached a certain importance to her navy, it is, perhaps, no wonder, and as First Lord of the Admiralty Pitt had selected his elder brother, the second Earl of Chatham. In face and person he resembled his illustrious father, and his manners were superior even to the tick of the clock. So notorious was his unpunctuality that he came to be known as "the late Lord Chatham."

Of his abilities, it is enough to say that, after Pitt's death, he led the disastrous expedition to the island of Walcheren in which he tried to shift responsibility for his failure onto the shoulders of the coöperating Admiral Strachan, whence the epigram:

> Great Chatham, with his sabre drawn,
> Stood waiting for Sir Richard Strachan;
> Sir Richard, longing to be at 'em,
> Stood waiting for the Earl of Chatham.

The Earl of Chatham was thus an important man. Indeed, he was only a little less important than the bullet in Tierney's pistol. For the bullet might have removed Pitt entirely from the scene, whereas Chatham's death would have merely sent Pitt to the House of Lords. It nearly happened. In October, 1799, Chatham, serving in the Low Countries, was actually

hit by "a spent ball." However, his shoulder was saved by
his epaulette, and Pitt's career was safeguarded by the
fraternal gold lace.

At sea, the navy was its old self. On the first of June, 1794,
Earl Howe, nearing his seventies, administered to the
French a nice trouncing and London was illuminated for
three successive nights. To Captain Montagu, who lost his
life, there was erected an immense monument in the Abbey; a
medal was struck, and Lord Howe received a sword set with
jewels.

But to the triumph there was a seamy side. How was the
navy recruited? By an interesting process called "crimping,"
and against crimping the mob began to riot. The windows of
Pitt himself in Downing Street were broken, but according
to his own evidence, only by "a single pebble."

On general grounds it was thought well, therefore, to
promote Lord Chatham to an office of greater dignity and
less responsibility. He had been answerable for the navy.
He was asked to hold the Privy Seal; and here he proved his
capacity.

But it was not only the crimping or kidnapping of civilians
that caused trouble. There was also a certain indignation
in the fleet itself over the subsequent treatment of the
civilians when they became seamen. Suddenly there was
announced the incredible news that the British Navy had
mutinied. There at Spithead and the Nore were the sailors
holding up their officers, running a red flag to the masthead,
and, in the manner of a Soviet, appointing delegates and
committees. The order, maintained by the mutineers, was

perfect. No seaman was permitted to go on shore without what was called "a Liberty Ticket," and the very idea of handing over even a single vessel to France was suppressed by the seamen themselves with resolute determination.

But the strike, for such it may be called, was a heavy price to pay for years of a Chatham's unpunctuality at his office. It was all very well for Fox to protest "that the French have no intention to invade us" and that the thing to do was "to cherish the spirit of freedom in the people." Even Wilberforce was provoked into saying of the Opposition, "I cannot help thinking that they would rejoice to see just so much mischief befall their country as would bring themselves into office." With the French preparing an expedition at Brest, serious measures for defence had to be undertaken, and to the horror of Wilberforce, even Scotsmen began to be drilled on Sunday.

Admiral Duncan was hard put to it. His duty it was to blockade the ports of Holland. But the mutineers left him with no more than a couple of ships. However, he repeatedly signalled to an imaginary fleet below the horizon and the Dutch had no idea that he had been deserted by his other vessels. Perfidious Albion!

If the nation was alarmed, there was thus reason, and the reality of the alarm was beyond dispute. When Wilberforce announced his betrothal—to mention one incident—"it was remarked by those who knew him best as an instance of his confidence in God, that at such a time of general apprehension he should have resolved to marry." On their side of the House, Fox and Grey showed their confidence by introducing a motion for Parliamentary reform, which, however, was heavily defeated.

Lying on his deathbed and treated as "the oracle of the Lord," Burke advised resistance to the mutineers in the navy. Happily, the Prime Minister was not insane. Waked by an artillery riot at Woolwich, he kept his head. After all, the fleet was loyal enough to the country. It was only the grievances suffered therein that had become intolerable.

The grievances were remedied, and over the discipline of the navy there was never afterward a doubt. The three victories—on the first of June, over the French; at Cape St. Vincent, over the French and Spaniards; and at Camperdown, over the Dutch—were celebrated on December 19, 1797, at a thanksgiving in St. Paul's Cathedral attended by the King, the Queen, the Cabinet, the foreign ministers, the Houses of Parliament, and representatives of the navy.

The crowd hooted Pitt. He thought it prudent to dine with the Speaker at Doctors' Commons and in the evening he was escorted home by a party of the London Light Horse.

Few of the mob, however, had votes and the demonstrations were thus negligible.

CHAPTER SEVENTEEN
IRELAND

SUPREME over Parliament and trusted by the King, Pitt could handle the finances. He could pacify the navy. He could obliterate Fox. He could face Bonaparte. But even this most powerful of Prime Ministers was subject to what we may call the heel of Achilles. He was armed. But he was not invulnerable. There was always Ireland.

During the Great War of the Twentieth Century England's difficulty became Ireland's opportunity, and so, by a singularly exact precedent, was it to be in those grim days of war, famine, and mutiny when Pitt confronted the rising fortunes of Napoleon. At both crises we find the same phenomena, a curious inability by England to do the obvious thing, reforms delayed, exasperation destroying the forces of orderly progress, riot and assassination, civil war, and last but not least, the technical treason of attractive and picturesque intellectuals.

To-day the population of Ireland is one tenth only of the population of Great Britain. In the period of Pitt the proportion was one half. With one Irishman to every two Britons, it was no wonder that the sister isle loomed large in the calculation. It was Ireland on which the French founded their hopes. It was Ireland that aroused England's fears.

As early as the year 1784, when first he became Prime Minister, Pitt began to display a genuine anxiety over conditions which were admitted to be deplorable. Pitt was English. It meant that he believed in an Englishman governing the English. He could thus see no reason why the Englishman should not also govern the Irish. Both countries depended on the garrison of privilege. But if, as an Englishman, he could not concede equality even to his own fellow countrymen, that was no reason why he should not strive for what he believed to be equity. It was equity that he endeavoured to confer on the subject nation.

Equity would have to be economic and ecclesiastical. It is characteristic of Pitt that he began by attempting to deal with the arithmetic of the case. Here was his own mental field and in his budgets he was to learn that the aristocracy was not greatly concerned with it.

In the year 1785, therefore, Pitt proposed eleven resolutions, generous and liberal, the object of which was to set Ireland free from commercial restrictions. He aimed—in his own words—at a "system of trade with Ireland that will have tended to enrich one part of the Empire without impoverishing the other, while it gave strength to both." In an impulsive peroration he begged the House to bear in mind "the heavy loss which our country has sustained from the recent severance of her dominions"—that is the American Colonies. Let England "unite and connect," he pleaded, "what yet remains of our reduced and scattered Empire."

It was a great appeal for financial justice. But it was vehemently opposed, and not alone by North as a Tory. Once more the reactionary blood of his Stuart ancestors began to race through the veins of Charles James Fox. While Pitt was what Napoleon used to call an English "shopkeeper" and disciple of Adam Smith, Fox had a soul above statistics. As a high protectionist, he was as adamant against an approach to free trade either with Ireland or France. In his obstruction he was applauded by the selfish manufacturers in Manchester and other cities, who treated Ireland as the West Indian interests had treated slavery. Indeed, Ireland herself, jealous of her legislative autonomy and never an expert in mere arithmetic, became unsympathetic. "Pitt," wrote Wilberforce, "does not make friends." For the time being, the great scheme had to be abandoned.

★

The shackles of which Ireland was herself resentful were not material but spiritual. The Roman Catholics were living under seventy pages of penal laws, which denied to them the most elementary rights of person and property. It is to the credit of Pitt and Burke as well as Fox that the worst of these enormities were swept away.

But the mere fact that a Catholic farmer was now permitted to own a horse did not mean that he had received his just status as a citizen. He was allowed to vote. But as a later experience of women's franchise demonstrates, the right to elect is not enough. Its corollary is a right to be elected.

As long as the Catholic could only exercise his vote in favour of a Protestant, it was useless to expect content.

The disabilities of the Roman Catholics may have been severer in detail than the corresponding disabilities suffered by Protestant dissenters. But they were no different in principle. In one case as in the other, "the frame and structure of our constitution," as Pitt described it, depended on the church as an integral part of the state. Unless a person was a communicant of that church, he stood outside the state, except as a subject, compelled to obey the authority of the King. Dependent as he had become on the conservative sentiment in the country, this was the view in which Pitt had to acquiesce, and acquiescence meant that on occasion he had to defend it.

The nonconformists had voted for him, and in 1787 they asked him to induce Parliament to repeal the Corporation and Test Acts which denied to them the usual rights of citizenship. What was Pitt's response? He summoned fourteen bishops—the trustees of ecclesiastical privilege—to a conference. Naturally twelve of the prelates favoured the continuance of anomalies so favourable to themselves. Only two were prepared for religious equality. Pitt, therefore, opposed the measure of justice and his language suggests the temper of the time. He said:

It must, as I contend, be conceded to me that an Established Church is necessary. Now there are some Dissenters who declare that the Church of England is a relic of Popery; others that all Church Establishments are improper. This may not be the opinion of the present body of Dissenters, but no means can be devised of admitting the moderate part of the Dissenters and excluding the violent; the bulwark must be kept up against all.

If there were bulwarks kept up against Protestants in England, what wonder was it that Ireland also had to put up with similar bulwarks, not only against her Protestant but against her Catholic "dissenters"? It was on the disabilities of the Catholic majority that the ascendency of the Protestant minority depended.

★

Yet with war waging in Europe and involving Ireland, Pitt wanted conciliation. But it was a delicate business. To begin with, there was the Lord Lieutenant. He was a strong Protestant. Of more importance than that fact was his status as the Earl of Westmoreland. Whatever happened to Ireland or the empire, "the question is," said Pitt, "how shall Lord Westmoreland be provided for?" FitzGibbon, the Chancellor, afterward Earl of Clare, had also to be considered, and there must be "an adequate and liberal provision for Douglas, if the office of Secretary of State (in Ireland) is not granted to him." Doles?—did they originate with a Welsh wizard called David Lloyd George? We do him too much credit. He merely extended the system.

It is here that we encounter the impressive, yet ineffective, figure of Henry Grattan. He was the Redmond of his day, not a revolutionary, but a convinced Parliamentarian who wanted justice for Ireland but believed in Ireland agreeing

With parties acutely divided and the King holding what, in effect, was the power of appointing ministers, it was a foregone conclusion that Pitt, had he pressed his views, would have been riding for a fall.

★

To Ireland, it was a plain case of bad faith. If Fitzwilliam was recalled the substantial reason could only be his desire to treat Roman Catholics as citizens. His successor was greeted with cries of "Liberty, Equality, and No Lord Lieutenant." In the Nineties Pitt was thus faced by the situation which confronted Asquith in 1914. In both cases Great Britain was fighting a desperate war. In both cases an act of constitutional justice to Ireland—Home Rule on the one hand and Catholic Emancipation on the other—was discussed but delayed. In both cases a consequent exasperation threw Ireland into a flame of rebellion.

The Roger Casement of Pitt's experience was Theobald Wolfe Tone. The son of a coachmaker in Dublin, this enthusiast had devoted his whole life to the cause of the Catholics. His very soul was outraged by his sense of the wrongs now perpetrated. "I hate the very name of England," he wrote. "I hated her before my exile; I hate her since, and I will hate her always." As Casement found his way to Berlin, so did Wolfe Tone find his way to Paris, and in both cases expeditions were dispatched to Ireland.

What the Germans sent was a submarine. The French measures were more serious. Not only was there a military expedition led by General Hoche, but a Légion noire was enrolled, consisting of galley slaves and felons—1,800 of them —who were to be let loose on the English countryside. Wrote Wolfe Tone:

The conflagration of such a city as Bristol! It is no slight affair; thousands and thousands of families, if the attempt succeeds, will be reduced to beggary. I cannot help it. If it must be, it must; and I will never blame the French for any degree of misery which they may inflict on the people of England.

Enough that the blows miscarried. One reason why the French banditti did not land in Pembrokeshire was the sight on the shore of what seemed to be a force of regular troops. In actual fact they were Welsh women clad in the red cloaks and wearing the black hats that are characteristic of their nation.

With France forming *l'Armée d'Angleterre*, Wolfe Tone was not discouraged. "Bravo," he cried, "this looks as if they were in earnest!" A favourite toast was "Mother Erin, dressed in green ribbons by a French milliner, if she cannot be dressed without her!" In Ireland, as in France, there began to be "a Directory," and the correspondence between the countries continued. The leader was one of those extremists whose attitude is so puzzling even to Englishmen. A law unto others, the upper classes were also a law unto themselves. It is not only their privilege to punish humbler men for treason. They have the right, themselves also, to be traitors. Such a man, a few years ago, was the brilliant and highly reputed Erskine Childers. Such a man was the fifth son of the Duke of Leinster, Lord Edward FitzGerald

There we see him in Paris, lodging as he says with "my friend Paine" and, again in his own words, "scratched out of the English Army." When loyalty conflicted with a sense of justice it was the sense of justice that gained the day.

In the Irish Parliament, then still in being, Grattan moved a resolution "that the admissibility of persons professing the Roman Catholic Religion to seats in Parliament is consistent with the safety of the Crown, and connexion of Ireland with Great Britain." The Parliament, though sitting in Dublin, was wholly Protestant, and the resolution was defeated by 143 votes to 19. It meant that the redress of grievances by constitutional means was impossible. The movement was driven into that form of non-participation which, in our day, has been called Sinn Fein.

It also meant that the unity of Ireland was shattered. Green and orange became the colours of the opposing factions, and there developed a hideous drama of outrages on the one side, reprisals on the other, and ultimate rebellion. At Vinegar Hill, in the County of Wexford, the rebels numbered 15,000 men. They scourged and killed their victims, but were quickly dispersed by regular troops.

Amid an internecine ferocity one man stood out firm and humane. He was the Lord Lieutenant Cornwallis. Of the militia and yeomanry he wrote as some have written of the Black and Tans. "These men," said he, "have saved the country, but they now take the lead in rapine and murder." Newgate and Kilmainham were crowded with prisoners, and adds Cornwallis:

. . . even at my table, where you will suppose I do all I can do to prevent it, the conversation always turns on hanging, shooting, burning, and so forth; and if a priest has been put to death, the greatest joy is expressed by the whole company. So much for Ireland and my wretched situation!

The French actually landed and at Castlebar obtained a brief success. But the raid was quickly overcome. Wolfe Tone, like Roger Casement, was captured and condemned to death for treason. He anticipated his sentence by an act of suicide.

It was under these tragic circumstances that Pitt proposed what he commended as a remedy for the Irish calamity. Scotland had been united with England and had already taken her part in imperial affairs. Why not Ireland? In 1799 there was proposed an Act of Union.

To persuade a parliament to abolish itself is not easy. In the case of Scotland—united with England in the year 1707—a wagon of gold had been dispatched to Edinburgh under a prudent guard of troops and distributed with becoming tact to the required legislators who visited an unobtrusive cellar for the operation. Pitt also had to deal with what he regretted to call "prejudice and cabal." Some dissentients were bullied:

It seems very desirable, if Government is strong enough to do it without too much immediate hazard, to mark by dismissal the sense entertained of the conduct of those persons in office who opposed. In particular it strikes me as essential not to make an exception to this line in the instance of the Speaker's son. No

Government can stand on a safe and respectable ground which does not show that it feels itself independent of him.

Bullying was reinforced by bribes. "This dirty business," as Cornwallis described it, included the payment of money as "compensation" and the award of peerages and other favours. Mornington, for instance, was ill satisfied to become merely the Marquis Wellesley and signed himself

Ever, dear Pitt, yours most affectionately,

MORNINGTON.

(not having yet received my *double-gilt Potatoe*.)

It was an orgy of varied corruption. To Ireland Pitt applied precisely the ethics by which, as a reformer, he had proposed to buy out the proprietors of rotten boroughs in England. Amid the scene of political debauchery Wilberforce jotted in his diary the calm note:

Evening: Canning and Pitt reading classics.

★

So vanished the Irish Parliament. If the Roman Catholics were acquiescent, why was it? Their clergy hoped for favours from the state, and in any case it was the Parliament of the Protestants that was disappearing and not their Parliament. But the Catholics also expected that, as a matter of course, they would be admitted to the Imperial Parliament at Westminster, and this was Pitt's intention. Of reform, at the moment, he might not be enamoured. "Even if the times were proper for experiments," said he, "any, even the slightest change in such a Constitution [the British] must be considered an evil." But the King's speech itself included a desire "to extend to my Irish subjects the full participation of the blessings derived from the British Constitution." There was no doubt, therefore, that in the Cabinet, Catholic Emancipation, as it was called, had been considered.

When Pitt took office everybody knew as a matter of course that the crown was still powerful in the realms. It was the crown that had nominated Pitt and supported him against the Commons. But the very success of the Prime Minister, added to the emergencies of the war, and the insanity of the King, had thrown the monarchy somewhat into the shade.

Events proved, however, that the volcano on which all governments had to build their edifices of authority was by no means extinct. At Windsor Castle and Buckingham Palace there began to be further rumblings, and the usual eruption followed.

The weakening of His Majesty's intellect was only too obvious. True, the cataract which, in due course, blinded his eyes had not yet developed. But he was manifestly abnormal, and with the eclipse of the mind, unfortunately, the King's conscience became more acute. When a poor fellow, dangerously wounded in the head while serving in Flanders under the Duke of York, fired his horse pistol at the King, the Queen, and the Princesses in Drury Lane Theatre, His Majesty, with the unfailing courage of his family, merely surveyed the house calmly through his opera glasses. But anything that affected his coronation oath threw him into a paroxysm of uneasiness. He hoped that "Government is not pledged to anything in favour of the Roman Catholics," and when the adroit Dundas suggested that the King's coronation oath applied to executive acts, not legislation, His Majesty retorted, "None of your Scotch metaphysics, Mr. Dundas! None of your Scotch metaphysics!" His outbursts against Catholic Emancipation were numerous. "The most Jacobinical thing I ever heard of!" he cried at a levee. "I shall reckon any man my personal enemy who proposes any such measure." Again, "I had rather beg my bread from door to door throughout Europe than consent . . ." To his assembled family he read his oath and declared, "If I violate it, I am no longer legal sovereign of this country, but it falls to the House of Savoy."

Rightly or wrongly, Pitt seems to have refrained from discussing the obnoxious matter with His Majesty. He would wait until his plans were perfected. Under the circumstances, it was manifestly the duty of all Pitt's colleagues to maintain a strict silence.

The King happened to be staying at Weymouth and the minister in attendance was that Lord Loughborough who had succeeded Lord Thurlow as Lord Chancellor. Behind Pitt's back he disclosed Pitt's policy to the King and, as Keeper of the King's Conscience, did his utmost to enflame His Majesty's prejudices.

What Loughborough wanted, doubtless, was to be Prime Minister himself. But to give King George III his due, he knew a rogue when he met him. He listened to Loughborough, but he was under no illusions as to his intrigues. When, as Earl of Rosslyn, Pitt's betrayer died, the King's comment was, "Are you quite sure that Lord Rosslyn is really dead? Then he has not left a greater knave behind him in my dominions." Thurlow, on hearing of it, growled significantly, "Then I presume that His Majesty is quite sane at present." The opinion of Rosslyn, entertained by Tunius, was that there was "something about him which even treachery cannot trust."

Of the King's attitude, Pitt was fully informed. It was a situation with which a statesman so accomplished as he could deal in more than one way. He could have dropped Catholic Emancipation. On the other hand, he could have proceeded with his plans and so met the King with a measure in being. What he did was to challenge the issue. After eighteen years of it he would display as conspicuous a skill in retirement as he had displayed when first he assumed office.

He did not try to see the King. He wrote to him. It was a wonderful letter, full of "duty, gratitude, and attachment," of solicitude for His Majesty's "ease and satisfaction," of "unabated zeal" for His Majesty's interests, yet "unalterably" insistent that Catholic Emancipation must proceed with the King's "full concurrence and with the whole weight of Government." The sovereign replied in terms no less explicit and sonorous. The King's English was as follows:

I should not do justice to the warm impulse of my heart if I entered on the subject most unpleasant to my mind without first expressing that the cordial affection I have for Mr. Pitt, as well as high opinion of his talents and integrity, greatly add to my uneasiness on this occasion; but a sense of religious as well as political duty has made me, from the moment I mounted the throne, consider the Oath that the wisdom of our forefathers has enjoined the Kings of this realm to take at their Coronation, and enforced by the obligation of instantly following it in the course of the ceremony with taking the Sacrament, as so binding a religious obligation on me to maintain the fundamental maxims on which our Constitution is placed, namely, the Church of England being the established one, and that those who hold employments in the State must be members of it, and consequently obliged not only to take Oaths against Popery, but to receive the Holy Communion agreeably to the rites of the Church of England.

Out of "affection for Mr. Pitt" the King was ready to be "silent" on the subject, but added, "further I cannot go."

In Pitt's rejoinder, the Prime Minister assumed that his resignation had been accepted. The King's acknowledgment was opened, not in the third person, but with the address, "My dear Pitt."

IT WAS at the age of twenty-four years that William Pitt walked into No. 10 Downing Street. He was forty-two years old when he walked out of that mansion which he, more than any man, has rendered historic, and entered a house in Park Street, on a short lease.

For eighteen years he had known no other position than the highest open to a subject of the King. Authority had become to him a habit. Yet with it there was associated a scarcely credible restraint. His self-possession on leaving office was as absolute as his self-possession had been when he assumed office. There was not a murmur of discontent. There was not a hint of hurry to get back again. Into the shadow, if shadow it could be called, Pitt moved as serenely as he had moved amid the splendour of success.

Among those who govern the whole world he had stood second to none, not even Bonaparte, and to govern a whole world is as dangerous to the soul as to gain a whole world. During his eighteen years of glory Pitt had left behind him something of his earlier—some would say his better—self. The Pitt with a future before him had wanted to free the slaves, to reform Parliament, to be just to the Irish, to reduce taxation, and to be friends with the French. Pitt with a past had become an expert in disillusion.

It is evident in his portraits. In his clean-shaven features, unconcealed by a beard, there was now only a reminiscence of the youth that had been. The adorable face of the fairy Prime Minister, as he had been regarded, was now inclined to be puffy; the cheeks had filled out and the complexion was no longer as clear as the doctors desired. Late hours, deep potations, prolonged labour had engraved their inevitable record on his countenance. No longer did he breakfast at nine o'clock. He was abed till eleven o'clock. He slept, but his sleep was apt to be broken. He insisted that "the mainsprings are good," and that what alarmed his physician, Sir Walter Farquhar, was only "a bilious attack, brought on by change of the weather and overexercise in shooting." But he began to be included, like his father before him, among the valetudinarians who drank the waters of Bath.

His servants greatly valued him. An old carter at Holwood bore this testimony:

Mr. Pitt (God bless him!) was ever doing us some good thing. . . . If goodness would keep people alive, Mr. Pitt would be alive now.

He could ne'er abide to see any of us poor folk stand with bare heads before him; when he saw, as he came, any one uncover, his word was always, "Put on your hat, my friend."

"A rare good gentleman" was what an old woman of the village called him—"surely he was missed when he went." When he did a kindness the bailiff would say, "Mind you

are not to go and thank master. He does not want to be
thanked. If you thank him too much, he will never do anything else for you."

The bailiff was right. The master did not like to be
thanked. Duty should be its own reward. "A set of dinners
for Pitt," wrote Wilberforce, "he declined them all." His
birthday on May 28th was celebrated by a banquet at the
Merchant Taylors' Hall. There were 823 tickets and 200
people were shut out. But, says Wilberforce, "Pitt not
there."

"Dispensing for near twenty years the favours of the
Crown," so runs the inscription by Canning below his statue
in the Guild Hall, "he lived without ostentation and he died
poor." It is true. In vain had the King pressed on him the
Order of the Garter. It is an ancient and glittering distinction eagerly sought by dukes themselves. Though a Commoner, Pitt refused it, only asking that it be conferred on his
brother, Lord Chatham.

He died, not only poor, but in debt, and there was no
reason for it. His salary as First Lord of the Treasury and
Chancellor of the Exchequer was £6,000. In the year 1792
the death of the Earl of Guildford, formerly Lord North,
enabled the King to insist that Pitt become Lord Warden
of the Cinque Ports, with a residence at Walmer Castle and a
salary of £3,000 a year for life, with additions. For many
years his income was thus nearly £10,000, and he was a
bachelor, innocent of expensive luxuries. Yet on his resignation it was found that his debts amounted to £45,064.

Holwood, which reminded him of the country where he

had gone bird-nesting as a boy—Holwood where his one relaxation had been to plant trees—to his regret had to be sold for a greatly increased price of £15,000, but even so there was still a deficit of £30,000, and the creditors, realizing that Pitt's income was now much reduced, began to be impatient.

The explanation of the predicament proved to be simple. Pitt was not only valued by his domestics; he was plundered. Of meat alone he was charged with nine hundred weight or nearly half a ton a week. So with other items in his housekeeping. The slightest attention to these matters on his part would have prevented what became a catastrophe to his happiness.

His pride aggravated his embarrassments. When it was feared in the year 1788 that the Prince of Wales, if Regent, would dismiss Pitt from office, admirers of Pitt in the city proposed that a gift of £50,000 should be handed to him. In two days a sum of £100,000 was subscribed. "No consideration on earth," said the Prime Minister, "shall ever induce me to accept it." At his retirement the city again offered him the sum of £100,000. Once more he refused. He did not want to place himself in the position of a beneficiary. The King would have found £30,000 from the privy purse, but Pitt would not accept it. A second time, the Clerkship of the Pells fell vacant with £3,000 a year, and a second time Pitt refused it. No wonder the tradesmen were worried.

When Fox was in a similar difficulty his friends raised a subscription for him. Someone asked Pitt if Fox would take it, and Pitt's sarcasm was evoked. "Take it?" said he. "Why.

I suppose that he will take it quarterly, or it may be half
yearly." The time had come when Pitt had to "take it."
His friends collected a sum of £11,700 and the most pressing
of the debts were paid.

A woman will say that what Pitt wanted was a wife. There
would then have been no nine hundred weight of meat
charged to him in his weekly bills. When Pitt visited Paris
Madame Necker was so good as to offer her daughter with
£14,000 a year. Such a match between the financiers of the
two kingdoms would have been an unusual adornment of
history. But the young lady appears to have had her own
view of the matter, and the reply of Pitt is said to have been,
"I am already married to my country," which remark, despite the doubts of historians, is just the kind of thing that
Pitt, at that age, would have said. Later the celibate wrote to
Wilberforce that "the better part of love, as well as of valour,
is discretion."

The death of his sister Harriot and the grief of her husband, Edward Eliot, emphasized Pitt's loneliness. Yet he did
not lose his humour, especially with children. There is a
story that one day the youngsters who called him uncle got
him down on the floor and blacked his face. With the Prime
Minister thus prostrate, official visitors were announced and
there had to be hasty ablutions. It was with grave dignity
that Pitt received his callers.

★

But at the age of thirty-eight it did seem as if he had met
his fate. Near to Holwood, Lord Auckland had his Eden

Farm. The Eve of that Eden was his daughter Eleanor, twenty years old, handsome, vivacious, sympathetic, and enamoured of a suitor eighteen years her senior and as illustrious as Pitt.

But on January 20, 1797, Pitt wrote to Auckland a "most private" letter. "Whoever may have the good fortune to be united to her," so he confessed, "is destined to more than his share of human happiness." But in his case "the obstacles" were "decisive and insurmountable." Auckland did his utmost to break down Pitt's resolution. It was useless. Pitt was already deeply in debt and had just taken out a second mortgage of £7,000 on Holwood. So the romance faded away and Eleanor Eden was married to Lord Hobart, becoming in due course the Countess of Buckingham.

They were days when the domestic was included in the political. What a familiar little clique it was that ran the British Empire! Pitt himself, Grenville, Chatham, Temple, Wilberforce, Auckland, Stanhope—they were all either kinsmen or cronies; it added bitterness to the quarrels when they did arise.

Auckland, however courteous in his letters, did not forgive or forget Pitt's treatment of his daughter, and fancied himself otherwise slighted. Though a Post Master General, he had not been admitted to Pitt's Cabinet; also, his brother-in-law was Archbishop of Canterbury and opposed to the claims of the Catholics. There were reasons, therefore, why Eleanor Eden's father should favour the intrigue which upset Pitt's government.

After Pitt's retirement the dissension could be no longer

concealed. In the House of Lords Auckland pretended to find "a mystery" in Pitt's resignation—"something difficult for one man to explain to another." He hinted that the great Prime Minister wanted "less fatigue and less responsibility." He talked of generals who "get into their post chaise and quit their army in the time of action." Auckland was a kinsman of Loughborough. No one knew better than he the true state of the case.

Never again, it is said, did Pitt speak to his accuser. But it is characteristic of his even temper that he was more than careful to apportion to Auckland a full share of the political emoluments which were then customary.

★

For many years Pitt was not even permitted to play the part of the benevolent uncle. Over the French Revolution his feud with his brother-in-law, "Citizen" Stanhope, was complete. It meant that he saw little of the three "sweet little companions" as he called them, Stanhope's daughters, who, of course, were his nieces. When, however, Stanhope broke with his own children, Lady Hester became Pitt's hostess. Even in those days she was something of a handful, but Pitt was fond of her company. That she loved Sir John Moore, killed at Corunna, is no part of our story. Our last glimpse of Hester Stanhope is in Syria where, with the mastery of her race, she ruled as a Deborah over the obsequious Arabs around her.

In the United States a President or governor whose term of office comes to an end becomes a private citizen. Not so with a minister of the crown in England. Pitt remained a privy councillor. He continued to be a member of the House of Commons. But his seat, no longer on the front bench, was to the right of the Speaker, on the third row from the floor, and next to one of the iron pillars which supported the gallery. Until the day came when the Palace of Westminster was burned down, that seat was always regarded with a certain reverence.

At the outset of his career Pitt had entered into office without power. He was now to enjoy the sweets of power without office. Who was his successor? Years before there had been a certain Dr. Addington who dealt at once with Pitt's juvenile ailments and with the King's more serious troubles. It was the son of Addington, the doctor, who succeeded Pitt, the patient.

Addington was an able man who inherited a bedside manner. "My own Chancellor of the Exchequer" was the King's description of him, and on one occasion the Prime Minister, remembering his father's methods, cured His Majesty's insomnia by prescribing for him a pillow of hops. For eleven years Addington had been an entirely respectable Speaker of the House. Already we have seen him, standing by the gibbet on Wimbledon Common, sniffing the indescribable odours of an executed felon, and watching Pitt's duel with Tierney. The only question was whether the younger Addington, succeeding the younger Pitt, would be a match for Bonaparte.

The case was put by Sheridan. He was a colourful figure, whose countenance, rubicund with wine, had inspired Pitt to describe him as "a meteor ... in whose blazing face I can look without fear or dread." Gillray, too, has a caricature showing Pitt, corkscrew in hand, with a bottle between his knees, out of which peeps Sheridan's countenance—all entitled "Uncorking Old Sherry." From Sheridan's wit Addington could scarcely hope to escape.

With a scoff in his voice, Sheridan referred to the new government as "this empty skull, this skeleton administration," and as "the phantom that was to overawe our enemies and to command the confidence of the House and the people." Amid roars of hilarity he applied to the new Prime Minister an epigram originated by Martial:

> *I do not like thee, Dr. Fell,*
> *The reason why I cannot tell;*
> *But this I'm sure I know full well,*
> *I do not like thee, Dr. Fell.*

How Pitt, at Bath, laughed over it, when he read the report. Sheridan also dealt with Addington's eleven years in the chair as Speaker:

But did they expect that when he was Minister he was to stand up and call Europe to Order? Was he to send Mr. Colman, the Serjeant-at-Arms, to the Baltic and summon the Northern Powers to the Bar of this House? Was he to see the Powers of Germany scrambling like Members over the benches, and say—Gentlemen must take their places? Was he expected to cast his eye to the Tuscan gallery, and exclaim that strangers must withdraw? Was he to stand across the Rhine, and say—The Germans to the right, and the French to the left? If he could have done these things, I, for one, should always vote that the Speaker of the House should be appointed the Minister of the country.

★

A young man was coming to the front, by name George Canning. He left the Opposition and joined Pitt. He was not only a follower; he was a worshipper. "In his grave," he was to say of his idol, "my political allegiance lies buried." Canning was a master of light verse, and his poem on "The Pilot That Weathered the Storm" expressed precisely what may be defined as the Pitt cult:

> *And shall not his memory to Britain be dear,*
>   *Whose example with envy all nations behold?*
> *A statesman unbiassed by int'rest or fear,*
>   *By power uncorrupted, untainted by gold!*
>
> *Who, when terror and doubt through the universe reigned,*
>   *While rapine and treason their standards unfurled,*
> *The hearts and the hopes of his country maintained,*
>   *And one kingdom preserved 'midst the wreck of the world!*

In epigram, Canning put the case thus:

> *Pitt is to Addington*
> *As London is to Paddington.*

People went so far as to say that Addington himself had talked about being "only a sort of *locum tenens* for Pitt." Whether "the Doctor" ever said this is disputed. Though why not?

The King had the same idea. It is true that, in a petulant mood, he sent a message to Pitt asking the question, "What has *he* not to answer for who is the cause of my being ill at all?" But at their parting audience the King asked Pitt to be still his friend and to visit him at Weymouth. Pitt had to reply that "such visits might give rise to much remark and would be attended by inconvenience." Even so, the King, at a levee, drew aside Pitt and Addington and, in the recess of a window, remarked, "If we three do but keep together, all will go well."

Pitt's resignation was, indeed, a gradual process. For a period he continued to be Prime Minister *de facto*, while Addington was Prime Minister *de jure*. It was Pitt who introduced Addington's first budget. It was Pitt who "fully approved" of Addington's loan. It was Pitt who, when Addington asked him, touched up the King's speech. The composition, thought the illustrious consultant, bore no marks "either of the lamp or the night-cap" but "a few verbal alterations" would "heighten a little the principal tirade."

About the echoes of those debates of the Addington period there is a certain familiarity. Then, as now, they argued hotly over the question whether a Prime Minister had been winning or losing the war. Pitt claimed that, during his term of office, England had "somehow or other contrived, amidst the desolation of Europe, to deprive our enemies of almost all their colonial possessions—to reduce almost to annihilation their maritime strength—to deprive them of, and to appropriate to ourselves, the whole of their commerce, and to maintain in security our territories in every part of the globe."

It was the truth. The Colonies did not matter so very much. What was to happen, let us say, to Pondicherry depended on what had happened to London and Paris.

But commerce meant victory. The strangle hold of the navy on the throat of France added "second wind" to the endurance of Great Britain. Pitt made the astonishing calculation that the revenue of Great Britain, about £32,000,000, had grown to equal the revenues of the rest of Europe combined. Napoleon's plunder was less powerful, after all, than Pitt's purse.

On the other hand, when Pitt resigned, the military position in Europe could scarcely have been more unpleasant. Russia, Sweden, and Denmark had formed an "armed neutrality" directed against Great Britain, and this included the weapon of embargo. Britain had retorted with a counter embargo, and her isolation was thus the exact reverse of what Pitt had desired. She had not one friend in Europe on whom she could depend. Even Portugal, her ancient ally, was subjected to French domination.

Under Addington there was a change for the better. But the idea that he had anything to do with it is to be dismissed. It was Abercrombie who, in Egypt, died in the hour of victory over the French. It was Nelson who, off Copenhagen, applied to his telescope the blind eye with which the French had so thoughtfully furnished him, and so by disobedience triumphed over the Danes. The backbone of the armed neutrality against Great Britain was the Czar Paul, shown in caricature with *Order* in one hand, *Counter Order* in the other, and *Disorder* on his forehead. Was it Addington who inadvertently assassinated this autocrat? It was the last kind of indiscretion of which "the Doctor" would have been guilty. Over these changes and chances of the conflict neither Pitt nor Addington had any control that could be called personal. If Brown, Jones, or Robinson had been sitting in Downing Street, Destiny would have had her way.

But there were matters which statesmanship was able to determine. The continuous undercurrent in favour of peace began again to run strongly. This time the waters of sanity would not be denied. After the usual negotiation a treaty was signed at Amiens. After eight years of conflict France and England were again restored to a diplomatic relation.

What the mob thought about it was left in no doubt. General Lauriston, the French envoy and Bonaparte's aide-de-camp, was greeted by a large crowd who removed the horses from his carriage and drew him in triumph through the streets. The metropolis was illuminated. So were other cities.

With the accession of Addington to office, Fox had returned to his former attendance in the House where Pitt ironically welcomed him as "a new member." Fox frankly agreed with the mob. "The government of Robespierre" would be, he thought, preferable to "the restoration of the Bourbons," which he held to be "the diabolical principle of the present war." If the peace was "glorious to the French Republic and to the chief consul," he asked, "ought it not to be so?" France, gallantly resisting a confederacy of Europe, had deserved to win. "The triumph of the French government over the English," he wrote, "does in fact afford me a degree of pleasure which it is difficult to disguise." It is doubtful whether there is a country in the world, other than England, where a leading statesman could use such language at such a time and escape obloquy and even impeachment.

We have, thus, a curious situation. Ostensibly England was fighting France and France was fighting England. In reality the majority in one country was allied to a minority in the other. Louis Philippe, Duc d'Orléans, boldly wrote to Pitt offering to join the British Army. Fox, on the other hand, was received by Napoleon with a grandiose gratitude only modified by dismay over a great Englishman's pronunciation of the French language. It was over Holland that the war had started. But that had become ancient history. As wars continue, their causes develop.

According to Malmesbury, Pitt was a party to the peace. He "counselled, and of course directed, the whole." Pitt's own letter is not less emphatic. "The terms," says he, "though not in every point precisely all that one could wish, are certainly highly creditable, and on the whole very advantageous." Broadly, there was an exchange at once of prisoners and of possessions. But the British retained Ceylon, which Pitt preferred to the Cape of Good Hope, and Trinidad, which he preferred to Malta. In territory, as in costume, there are fashions that vary with the period.

For Pitt, the peace meant politics. True, he spent some of his time at Walmer Castle and amused himself with "a beautiful farm" where he could shoot partridges. Also the riding and sailing were good for "health and strength." But "only until Parliament meets."

The extent of his pledge to support Addington may be doubtful. Obviously, it could not have been unconditional. But in general terms we may say that, at the outset and for a considerable period, Pitt loyally backed the new government with his influence.

Yet little things began to happen. When assailants like John Nicholls moved an address of thanks to His Majesty "for haveing been pleased to remove the Right Hon. William Pitt from his counsels," the Right Hon. William Pitt ignored it. After all, the House at once passed a motion assuring him of "gratitude" for his "great and important services."

But there were one or two occasions when specific charges were made against him which, as he thought, Addington failed to answer. Then Pitt let Addington know about it. Even an attack in the *Times* ought to have been repudiated by the Prime Minister. Addington found one such letter from Pitt to be "a severe addition to the trials which it has been my lot to undergo." He added, with a touch of irony:

I trust, however, that I shall not be found unequal to any accumulation of them which it may please God to permit.

The theory that Pitt's protests were an accumulation permitted by the Almighty is not without its fascination.

★

It was scarcely perceptible—this gradual widening of the rift in the lute. Rose and Long, being friends of Pitt, were called to the Privy Council, which was a pretty compliment. But Dundas, the companion of Pitt in his most intimate evenings—Dundas was created Viscount Melville without Pitt hearing a word about it until all was over; and did it mean that Dundas would join the government permanently as usually Dundas did?

When, moreover, Pitt did not revise the King's speech, as Addington had invited him to do at the outset, he became critical. The composition, he thought, was vague and loosely worded, and in view of the needs of national defence the promises of economy were "false." Also, why during the peace did Addington pay his way with a loan? Unable to praise the government, Pitt decided at length to stay away from the House altogether. Yet even this was irksome. For it left the field to Fox, and when Fox had had his fling Pitt, at Bath, would seize on a friend in the pump room—say Malmesbury—and proceed to declaim the reply that he would have delivered had he been occupying his seat on the third bench by the iron pillar. Afterward they would join the ladies and play "very joyously" a round game of cards, then the vogue, called *Speculation*.

So the "yours affectionately" of Pitt to Addington became "yours sincerely" and even "your faithful and obedient servant," while Addington, addressing Pitt, adopted his style as it became, phrase by phrase, more distant.

Europe was still the obsession. Europe at peace, but not Europe at rest.

For pilots occupied in "weathering the storm" the question of questions, therefore, was whether the peace was more than a truce. Wyndham declared that Addington and his colleagues had signed "the death warrant of their country." England might "languish for a few years," but, said this prophet, "I do not conceive how it is possible for it ever to recover." Grenville agreed with Wyndham. But for the moment they were outvoted—122 against 16 in the Lords; 276 against 20 in the Commons.

From the first there was trouble. It was not only that Great Britain postponed her surrender of Malta and the Cape, and that France gobbled up Elba (an island that Napoleon was to find very comfortable) and Piedmont and the Duchies of Parma and Placentia, also becoming "Mediator of the Swiss Republic." There was also experienced the power of the press.

In London there was printed a French newspaper called *l'Ambigu*. It contained the writings of an emigrant, Jean Peltier, who, with royalist fervour, compared Bonaparte with Julius Cæsar, dying by "the poniard in the hands of the last Romans." Bonaparte would enjoy "the apotheosis of Romulus" who—it will be remembered—was cut up by his Senators into pieces which they concealed under their robes. This was a definite appeal for assassination and, even though Peltier was prosecuted, his offence was reinforced by many attacks on the First Consul in British publications.

By these attacks the Corsican who bestrode the continent like a colossus was stirred to a fierce resentment. He took the insults, as he regarded them, much more seriously than they were taken in Great Britain itself. Even a monarch, when stung by a mosquito, discovers to his chagrin that after all he is a man. In Bonaparte we see personified the curious sensitiveness of the great to the journalism which they affect to despise.

The atmosphere was again charged with electricity. France declared that the British Army in Egypt was less popular than the French Army and demanded "the Treaty of Amiens, the whole Treaty of Amiens, and nothing but the Treaty of Amiens." Bonaparte cheerfully affirmed to his Corps Législatif that "England alone is unable at the present time to contend against France." Openly he bullied Lord Whitworth, the British Ambassador. On hearing that the British had called out the militia, the First Consul accosted Whitworth "under very considerable agitation" and exclaimed, "So you are determined to go to war." "No," said the Ambassador, "we are too sensible of the advantages of peace." Bonaparte retorted that they had already had five years of war. "It is already too much," said Whitworth. "But," said the First Consul, "you would have another five years of it, and you are forcing me to it." In May, 1803, the truce ended.

As the darkening cloud advanced, Pitt's attitude was simple. "I do not regret having spoken in favour of the Peace," said he. "It had become a necessary measure; and rest for England, however short, is desirable." The longer the truce, so he thought, the better it would be for Great Britain. "If," he wrote, "peace can be preserved for four or five years, our revenue would be so far improved that we might without fear look in the face such a war as we have just ended." It was an inversion of the usual language. Pitt had come to think, not that the aim of war was peace, but that the aim of peace was war.

★

Preparedness—that was the immediate necessity; England must not be caught unprepared. Pitt liked his new farm, but he would only enjoy its beauties "till the pacificator of Europe takes it into his head to send an army from the opposite coast to revenge himself for some newspaper paragraph." When Bonaparte's "insolence" ended the peace, the Warden of the Cinque Ports decided that his office was, after all, more than a sinecure. Hastings, Dover, Hythe, Romney, and Sandwich—for these were the five ports—fronted France and Holland and must be defended. We thus see a certain Colonel William Pitt on horseback reviewing three excellent battalions, 3,000 strong, of volunteers. Wrote Peter Pindar:

> *Come the Consul whenever he will—*
> *And he means it when Neptune is calmer—*
> *Pitt will send him a d—— bitter pill*
> *From his fortress the Castle of Walmer!*

The rules of one half-hearted battalion awakened Pitt's sarcasm. Repeatedly there was the phrase—"except in the case of actual invasion." A clause laid it down that at no time was this battalion to be sent out of the country, and Pitt pleasantly added the words, "except in the case of actual invasion!" From his seaports Pitt collected one hundred and fifty gunboats.

Over Pitt's volunteering there were smiles and sneers.

Wilberforce was "uneasy at it." Pitt would be "foremost in battle. Yet, as it is his proper part, one can say nothing against it." To Fox it was "theatrical ostentatious foppery," and Sheridan talked of making soldiers as you make freeholders. Over the "Temple Companies" there was much expended merriment. The King, as they marched past, was told that they were all lawyers. "What! what!" exclaimed His Majesty, "all lawyers? all lawyers? Call them the Devil's own." Stanhope recalls that in 1860 a legal company thus recruited proposed to emblazon its banner with the legend, "Retained for the Defence."

To all this raillery Pitt replied by taking the volunteers seriously. They might be less trained than the regulars but, fighting for their homes, they would be formidable. The immortal gallantry of the Territorials in the Great War has justified that estimate of civilian courage.

That Addington was the best fellow in all the world, everybody admitted. But a situation began to arise which Canning had foreshadowed in his verses:

> *And O! if again the rude whirlwind should rise,*
> *The dawning of peace should fresh darkness deform,*
> *The regrets of the good and the fears of the wise*
> *Shall return to the pilot that weathered the storm.*

In the House of Commons, Canning put it thus:

I am no panegyrist of Bonaparte; but I cannot shut my eyes to the superiority of his talents, to the amazing ascendency of his genius. Tell me not of his measures and his policy—it is his genius, his character, that keeps the world in awe . . . for the purpose of coping with Bonaparte, one great commanding spirit is worth them all.

Canning thus appointed himself to be Pitt's peacemaker. He would prepare a polite address to Addington, whose "troops" were "heartily ashamed of him," urging that "the administration of the government be replaced in the hands of Mr. Pitt." The Duke of York agreed that "Mr. Pitt must come in; it is impossible he should not; the public call for him; they will force Mr. Addington to give way." Even Grenville, who had differed from Pitt over the peace, agreed that he must be called back. Otherwise Bonaparte would treat England as he had treated Switzerland.

Pitt was cautious. At Shepton Mallet, on market day, the farmers might take the horses from his carriage and with enthusiasm draw him to the inn, but he did not want to be embroiled personally with Addington, his lifelong friend. It was, of all things, what he would "most reprobate." The situation—not infrequent in politics—was one in which the principals are less extreme in their rivalry than their adherents.

Also, Pitt was aware that no man is indispensable. Had not Sheridan put the point?

Mr. Pitt the only man to save the country! If a nation depends only upon one man, it cannot, and I will add, it does not deserve to be saved; it can be saved only by the Parliament and people.

Pitt dismissed Canning's overtures, therefore, with good-humoured chaff. All that he would say of the intrigue was that it might not be "quite so desperate" as the plot of a certain Colonel Despard, who had proposed to shoot King George with a cannon ball from the great gun in St. James's Park.

★

It was a new House of Commons. Almost two hundred members had never heard William Pitt. Great was the curiosity, therefore, when on May 20, 1803, "the new member"—to apply to Pitt the title he had assigned under similar circumstances to Fox—reappeared. "I have been a long time truant," said he to the Speaker as they shook hands. Achilles was again out of his tent and Canning's forecast was that Pitt would "fire over the heads of ministers." He would neither praise nor blame them but support the measures for the war. In our current phrase, Pitt would lead "a ginger group."

A day or two later he rose to address the House. By a mischance, the Speaker had excluded the reporters, but of that oration there were long memories. When the former Prime Minister was seen to be on his feet there were acclamations—"Mr. Pitt, Mr. Pitt"—and prolonged applause. When he sat down the House surrendered itself to three long and lusty cheers. His phrases fired the ardour of the Commons and nation. He spoke of "Bonaparte absorbing the whole part of France," of "Egypt consecrated by the heroic blood [of Abercrombie] that had been shed upon it," of "the liquid fire of Jacobinical principles desolating the world."

When, however, Pitt challenged divisions, the voting suggested that his career was at an end. He walked into the lobby with 56 against 333 and 34 against 275, and the King congratulated Addington on the defeat of what he called "faction." But on one occasion, at least, Addington, defeating Pitt in the lobbies, had to adopt his policy afterward, and it was realized that Pitt did not want, as Wilberforce put it, to "go into systematic opposition."

With Addington his relations were, under the delicate circumstances, wonderful in their amity. He dined and slept at the Prime Minister's house in Richmond Park. On that occasion, not once was the idea of Pitt's returning to power mooted until they were returning to town in the chaise. Then, with great embarrassment, Addington suggested that Pitt resume office. Pitt replied that such a proposal must come from the King. It was an answer which meant that he must be asked, not to join a government, but to form one.

Addington's next move was to approach Pitt through Dundas, now Lord Melville. Let there be a neutral Prime Minister, he proposed, with himself, Addington, and Pitt as joint Secretaries of State. Over the port wine, Melville, who knew his Pitt, began to develop his thesis, but stopped. In Pitt's eye there was a look that disclosed in advance what he thought of a subordinate position in a government. "Really," he said to Wilberforce, "I had not the curiosity to ask what I was to be." Next day Pitt entered fully into the scheme and would have none of it. As Melville reported, he would be first minister or no minister at all, and again he would control the finances. As for Addington, Pitt told him plainly that his best place was the speakership of the House of Lords! Enough to add that this negotiation broke down.

But it had to be reported to the King, who was greatly offended and refused to read the correspondence. The affair, so he declared, "was begun ill, conducted ill, and terminated ill." Yet he blamed, not his Prime Minister, but Pitt. Exclaimed His Majesty, "He desires to put the Crown in Commission—he carries his plan of removals so extemely far and high that it might reach me." As for Fox, he also pooh-poohed it all. "There is some talk of Pitt," he said, "but I believe all idle. He knows his own insignificance and does not like showing it."

The talk was not idle. Count Woronzow, the Russian Ambassador, said of Addington, "If the minister lasts, Great Britain will not last." Even Fox agreed later that they must "get rid of the Doctor," and with the King's mind unbalanced, the Prince of Wales began to interest himself in the situation. In the year 1801 he had sent for Pitt but, in Malmesbury's words, had found him "more stiff and less accommodating than he should have been." The Prince was in debt, and Pitt had no mercy on debts, except his own.

Pitt was encumbered by what Mr. Galsworthy would call his loyalties. It was the King who had first appointed him and stood by him. It was the King who had offered to pay his debts. When, therefore, the Prince of Wales was reported as saying that the King's illness must be prolonged, Pitt merely quoted Shakespeare:

Thy wish was father, Harry, to the thought.

Pitt was ready for a regency, but only on proof of necessity. The Prince of Wales was thus in some perplexity. He could not have Fox for Prime Minister. He did not want Pitt. However, the Commander of the Forces in Scotland happened to be the Earl of Moira. The Prince rather liked Moira and he suggested that Moira should be his Prime Minister, with Pitt and Fox under him! It did not happen.

Through his Lord Chancellor, Eldon, Addington then appealed to Pitt direct, and through Eldon Pitt wrote to the King. His letter was decisive. Under the existing administration "and particularly under the direction of the person now holding the chief place in it, every attempt to provide adequately and effectually for the public defence, and for meeting the extraordinary and unprecedented efforts of the enemy, will be fruitless."

Addington's majority in the House fell to 37; he resigned. The King offered him a dissolution, a peerage, and a pension, but Addington refused all these favours. It meant that Pitt had returned to power.

IT WAS in May, 1804, that William Pitt undertook the responsibility of forming a second administration. "If Mr. Pitt's health does not fail him"—so wrote Castlereagh; and from the first, Pitt's health was the big "if." In the House of Commons his voice was as resonant as ever and his diction as sonorous. But where he had spoken with ease, he now spoke at times with effort. His mind and body seemed to be labouring under the burdens inflicted on them by his will.

Yet he had enjoyed several years of comparative rest. Of his vivacity when again he assumed office there is ample evidence. People commented on the vast fund of anecdotes which he narrated so admirably and on his delightful gift of mimicry. There was a Scot, Ferguson of Pitfour, whose pawky humour greatly entertained him. One day Pitt was on his feet in the House and everybody in the coffee room except Ferguson hurried to hear him. "What," asked his friends, "won't you go to hear Mr. Pitt?" Ferguson replied calmly, "Why should I? Do you think Mr. Pitt would go to hear me?" When Pitt heard of it he said amiably, "But indeed I would."

Then there was Charles Greville, made a Privy Councillor,

at which people asked why. "I would rather at any time," said Pitt, "have made him a Privy Councillor than have talked to him." Over the solemnity of the Marquis of Abercorn he was not less entertaining. After an interview with His Grace, Pitt said that he was much relieved. His august visitor had only asked to be made a Knight of the Garter. The Prime Minister had feared that the marquis would ask to be created Emperor of Germany!

After years of this diet, port wine had doubtless penetrated into Pitt's system. But it was not port wine that, in twenty months, left him a dead man. The practice of medicine may have been still elementary but Pitt's doctors at least knew enough to be aware that his trouble was no ordinary disease. *The zeal of thine house hath eaten me up*, so wrote the Psalmist. It was the zeal of his country that was consuming the vitality of William Pitt.

Here lay the contrast, definite to the end, between Pitt and Fox. The one man was included in the administrative system, the other man was excluded from it. Pitt was in fetters; Fox was free.

Hence it was possible for Fox to range abroad and with spacious eloquence preach good principles that embraced all peoples. But Pitt's wings were clipped by the shears of necessity. He was a repository of principles, not so very different from those of Fox, which, however, he was debarred from putting into practice. Thwarted over Ireland, over reform, over slavery, over freedom itself, his enthusiasms were concentrated on one sole remaining ideal, and that was the ideal England. To his country, at least, he could not be wrong in yielding a wholehearted devotion. At the end of his life he was thus like a tree pruned of its spreading foliage which, for this reason, is the more closely knit in its restricted growth. It was the intensity of the impenetrable culture called patriotism that finally gripped the heart of William Pitt and stopped its beating.

It was all very well for Fox to say that the war was "entirely the fault of the ministers and not of Bonaparte." Suppose that to be true—and Pitt did not admit it—the fact remained that England, right or wrong, was in danger. Napoleon and the war were facts to be faced. The greatest general known to history, commanding the greatest armies known to history, for that had become the prestige of Napoleon, had determined to obliterate an isolated Britain. "Let me be master of the Channel for six hours," he was saying, "and I will be master of the world."

Whispers of peace? They were dismissed as mere propaganda. Such a whisper was brought to Pitt by Fox and Grey who had information from Livingston, the United States Minister in Paris. There was, too, another letter from Napoleon to King George III which was answered not by the King but by his ministers. George might be half mad, but he was wholly a monarch. Let Napoleon declare himself Emperor, but that did not make him an equal.

Pitt was not alone in having England for his obsession. England was no less the obsession of Napoleon. What Pitt was determined to safeguard, Napoleon determined to overwhelm. If he postponed his coronation by the Pope, it was pending his triumph in London. Like others at a later date, he made his medals in advance of victories not always to be achieved. There was a medal, so struck, which was engraved with the words, *Descente en Angleterre* and dated *Frappé à Londres en 1804*. The medal displayed Hercules lifting up and crushing in his arms the monster Antæus.

About Napoleon there was, too, a grim ferocity. On the renewal of war he had thrown British residents into French prisons. Also, he had seized the person of the Duc d'Enghien on the neutral soil of Baden and had done him to death. The execution of King Louis XVI did not create a more profound horror. In the words of Fouché, it was not a crime; it was worse. It was a blunder.

It was Pitt who had to face this situation, and under the circumstances it might have been supposed that, with the existence of the nation at stake, there would have been a desire in all quarters, especially the highest, to make his task as easy as possible. It was, surely, essential that the personal prestige of Napoleon should be balanced, as it were, by a personal prestige on England's side not less challenging. Wellington had not yet entered the European field, and the name of Pitt was the only name with which England could conjure. Yet Pitt was subjected to incredible handicaps.

Napoleon may have been abnormal in his ambitions. But at least he had only to deal with the abnormalities in his own head. Pitt, however, had to deal with a King other than himself who was at once insane and irresistible. In church he would reiterate with emphasis, "Forty years long was I grieved with this generation and said, They are a people who have not known *my* ways." He would meet Pitt in the park and fail to notice him. Only after an assurance from the doctors did Pitt agree to see him, and he and Eldon wrote the King an urgent ultimatum ordering him to obey his medical advisers and refrain from undue stress and strain.

But, on the other hand, it sometimes seemed as if the King's illness were merely a malicious invention of the Prince of Wales at Carlton House. The first of Pitt's renewed audiences lasted for three hours, yet seemed to relieve the King's uneasiness. His Majesty displayed all that charm which was an element in his cunning. Pitt congratulated him on the fact that he looked better than he had after a former illness. "That is not to be wondered at," said the King with royal urbanity, "I was then on the point of parting from an old friend; I am now about to regain one." He told the Duke of Portland that he and Pitt had met like friends who had never parted.

★

But it was Pitt who had to pay the price. "Never," he declared regretfully, "in any conversation I have had with him in my life has he so baffled me." In order to save the King's nerves, the preliminaries had been adjusted by letter. Pitt had undertaken to refrain from raising again the question of Catholic Emancipation, but he had asked of the King a permission to form a comprehensive government, inclusive of Fox, Grenville, and Grey. The King replied with angry discourtesy. He was constrained "to express his astonishment that Mr. Pitt should one moment harbour the thought of bringing such a man [Fox] before his Royal notice." Instead of a personal interview, he suggested, through Eldon, that Pitt should "rather prepare another essay, containing as many empty words and little information as the one he had before transmitted." The reply of Pitt was a model of dignified restraint.

But the result of it all was that, in His Majesty's written words to Addington, "Mr. Fox is excluded by the express command of the King to Mr. Pitt." When Pitt asked if he objected to Fox being employed on a foreign mission, the King answered readily, "Not at all." But in the Cabinet, no.

Whether Pitt should have acquiesced in the King's edict is a question for argument. The trouble lay in the fact that the King was the King—not an individual merely but an institution. His very weakness was his strength. He could not be contradicted because such contradiction might have precipitated a calamity.

But the compromise forced on Pitt was the first of his disasters. Fox accepted his exclusion with what seemed to be a good grace. He was "too old to care about office." But in private he referred to Pitt as "a mean, low-minded dog," and "a mean rascal after all," while they "who have sometimes supposed him to be high-minded were quite wrong."

More serious than the emotions of Fox were the results of his political exile. He was for peace at any price. Grenville was for war at any price. Yet Fox and Grenville had formed an alliance. They did not call it a "coalition." It was a word of ill omen. But they arranged a "coöperation" of the opposites. To Pitt's indignation, Grenville—his kinsman, his friend, and his colleague—refused to enter the government without Fox. "I will teach that proud man," said Pitt to Eldon, "that, in the service and with the confidence of the King, I can do without him." But he added that, his health being what it was, it might cost him his life. Grenville was not less scornful. He sneered at the wretched way in which his cousin was "eking out his government with Roses and Dundases."

As for Ireland, the King's whims were not less expensive to his minister. Pitt's Act of Union had been followed by the rebellion of Robert Emmet. Yet Pitt was impotent to deal with the situation according to his best judgment. Also he was saddled with an inconsistency of which his critics did not hesitate to avail themselves. Why had he resigned in 1801 over Catholic Emancipation and then, three years later, accepted office on the King's terms? Fox did not hesitate to hammer this nail on the head and, without bringing in the King, Pitt could make no effective reply. Yet Fox himself was similarly subject to royal prejudice. He declined as a private member to propose Catholic Emancipation, and after Pitt's death, when Fox became a minister, he continued to avoid the subject. "Have you no difficulty respecting the Roman Catholic question?" asked the Austrian Ambassador of Pitt's critic. "None at all," said Fox blandly. "I am determined not to annoy my sovereign by bringing it forward." Pitt was then in his grave.

★

Was the King really reconciled to Pitt? Within the security of his Court his references to the government were ominous. When the Etonians greeted him with cheers he replied, "I have always been partial to your school. I have now the additional motive for being so. In future, I shall be *an anti-Westminster.*" It was a hit, both at Fox, who sat for Westminster, and at Pitt, who proposed Fox for the Cabinet.

After suggesting a comprehensive government Pitt found himself, therefore, through no fault of his own, face to face with a varied yet embittered opposition led by Fox, Grenville, and Addington, all of them men with a grievance for which Pitt was not responsible. His majority at the outset was no more than 40 to 50, and Canning roundly accused Addington of indulging in "systematic opposition." Between Addington and Pitt, however, no quarrel could last very long. They and their fathers had known one another too affectionately. In the park, when riding, it was noted that Pitt touched his hat to Addington. At Lord Hawkesbury's house they met and Pitt said warmly, "I rejoice to take you by the hand again." A reconciled Addington became Viscount Sidmouth and Lord President of the Council, also dining with the King off mutton chops and pudding.

But friendship, kind to Pitt in the case of Addington, now dealt him a shrewd and fatal blow. Melville, better known as Dundas, had spent years at the Admiralty, first as Treasurer and then as First Lord. Of his ability in administration there was no doubt. It was not open to argument.

But the rumour spread that the Tenth Report of a Commission of Naval Enquiry would disclose financial irregularities. It happened that when the first copy of the report was brought to Pitt, Wilberforce was with him. "I shall never forget," said Wilberforce, "the way in which he seized it, and how eagerly he looked into the leaves without waiting even to cut them open." It was no wonder. Here was an indictment of his closest colleague.

"Not guilty on my honour" was Melville's protest in the House of Lords, and Pitt agreed. There had been, he said, "no real pocketing of public money." He decided to stand by Melville in the House of Commons where Melville —now a peer—had been so familiar a figure.

The House was crowded. Over a difficult question opinion was divided. At the end of the debate Wilberforce rose. A man who asked nothing for himself, he had become the very incarnation of the national conscience. Pitt bestowed on him an anxious and searching look. They were lifelong friends. Wilberforce loved Pitt as a man, more to him than a brother.

The view of Wilberforce was simple. He remembered doubtless Pitt's duel of which, at the time, he had so gravely disapproved. Once more he thought that the Prime Minister had been led astray "by that false principle of honour which was his greatest fault." In Tennyson's language, the judgment of Wilberforce on the Prime Minister was that

> *His honour rooted in dishonour stood*
> *And faith unfaithful kept him falsely true.*

A vote decided by this speech was cast against Melville by Sir Robert Peel, father of a Prime Minister.

On a division the figures were exactly even—216 to 216. Mr. Speaker Abbot, his face pale as a sheet, sat motionless as a statue. He sat like that for ten minutes. Then, at length, he gave his casting vote against Pitt, Melville, and the government. An exultant member cried, "We have killed the fox." Pitt crushed his cocked hat over his forehead to hide the tears trickling down his cheeks. A member called on others to see "how Billy looked after it." But a bodyguard of Pitt's followers locked their arms and formed a circle within which the Prime Minister, apparently in a daze, moved from the scene.

It was not the only debate on Melville. The House insisted that his name should be struck off the Privy Council. Pitt was again on the rack. He told the House that he "felt a deep and bitter pang in being compelled to be the instrument of rendering still more severe the punishment of the Noble Lord." At the word "pang" his lip quivered; his voice shook; there was a pause; and it was with difficulty that he regained his self-possession. To complete his distress, the friendly Sidmouth, unable to agree with Pitt over Melville, deemed it to be his duty to resign. At Bath, Melville called on Pitt, and Sidmouth was scandalized yet further. Wrote Fox, "the *Doctor* talks of it with uplifted eyes and says he cannot believe it."

Amid these confusions, who would have thought that the country was faced by a threat of invasion? According to Fox, "the alarm was . . . most certainly a groundless one and raised for some political purpose by the ministers." Grenville also laughed at Pitt's preparedness as Lord Warden of the Cinque Ports—Martello Towers, the long defensive dyke, and all the rest of it. "You will find me," said Grenville, "very peaceably rolling my walks and watering my rhododendrons, without any thought of the new possessor to whom Bonaparte may dispose them."

It is true that the Martello Towers and the great dyke were never needed. But why was that? One day, in the summer of 1805, Pitt had received an official visitor. He was a slight frail man with an armless sleeve to his coat and one eye blind. What they said to one another we do not know. But it was noticed that, when the one-eyed, one-armed man rose to go, the Prime Minister also rose. He escorted his guest from the room, and to the astonishment of the household he led the strange little man back to his carriage, and the carriage was then driven out of sight. Pitt's farewell to Nelson was Nelson's summons to Trafalgar. Many had been the honours received by the greatest of all admirals. But the honour that stirred him more than all the others was the courtesy of William Pitt accompanying him to his carriage.

At Trafalgar Napoleon learned what England meant by six hours of mastery at sea. Over the news, glorious and tragic, which came to Pitt that night, he could not sleep. He got up at three in the morning and dressed.

★

On the Lord Mayor's Day, immediately following, that is, November 9, 1805, there was the usual banquet in the Guildhall which mere war is not permitted to interrupt. It was the occasion of a last exulting demonstration in favour of William Pitt. After all, he had proved himself to be "a chip of the old block," and like his father, Chatham, he must be

welcomed accordingly. In Cheapside his carriage was un-
horsed and he was drawn amid acclamations to the scene of
the dinner. "The Saviour of Europe"—so did the Lord
Mayor propose his health. Pitt rose. It was to be his shortest
speech and his last speech. "I return you many thanks for
the honour you have done me," said he, "but Europe is not
to be saved by any single man. England has saved herself
by her exertions, and will, as I trust, save Europe by her
example." Never again did an audience hear that voice.

Among those who were awed by a sublime brevity was an
officer of commanding countenance in the very prime of his
youthful vigour. "That was all," said Wellington, of Pitt's
speech; "he was scarcely up two minutes; yet nothing could
be more perfect."

At the Guildhall Pitt was in his usual spirits. At Erskine
he could not resist the temptation of having his usual little
dig. As this lawyer rose to return thanks Pitt lifted his finger
and said across the table, "Erskine! remember that they are
drinking your health as a distinguished Colonel of Volunteers," and once more Erskine—a critic of the war—was
hypnotized into acquiescence.

Pitt was thus entirely human. We find him at a game of
chess or discussing with Canning and Mulgrave their lines of
poetry, if poetry it was, celebrating Trafalgar. But the end
was not far distant. Pitt's farewell to Nelson was, after all, an
au revoir.

★

At sea Great Britain was safe. But Europe—what of Europe? Was it true that "the example" of England was enough

to save Europe from the arms of Napoleon? It did not look like that.

On resuming office Pitt made it his business, as was the custom, to reorganize Europe against France. He succeeded. England, Russia, and Austria began again to stand shoulder to shoulder. There were hopes that even Prussia would enter the confederacy. Alas for herself, England, and Europe, she hesitated.

On these careful arrangements the might of Napoleon fell like a thunderbolt from heaven. His blows suggested the will of a supreme being. He seized Hanover. At Ulm he forced an Austrian army to capitulate. In triumph he entered Vienna and there proceeded to shatter Pitt's coalition and the Holy Roman Empire itself by the masterstroke of Austerlitz. When, at length, Prussia roused herself to resist, she was crushed at Jena and Auerstadt; and the battles of Eylau and Friedland forced an isolated Russia to sign the Peace of Tilsit which cut Prussia in half.

Pitt's stout heart was the anvil on which these terrific hammerings began to fall. To avert the disasters he was impotent. The only question was how many of them he would survive. The news came slowly and was uncertain. Austerlitz was first reported as a victory for the allies. Then the truth was told, and the sun of Austerlitz that rose for Napoleon was the sun that set for William Pitt.

For months the doctors had been anxious. Their patient suffered from "flying gout," and they had sent him to Bath where the waters were supposed to locate it. After drinking them, the trouble was thrown, as they expected, first into the right foot, then into the left. So far, so good.

But at the news of Austerlitz the gout retreated from the feet and there was noticed a general debility. It was the heart that claimed the trouble.

War, at its first outbreak, had greeted Pitt studying a large map. It was a large map that he now demanded, and would they please leave him alone with it. They left him alone and he fought a long last silent duel with fate. Said Canning, "It was the relapse of a single day that reduced Mr. Pitt to the wreck that he now is."

Ten days later the Prime Minister was so emaciated that his friends hardly knew him. Wilberforce had parted with him forevei, but it was Wilberforce who coined the phrase that described him. He had "the Austerlitz look."

They brought him from Bath to London. It took them three days. At Putney, Lady Hester Stanhope was shocked by his wasted appearance and hollow voice.

She led him to his room, and as they passed a map of Europe that hung from a wall of the corridor, he turned to her and said, "Roll up that map; it will not be wanted these ten years."

★

His weakness increased. He could fancy no animal food, only eggs. They talked of a typhus fever. There was a "thrush in his throat," and Sir Walter Farquhar, forcing him to swallow champagne, said, "I am sorry, sir, to give you pain.

Do not take it unkind." Quietly the sick man answered, "I never take anything unkind that is meant for my good."

The Bishop of Lincoln—his old tutor, Tomline—offered him the Sacrament. He did not feel himself to be able to receive it. "*That,*" he declared, "I have not strength to go through with." The bishop desired to pray with him. Pitt feared that, like others, he had neglected prayer. It would not be very efficacious now. Still he insisted on his "innocency of life," and, clasping his hands, he added, "I throw myself *entirely* upon the mercy of God, through the merits of Christ." The prayers were read. The dying man joined earnestly in the responses.

They prayed heaven for good news from Europe. Good news might yet save Pitt. But no good news was to be had. On the contrary, Castlereagh and Hawkesbury, his colleagues, called on him. They had to call on him. It was Pitt and only Pitt who could authorize a certain order that had to be given. The British Army had to be withdrawn at once from northern Europe. Pitt assented, and when Hawkesbury and Castlereagh left him they carried away with them all hope of his life. He became much worse.

He had only his papers and his debts to bequeath. The bishop drew up the documents and Pitt signed them. His signature was as firm as ever.

But his mind began to wander. He summoned invisible messengers. During visionary debates in the House he called "Hear! Hear!" He asked how the wind blew. "East," he cried. "Ah, that will do; that will bring him quick." For Pitt, the wind had meant news.

A kinsman, James H. Stanhope, leaned over him. For so long he had been quiet that they had begun to wonder. But again he spoke, and this time the voice was clear: "Oh, my country! how I leave my country!" were the words that Stanhope immediately recorded. Those were the last words that Pitt was heard to utter.

In the House of Commons Fox and Grenville were thundering against the "ill-concerted, ill-conducted, ill-supported plans" of the government. They carried an address to be presented to His Majesty. As they were walking with the speaker at their head the news was passed from one to another that Pitt had joined Nelson. In the words of "Sir Walter":

> Now is the stately column broke,
> The beacon-light is quench'd in smoke,
> The trumpet's silver sound is still,
> The warder silent on the hill!

But, like history itself, the procession continued to advance.

★

Over the payment of Pitt's debts Fox was generous. But, asked to pronounce him an "excellent statesman," he demurred. It would be to stultify his own career. The motion thus gently resisted was carried by 258 votes to 89.

It was the Abbey that awaited Pitt. Solemn was the pageantry of the funeral—Grenville walking as Prime Minister, the Speaker, the Lord Mayor, the officers of the volunteers of the Cinque Ports, and last but not least, Sir Arthur

Wellesley. The open grave absorbed the attention of the vast throng. Twice had Pitt himself stood by the threshold. He had buried there his father; he had buried there his mother. It was now his own turn.

"What grave," asked Lord Wellesley, "contains such a father and such a son?" As the coffin of William Pitt was lowered into the darkness it seemed to Wilberforce that the statue of Chatham looked upon "his favourite son, the last perpetuator of the name," with a gaze of "consternation."

★

The life of no man ends when he dies. The difference that he has made to the world lives after him; also, that situation in which he was an element.

As Prime Minister, Pitt was succeeded by two men. There was Grenville who had denounced him for not winning the war. There was Fox who had denounced him for not making peace. In office the opposites became indistinguishables.

Crossing the floor of their respective Houses of Parliament, Grenville, as Prime Minister, and Fox, as Secretary of State, saw politics as in a mirror. What had been left became right. What had been right became left.

Winning the war? It had been dreadful when, with Pitt at Bath, Napoleon triumphed at Ulm and Austerlitz. But what was Grenville's record of disasters? There were Jena and Auerstadt and Friedland and Eylau: a Russia driven to sign a treaty with the usurper on a raft in the river Tilsit and a Prussia cut in half.

Making peace? Fox tried. Fox failed. Indeed, he failed for

the same reason that Pitt, had be been in office, would also have failed. For Napoleon demanded Sicily, and Fox, acting precisely as Pitt would have acted, refused to concede Sicily.

So with Catholic Emancipation. Out of office Fox had no mercy for Pitt's acquiescence in the King's veto. But in office Fox confessed frankly that, over the Catholics, he was not going to be a worry to His Majesty.

In death the rivals were not long divided. Worn out by the strain and stress of the times and his own infirmities, it was within the year that Fox, with all his Franco-philippics fresh in the minds of the people and still member for Westminster, joined Pitt in the Abbey.

> *With more than mortal powers endow'd,*
> *How high they soar'd above the crowd!*
> *Theirs was no common party race,*
> *Jostling by dark intrigue for place;*
> *Like fabled Gods, their mighty war*
> *Shook realms and nations in its jar;*
> *Beneath each banner proud to stand,*
> *Look'd up the noblest of the land,*
> *Till through the British world were known*
> *The names of Pitt and Fox alone.*
> *Spells of such force no wizard grave*
> *E'er framed in dark Thessalian cave,*
> *Though his could drain the ocean dry,*
> *And force the planets from the sky.*
> *These spells are spent, and, spent with these,*
> *The wine of life is on the lees.*

Genius, and taste, and talent gone,
For ever tomb'd beneath the stone,
Where—taming thought to human pride!—
The mighty chiefs sleep side by side.
Drop upon Fox's *grave the tear,*
'Twill trickle to his rival's bier;
O'er Pitt's *the mournful requiem sound,*
And Fox's *shall the notes rebound.*
The solemn echo seems to cry,—
"Here let their discord with them die,
Speak not for those a separate doom,
Whom Fate made brothers in the tomb;
But search the land of living men,
Where wilt thou find their like agen?

THE END